Praise for The Country Club Murders

"A sparkling comedy of errors tucked inside a clever mystery. I loved it!"

– Susan M. Boyer,
USA Today Bestselling Author of *Lowcountry Book Club*

"Readers who enjoy the novels of Susan Isaacs will love this series that blends a strong mystery with the demands of living in an exclusive society."

– *Kings River Life Magazine*

"From the first page to the last, Julie's mysteries grab the reader and don't let up."

– Sally Berneathy,
USA Today Bestselling Author of *The Ex Who Saw a Ghost*

"This book is fun! F-U-N Fun!...A delightful pleasure to read. I didn't want to put it down...Highly recommend."

– *Mysteries, etc.*

"Set in Kansas City, Missouri, in 1974, this cozy mystery effectively recreates the era through the details of down-to-earth Ellison's everyday life."

– *Booklist*

"Mulhern's lively, witty sequel to *The Deep End* finds Kansas City, Mo., socialite Ellison Russell reluctantly attending a high school football game...Cozy fans will eagerly await Ellison's further adventures."

– *Publishers Weekly*

"There's no way a lover of suspense could turn this book down because it's that much fun."

– *Suspense Magazine*

"Cleverly written with sharp wit and all the twists and turns of the best '70s primetime drama, Mulhern nails the fierce fraught mother-daughter relationship, fearlessly tackles what hides behind the Country Club façade, and serves up justice in bombshell fashion. A truly satisfying slightly twisted cozy."

– Gretchen Archer,
USA Today Bestselling Author of *Double Knot*

"Part mystery, part women's fiction, part poetry, Mulhern's debut, *The Deep End*, will draw you in with the first sentence and entrance you until the last. An engaging whodunit that kept me guessing until the end!"

– Tracy Weber,
Author of the Downward Dog Mysteries

"An impossible-to-put-down Harvey Wallbanger of a mystery. With a smart, funny protagonist who's learning to own her power as a woman, *Send in the Clowns* is one boss read."

– Ellen Byron,
Agatha Award-Nominated Author of *Plantation Shudders*

"The plot is well-structured and the characters drawn with a deft hand. Setting the story in the mid-1970s is an inspired touch...A fine start to this mystery series, one that is highly recommended."

– *Mysterious Reviews*

"What a fun read! Murder in the days before cell phones, the internet, DNA and AFIS."

– *Books for Avid Readers*

SHADOW DANCING

The Country Club Murders
by Julie Mulhern

Novels

THE DEEP END (#1)
GUARANTEED TO BLEED (#2)
CLOUDS IN MY COFFEE (#3)
SEND IN THE CLOWNS (#4)
WATCHING THE DETECTIVES (#5)
COLD AS ICE (#6)
SHADOW DANCING (#7)

Short Stories

DIAMOND GIRL
A Country Club Murder Short

SHADOW DANCING

THE COUNTRY CLUB MURDERS

JULIE MULHERN

HENERY PRESS

Copyright

SHADOW DANCING
The Country Club Murders
Part of the Henery Press Mystery Collection

First Edition | June 2018

Henery Press
www.henerypress.com

Trade Paperback ISBN-13: 978-1-63511-350-1
Digital epub ISBN-13: 978-1-63511-351-8
Kindle ISBN-13: 978-1-63511-352-5
Hardcover ISBN-13: 978-1-63511-353-2

Printed in the United States of America

To Poppe, Kappus, and Ruth—I miss you!

ACKNOWLEDGMENTS

Thanks to my wonderful editors at Henery Press, Rachel Jackson and Kendel Lynn, to my agent, Margaret Bail, and to my family. But, most of all, thank you to everyone who reads and loves the Country Club Murders—I am incredibly grateful.

ONE

February, 1975
Kansas City, Missouri

"You are surrounded by death."

Oh dear Lord. Libba's "medium" sat on one side of a small table. I sat on the other. I tugged against her vice-like grip on my hand.

When Libba had said "medium," I'd imagined a woman in a turban (royal purple or turquoise) and long, flowing robes who was surrounded by the scent of patchouli. Someone who spoke with a foreign accent. The reality was an older woman with a surprisingly strong grip, wispy white hair, creped skin, liver spots, and fire engine red lipstick that had bled into the wrinkles surrounding her mouth. As for that accent—pure Brooklyn.

"You cannot fight your fate." Madame Reyna stared at my trapped palm through rhinestone-speckled cat glasses as thick as Coke bottles. Those glasses made her eyes appear ten times larger than they actually were. Those eyes, dark and enormous, lent her an otherworldly air completely at odds with our surroundings—a gold brocade living room set covered with plastic slip covers, deep, recently raked shag carpet, macramé wall hangings, and a corduroy chair the size of Maryland. Dust motes waltzed through the half-hearted sunshine peeking through the curtains. The lingering scent of a late breakfast—bacon and fried eggs by the smell of it—hung in the air. Suburbia, not supernatural.

Again I pulled at my hand.

Madame Reyna held on. She leaned forward, peered more closely through her Coke-bottle glasses, and tsked. "So much death."

I shot Libba a look that should have killed her.

It didn't.

Instead, she perched on the edge of the plastic-covered couch like a curious robin, immune to my murderous glare.

Madame Reyna tsked again.

This was Libba's fault. She'd dragged me here, not kicking and screaming but almost.

"Everyone is going to her," she'd wheedled.

"No."

"She's the real deal, Ellison."

"No."

"She says Henry wants to communicate with you." Henry was my late husband.

"I don't want to communicate with him." Then, in case I'd been unclear, I added, "I'm not going."

Yet, here I sat.

Libba was nothing if not persuasive.

I shifted my gaze to Madame Reyna. Weren't mediums supposed to commune with the dead? Why was this one reading my palm? Again, I tugged at my hand.

This time, she released me. "Your late husband has spoken to me."

I offered up a sympathetic sigh. My life was much better now that Henry, a cheating, lying, barnacle-on-the-ass-of-humanity type of man, no longer spoke to me.

"Don't you want to know what he said?"

"Not particularly."

"I do," Libba chirped.

Madame Reyna's dark gaze traveled between Libba and me. I could almost see the cogs working in her medium's brain. Libba was hooked. A true believer. A rich true believer.

"He says that Mrs. Russell will find death."

"Poo," said Libba, unimpressed. "For a while there, Ellison was finding death every week."

Some people found pennies in parking lots. I found bodies. And not just in parking lots. I found bodies everywhere. But I'd made a New Year's resolution. No more bodies. Eight weeks into the new year, my resolution held firm. Not a single body. Not one. I wrinkled my nose and stuck my tongue out at Libba.

No, I didn't.

But I wanted to.

"He says she will find death again. Soon."

I rolled my eyes with elegance and aplomb. Watching Grace, my sixteen-year-old daughter, roll her baby blues has made me an expert.

Madame Reyna reached across the table and re-trapped my hand. "He says your daughter will be in danger and that salvation is in the safe."

My organs seized. Froze. No air in the lungs. No beat of the heart. No blink of the eyes. Grace in danger? Almost as worrisome, how could the woman across from me know anything about the contents of our safe?

"That's not amusing." There was a decided chill in Libba's voice. "Not remotely."

I didn't believe in mediums or fortune-tellers or any such hokum. I remembered that and my organs resumed operations. "What are you talking about?"

Madame Reyna closed her eyes for ten, maybe twenty, infinitely long seconds. "The spirit has gone. I can give you no other answer today."

Translation—I'd have to return to her ranch-style house and cross her palm with more silver if I wanted an answer.

I pushed away from the table.

"Wait!" she cried.

I paused.

"I saw something in your palm."

"Oh, please." My purse hung over the back of the chair. I

picked it up and slung it over my shoulder.

"It's important."

I raised a brow. Slowly. The effect was one of mild disdain. I was an ace at that expression, too. A lifetime of watching Mother raise her brow in extreme disdain had made me an expert.

"There is a man."

"Isn't there always." The way Libba said it, it wasn't a question.

"You have met the One and let him go."

"Just wait a few days, Ellison. Another One will come along before you know it." That was how things worked for Libba.

Madame Reyna glared at Libba. With the size of her eyes multiplied by ten due to her glasses, it was an impressive glare. A glare she transferred to my blameless palm. "You've let the One go but Mr. Right is still coming."

Libba lowered her chin and regarded Madame Reyna with frank disbelief. "A second soul mate? You mean marriage?"

Sean Connery could show up at Libba's door with a three-carat diamond, a marriage license, and deeds to his condo in Vail, house in Lyford Quay, and villa in Tuscany, and Libba would tell him she wasn't ready for a commitment. She had too much fun being single.

I too would send Sean Connery packing. But not because I enjoyed being single. I would send the Scotsman away because the mere thought of a commitment turned my toes to popsicles. "I'm not interested."

Madame Reyna's crimson lips thinned. "You are foolish."

Well! Insulting her customers was hardly the way to win repeat business.

"This relationship has the power to transform your life."

I wasn't sure I wanted my life transformed. What's more, the man who might have transformed said life had walked out of my house (and life) eight weeks ago without looking back. "Not interested." Nor was I interested in a new Mr. Right.

The medium rolled her eyes.

Was there a Mr. Reyna? If so, did his wife complain about her clients over cocktails? Two society women came in today. One didn't believe in me at all. The other mocked the idea of soul mates. I charged them double.

"Ellison, we should be going." Libba stared pointedly at her watch.

I wasn't about to argue.

"You'll be back." Madame Reyna looked almost smug.

Not likely. "It was a pleasure meeting you."

Libba and I stepped out into late February chill. The sun played hide and seek with scudding clouds and lost. Both of us pulled the collars of our coats tighter around our necks.

"I'm sorry about that." Libba jerked her chin toward the little ranch house and the medium inside.

"Don't worry about it. You had no idea she'd make up stuff about Grace being in danger."

"Still, I'm sorry." She actually sounded contrite.

"Grace is fine." I would not worry based on the warning of a bogus medium.

We walked toward our cars with our shoulders hunched against the cold, our hands jammed in our pockets, and our heads down spotting the slick spots on the sidewalk.

"You could call him." Libba's voice was soft, quiet, almost tentative.

Him. Detective Anarchy Jones. The One. "When pigs fly."

"You know, I don't think I've ever seen you be this stubborn."

Just because I gave in on things like visiting mediums or extending curfews didn't mean I couldn't dig my heels in. "Pfft."

"Seriously." Libba laid a gloved hand on my arm, stopping me. "You've changed."

Finding your husband murdered then finding umpteen other bodies will do that to a woman. "I had to."

"He's a good man."

"I know."

"He cares about you."

"You know why he's mad at me?"

"I do."

Of course she did, I'd told her at least fifty times. Some of those tellings blurred by wine, some sharpened by coffee.

"You know what I did?"

"I do." Libba let go of my arm and resumed walking.

I followed her. "If I had to do it all again—"

Libba held up her hands halting my words. "I know, I know. You'd still do almost exactly the same thing."

Perhaps I'd been a little boring on the subject. "You've been a good friend to listen to the same story so many times." Maybe I'd been a lot boring. "Never again. I promise. You won't hear me even mention the name Anarchy Jones." I traced an X over my heart.

Libba pulled her keys out of her handbag and shivered as a gust of wind buffeted against us. "Don't be silly. I'm happy to listen."

"I mean it Libba."

"If you say so." Was that a lilt in her voice? She glanced again at Madame Reyna's snug little house. "I'm not one to give advice, but—"

I refrained from comment. Barely.

"Either let this go—him, the anger, and all the other feelings—or fix it." She circled her car and opened the driver's side door. "I'll talk to you later. Toodles."

"Toodles." My voice lacked her verve. Mainly because she was right. Retelling (and retelling) my falling out with Anarchy was a way of holding on.

With a sigh, I settled into my car and started the engine. I sat for a moment, letting the engine warm and replaying Madame Reyna's words—you have met the One and let him go. The time had come to do just that—let Anarchy Jones go.

I drove toward home, my mind not on the road. Barry Manilow crooned "Mandy." I turned up the radio over the sound of the heat blasting. I touched my lips, remembering Anarchy's kiss. I dug in my purse for a tissue. Maybe that's why I didn't see her. Then again, she dashed out from between two parked cars. I slammed on the brakes. The tires screeched. The car slowed. Not fast enough.

The sickening thud of my front bumper meeting a human being reverberated through me. I threw the car into park and leapt out of my seat. "Are you all right?"

Of course she wasn't. I'd hit her.

The girl sat on the cold pavement looking dazed.

"Where are you hurt?" I demanded. And what was she doing outside without a coat? And why wasn't she in school?

She shook her head. "I'm not hurt. You weren't going very fast."

I'd hit her. With a car. Granted the car was a TR6 and not a Cadillac Fleetwood, but I'd still hit her. "Did you hit your head?"

"No." She glanced down at the cold pavement. "I landed on my bottom. I'm fine." She offered me a smile as if the curve of her lips could prove that all was well.

"Let me help you up." I extended a hand.

She stared at the navy leather of my glove for a few seconds before she accepted.

I pulled her to standing.

She was tiny with dark hair and a pixie face. Maybe fourteen. Possibly fifteen. A gamine.

"Shall we try and find a phone?" I asked.

"A phone?"

"To call the police. We need to file a report."

"No!" Her hands—no gloves—flew to her cheeks. "There's no need to file a report." Her words tumbled over each other in their hurry. "I told you, I'm fine. Let's just pretend this never happened."

"It did happen."

"But I'm fine. See?" She danced a little jig on the pavement. "Fine."

I remained unconvinced. "What are you doing out here? Why aren't you in school?"

She glanced over her shoulder as if she expected to find a truant officer lurking behind her. "I skipped."

Obviously. I waited. Silence was one of the tools Mother used on me in my youth. In turn, I've used it with Grace. People—especially teenage people—didn't like silence. They felt the need to fill it. And sometimes, they said more than they should.

The silence stretched.

"I skipped school and went to my boyfriend's house."

That didn't explain why she was wandering the streets in nothing but a pair of jeans and a sweater. "And?"

"And we had a fight." She glanced at the cold pavement and shifted her feet. "I ran away."

"Did he hurt you?"

Her face shuttered. I'd asked a question she didn't like. "Of course not."

I didn't believe her. I lived with a teenager. I could spot a lie at ten paces. "Get in the car, I'll take you home."

"No. I don't know you."

I raised a brow.

"My mother told me never to get in the car with a stranger."

"I'm Ellison Russell. What's your name?"

"Leslie." No last name.

"Leslie?"

"Smith." She'd told me another lie.

"Well, Leslie Smith, we're not strangers anymore."

That earned me an eye roll.

"I can't leave you out here in the cold with no coat. Besides, the car is warm."

Leslie shivered and glanced longingly at the car. "I live close by. I can walk."

"Where does your boyfriend live? Let's get your coat."

"No!" Dogs started barking at the pitch of her voice. "We had a fight." She rubbed her cheek. "I'm not going back there."

She looked away. Her sullen expression told me silence wouldn't work this time.

"I'll go with you," I offered.

"I'm not going back there."

"Then let me take you home."

"I'm fine."

She wasn't fine. She was freezing. And probably bruised from my bumper. And definitely bruised from whatever had transpired at her boyfriend's house. "Please, Leslie. Let me take you home."

"No." She crossed her arms and shivered.

Too bad I couldn't force her into the car. "Take my coat."

Her eyes widened. "What?"

I shrugged out of my pea coat; I'd had it for years and it had seen better days but it was warm. "Put this on."

"I couldn't." Her teeth chattered.

"You can. You're freezing." Now that I was without a coat, I understood just how cold she was. The wind cut through my heavy sweater as if I was wearing gauze and not four-ply cashmere. "I'm not leaving you here unless you take it."

"But—"

I held out the wool jacket and shook it until its sleeves danced. "No buts. Take the coat."

She took the coat. She slipped her arms in the sleeves and wrapped the front tight across her body. "Thank you."

"Gloves, too." I peeled my gloves off my hands and thrust them at her.

"Why are you doing this?"

"I have a daughter a little bit older than you. If she was wandering the streets without a coat, I'd want someone to help her."

Leslie wiped her eyes with the backs of her hands and accepted the gloves. "I'll return them. I promise. Where do you live?"

"I'll give you my address." I reached into the car, grabbed my purse, found an old Swanson's receipt, and jotted my name and address on the back.

She took the slip of paper and thrust it deep into the coat pocket. "Thank you."

"You're welcome. You're sure I can't take you home?"

An expression—sadness mixed with longing—flitted across her face. "I'm sure."

"I can take you someplace else."

"You're still a stranger."

True.

"You're positive you're not hurt?"

"I'm fine." She sounded almost exasperated and glanced over her shoulder as if she was still expecting the truant officer.

The wind cut through my sweater and the warmth of the car beckoned.

"Thank you for lending me your coat."

"Keep it."

"You're very kind." She sounded surprised, as if kindness was foreign to her. "Your daughter is lucky." Then Leslie turned her back on me and walked away. The opposite direction from which my car was pointed.

I watched her for a few seconds then hurried into the warmth of the car.

I drove three blocks. Was she really okay? Maybe I should follow her home. I reversed directions and backtracked. I drove past the spot where I'd hit her. She was nowhere in sight. I cruised the next few blocks but didn't spot her. Leslie Smith had disappeared.

TWO

I blasted the heat in my car and the vents did their level best but the cold still snuck through the cloth roof and down my neck. I hoped Leslie appreciated that coat because I missed its warmth.

When I pulled into the drive, I parked as close to the front door as possible, and, keys in hand, dashed to the door. It opened before I could even insert the key in the lock.

"Where's your coat?" Aggie, my housekeeper, asked.

"Long story."

"Your mother is on the phone."

"She is?"

"She's called six times in the past hour." Aggie eyed my cashmere sweater, which had proved unequal to the weather. "If you'd like to take the call in the study, I'll bring you hot coffee."

"Thank you." Coffee sounded better than heaven.

I shuffled into the study, rubbing my arms as I went. Six calls in an hour? Whatever Mother wanted, I wasn't going to like it. I picked up the phone. "Hello."

"Ellison!" Mother's voice was a mix of relief and exasperation. "Where have you been?"

Tell Mother I'd visited a medium? I'd rather hammer shims under my fingernails or wander around outside without my coat. "Out."

"I need you."

Time stopped. Mother never needed me. "What's wrong?"

"I need you." Apparently that was the only explanation I was getting. "Can you come over? Please?"

Please? What had happened? "Of course, I'll come. Are you okay?"

"Hurry." She hung up.

Aggie appeared in the doorway, a steaming mug of all-things-good in her hand.

"Would you please put that in a travel mug?" I asked.

"Of course. Problem?"

"She won't tell me what's wrong." Mother was not given to crying wolf. Whatever the issue was, it was big. A trickle of dread chilled my blood. "The ambiance committee is meeting here at three. I'll be back before then."

"I'll have everything ready." Aggie was indispensable. How we'd ever gotten along without her was a mystery. With her sproingy red hair, vivid kaftans, and outspoken ways, Aggie was not Mother's idea of a perfect housekeeper. Mother's opinion didn't matter. I thought Aggie was the best thing since sliced bread.

A moment later I was back in the car, snug in a fox jacket with matching hat. I settled the plastic travel mug filled with coffee between my thighs and wished I hadn't. The plastic was hot. I turned the key and ELO's "Can't Get It Out of My Head" nearly deafened me. I sympathized. Even with hitting a pedestrian and Mother's crisis, there was a man I couldn't get out of my head. I turned off the radio and motored down the drive.

Mother's door opened as soon as I pulled up in front of her house.

I took a quick gulp of coffee then hurried up the front walk. "What's wrong?"

Mother looked from left to right as if her neighbors were hanging around in the cold, waiting to eavesdrop. "Come in."

With the door safely closed behind me, Mother sighed.

"What? What's happened?"

The color had leeched from her skin and the perfect helmet of her hair was mussed. "I found a body."

Mother? A body? It was about time someone in this family besides me found a body. "Where?"

"In the closet." She lifted her hand and pointed at the hall closet, home to various umbrellas, two pairs of galoshes, the good coats, and two leaves for the dining room table. "It was on the shelf."

I closed my eyes and imagined a body pretzeled onto the small shelf. "Who?"

"I don't know."

I walked toward the closet. "Does Daddy know?"

"Your father is out of town."

So she'd called me. "You didn't call the police?"

"Of course not." She shuddered.

I took a deep breath and closed my hand around the knob. That Mother had closed the body back up in the closet didn't surprise me. She was an expert at hiding things she didn't want seen. I opened the door.

Nothing.

Nothing. Not a single coat or umbrella or galosh. The closet was empty. Mother had been joking. I knew it! I scowled at her. "Not funny."

"You didn't think I'd leave it in there?"

"That's precisely what I thought. The police take a dim view of moving bodies." I glanced again into the empty closet. "And evidence. They don't like it when you disturb evidence."

With the wave of her hand Mother brushed away my concerns. "Piffle."

"Piffle?" My voice might have jumped an octave. Or two.

"This way." She walked away from me. "I put it in the music room."

My brain struggled to process this announcement.

Mother looked over her shoulder. "Close your mouth before the flies buzz in."

"The body is in the music room?"

"That's what I said."

Strictly speaking, the music room was a sun porch. It had become the music room because it was the farthest room from

Mother's office. She'd disliked listening to her children practice their scales almost as much as we'd hated practicing them. The room contained an upright piano, my sister Marjorie's old guitar, a chaise longue that belonged to Daddy's mother, and one of my early paintings. In short, it was the room where she kept things she wanted to get rid of but couldn't. Including a body.

I followed Mother into the living room and paused, taking off my coat and hat and folding them over the back of a couch.

"Come along, Ellison." Impatience laced her tone.

I came.

We entered the music room. There was the piano and the guitar and the chaise. My painting still hung on the wall. No body.

"Mother." My voice had acquired an edge.

"On the chaise."

The only thing on the chaise was a box. Mahogany. Highly polished.

I stared at that box. "You don't mean?"

Mother nodded. "I'm afraid so."

Well at least it wasn't an actual body. "Who is it?"

"I have no idea."

I leaned against the door frame. "So someone came to your house with this, stuck it in the front closet, and left?"

Mother nodded.

I ventured into the music room and picked up the box. It was heavier than I expected. Not a single marking marred its shining surface. Carefully, I opened the lid. Inside was a sealed plastic bag.

I closed the lid. Harder than I'd intended.

"Careful," said Mother. "Don't break it."

I did not snap back a quick retort. Wanted to. Didn't. Instead, I put the box back on the chaise. "I need coffee."

"I figured you would. There's fresh in the kitchen."

Mother had a percolator and the coffee it produced was nowhere near as good as what Mr. Coffee made. I'd offered to buy her a Mr. Coffee. Multiple times. And she'd declined. She'd made coffee the same way for years. Why change now? What did it matter if the percolator could burn liquid? At that moment, I didn't care if the coffee was burnt. "Lead the way."

Mother's kitchen was built as a place for the help to prepare food. Aside from the occasional coat of fresh paint, it remained unchanged and original. There was no place to sit, no place to linger over coffee, no place to stare into space and wonder who sat on the chaise in the music room.

Mother poured two mugs of coffee. I added cream to mine. And together we trudged to the family room.

I settled onto a chintz-covered loveseat. "How long has it been since the closet was cleaned?"

Mother sat across from me. "Before it turned cold."

"So four months."

"How often do you clean your hall closet?" She sounded defensive.

Had I ever cleaned my hall closet? Had Aggie ever cleaned my hall closet? "I'm not passing judgment on how often your closet gets cleaned. I'm trying to figure out how long that box was there."

Mother sniffed.

"Who do we know who's died recently?"

Mother snorted.

Find a few bodies and Mother never let you forget a single one. I rephrased my question. "Who do we know who's died who has a relative who might have brought their ashes to a party at your house?"

"I have no idea.

Neither did I. "What are you going to do?"

"You can take the box home."

"No."

She raised her brows and looked down her nose. "No?"

"I am not taking home an anonymous box of ashes. Besides, at some point, the person who left them will realize they forgot Great Aunt Sally or whoever it is and come back here to claim them."

"Well, what am I supposed to do with them?"

"They weren't hurting anyone in the hall closet."

Mother glared at me.

"Maybe Daddy knows who it is."

"Why would your father know that?"

My father and his cronies played cards at the club. Often. If their game lasted longer than the club's hours, they came here. "One of the men he plays cards with might have brought it."

"But why bring the box into my house?"

"Maybe he didn't want to leave it in the car."

Mother pondered that suggestion.

I sipped my burnt coffee. Mother desperately needed a Mr. Coffee in her life.

"Your father won't know." She pursed her lips and glared at the Hassam that hung above the fireplace. "He pays no attention to things like this."

"I bet if you tell him you found unidentified ashes in the hall closet, he'll pay attention."

"And then he'll tell everyone he knows."

"That's probably the best way to identify the ashes."

"No. Absolutely not. Ours will not be the family that finds bodies."

If the shoe fit...

Mother must have read something in my face because she drew herself up in righteous indignation. "It's bad enough that you trip over bodies the way most people trip over shoe laces, now I'm finding them."

"It's not as if you've become embroiled in a murder investigation. You found a box of ashes."

Mother's perfect posture sagged—just for a second. If I hadn't been looking I would have missed it. She really was bothered by her discovery.

"Aside from taking the box home, which I won't, what do you want me to do?"

"Ask Aggie to find out who it is. We can return the box quietly. No one need ever know."

"Of course she'll look into it." The "but" that followed

remained unspoken. It was one thing to find a box of ashes and ask your friends if they were missing a scion, it was quite another to use a private investigator (Aggie's former job) to identify a body. Everyone would find out. The story was simply too good.

"I can't imagine someone caring so little." She shook her head. "If you cremate me and stick my ashes in a closet, I'll haunt you."

If I failed to give Mother the funeral of the decade, she'd haunt me. "You don't need to worry about that."

She sniffed and sipped her burnt coffee.

The first committee member arrived at five minutes till three. Beverly Jenkins was an unlikely committee member. She'd married Arnie Jenkins over her parents' objections—they said he'd never amount to anything—and produced a son who she named after her grandfather.

Sadly, Beverly's parents were right about Arnie. He'd failed to amount to a hill of beans. But rather than divorce him, she donned a tight smile and resigned herself to the outskirts of the life she expected. The only reason she'd been asked to serve on the committee was because her grandfather (who was old as Methuselah) sat on the museum board.

I liked Beverly. What she lacked in funds she made up for in enthusiasm.

I waved at her through one of the glass panels that flanked the front door and called, "Aggie is Max closed up in the kitchen?" Max, the Weimaraner with plans for world domination, had a habit of burying his nose in crotches. Not everyone enjoyed the sensation.

"Yes." The answer floated down the hall.

I opened the door. "Welcome. Come in out of the cold."

"Am I the first one here?" Beverly asked.

"You are but I'm sure everyone else will arrive soon." I took her wool coat and hung it in the closet. "We'll be meeting in the living room. Help yourself to coffee and a cookie."

She lingered in the front hall. "You have such a lovely home."

"Thank you. How's Major?"

She smiled brightly. "Loving his first year of high school."

According to the grapevine, Beverly's parents were paying for their grandson to attend Suncrest.

"So glad to hear that. And Arnie?"

Her smiled flickered. "Fine. He's fine. Is that one of yours?" She pointed to a painting hanging above a bombe chest.

"No. It's a Cassatt." A gift from my husband on our first anniversary, when he still found the idea of a woman artist charming.

Ding dong.

I opened the door to a bevy of committee members.

They crowded into the foyer, handed over their minks, and kissed the air next to my cheek.

"Living room, girls. There's fresh coffee and Aggie baked cookies."

"Is there wine?" asked Martha Coleman.

"No, but there will be as soon as we're done." Business meetings and wine didn't mix. "Who are we missing?"

"Jinx," said Cyd Higgins.

"We'll start without her. Living room." I spread my arms wide as if I could successfully corral a group of chattering women.

To my great surprise, they moved. Probably lured by Aggie's cookies.

Plates and cups were filled and we took our seats.

Of all the committees for the gala I was chairing, the ambiance committee was the most challenging. I blamed Cyd, the committee chairman.

Even now, she was throwing wrenches into the works. "I still think we should have the servers dress up as geishas."

"It's a Chinese exhibit," I explained. Not for the first time.

"So?"

"Geishas are Japanese."

"No one will know the difference."

"The dignitaries from China might," said Beverly.

Cyd cast a sneer in Beverly's direction.

In a weak moment, I'd agreed to chair the gala associated with a Chinese exhibit at The Nelson-Atkins Museum. The exhibit was visiting only three cities—Kansas City, Washington, D.C., and San Francisco—and expectations for the grand opening gala were high.

Thus far we'd agreed on the colors in Kirkwood Hall—crimson, gold and oxidized copper. The flowers—roses, peonies, orchids, and lilies. And the tablecloths—red with overlays embroidered with dragons. But final decisions on everything else were due. The time for discussion had ended.

"The service staff will wear black pants and white shirts," I said.

There were murmurs of agreement.

"I think Foo dogs flanking the entrance would have the biggest impact." I waited for Cyd to disagree.

She didn't.

Ding dong.

A moment later, Jinx breezed into the living room and took a seat near the door.

I nodded a welcome.

She mouthed, "Sorry."

"What about kimonos?" said Cyd. No wonder she hadn't argued about the lions. She was still on the staff's attire. "The staff can wear kimonos."

"Japanese," said Beverly.

I forced a smile and sent it Cyd's way. "Black pants. White shirts."

Cyd crossed her arms. "We're missing an opportunity."

We were missing an opportunity to offend Chinese guests.

"Duly noted. Let's move on. Where are we with logistics?"

Transforming Kirkwood Hall into a room reminiscent of the Forbidden City was no small feat.

Anne Smith, as practical as her name, checked her notebook. "The florist arrives at..."

Anne had everything scheduled to the minute. I had no

worries on that front. While she spoke I looked around my living room.

The women who gathered round my coffee table were well-dressed. One or two even had a sense of style. They were well-spoken. They were well-coiffed. Their make-up was applied with restraint. The fashion magazines might proclaim glittery turquoise eye shadow as all the rage but such a shade would never defile their lids.

They spent their days completing good works.

They spent their evenings pouring cocktails and getting dinner on the table.

By all appearances, they had trouble-free lives.

Appearances were deceiving. Jinx was fresh out of rehab. Beverly was dependent on her family. Cyd—who knew what Cyd was hiding? Anne kept chaos at bay through sheer will and world-class organizational skills. And the others, Avery and Martha and Gloria, their bored smiles hid secrets. I was sure of it.

I used to have the appearance of a trouble free life. I was a successful artist, my husband a successful banker. Our daughter was lovely and smart and nearly perfect. We skied in Vail, went to the beach in Biarritz, and paid our club bill on time. Also, we barely spoke. Henry cheated on me far and wide. And my being an artist, which began as a charming hobby, became a thorn—a sharp thorn that pierced the delicate hide of Henry's pride—when I earned more money than he did.

Appearances fell by the wayside when I found Henry's current inamorata floating in the club pool. Since then, I'd lost interest in keeping up the façade of perfection.

Life was messy. And sometimes painful. And often chaotic. Nothing—not beautiful clothes, not organizational skills that would make a blue-chip CEO jealous, not Valium, not sex—could keep the chaos at bay.

"What do you think, Ellison?" Anne looked at me as if she expected an answer. Too bad I had no idea of the question.

"What do you think?" I replied.

"I think two hours will be enough."

"Go with that." I had complete faith in Anne's skills.

She gave me a curt nod. Not because she was curt (she was) but because even her movements were deliberate and organized. "That concludes my report."

All gazes landed on me. I cleared my throat. "Thank you all, for all your hard work. This event is going to be simply fabulous. Just so you know, we have a handful of major sponsor tables remaining. And, of course, there's still an opportunity to come in as a benefactor." I avoided looking at Beverly, focusing instead on Avery Gant whose husband, if he'd been so inclined, could have underwritten the whole exhibit. "Invitations will drop later this week. I can't wait for you to see them. As for entertainment, the evening will begin with Chinese music. After dinner, a troupe will perform a dragon dance."

"What are we having for dinner?" asked Gloria Kimbrough. Gloria kept chaos at bay with food.

"I am not allowed to say." The food committee needed to make some decisions. Pronto. "Rest assured it will be delicious mix of Chinese and American flavors." My gaze traveled the room, pausing on women who'd yet to commit to a ticket level. "The hosts for the benefactors' party are Millicent and Major Barcroft. They have a fabulous evening planned and I do hope you'll all be there." We needed another ten benefactor couples to meet our financial goal. "If no one has anything else?" I crossed my fingers in my lap. "We can open a bottle of—"

"I do," said Cyd.

Dammit.

"I just want to thank you, Ellison, for stepping in at the last minute." Was she being sincere or reminding everyone in the room that I had not been the first choice to chair the event? The first choice had been murdered. "You are doing a marvelous job leading us all."

Were she not still seething over no geishas, I might have believed her.

"That's so kind of you, Cyd. Thank you. But everyone in this room knows the truth. It's the committee members and—" I nodded at Cyd "—committee chairmen who bring everything together. This is your event and because of you, it will be a night to remember."

"Is it time for wine?" asked Martha.

Everyone laughed and whatever petty dislikes or dark currents that had flowed through the meeting were forgotten in full glasses of chilled Blue Nun.

THREE

"Bye, Mom." Grace deposited her dirty cereal bowl in the sink, dropped a kiss on my cheek, and headed for the back door.

"Dishwasher?"

With a dramatic sigh, she returned to the counter and moved the bowl from sink to dishwasher.

"Are you home for dinner?" I asked.

"Yeah." She buttoned her coat and disappeared into the cold.

"Love you," I called after her.

Max stood, stretched, yawned, and returned to his bed.

I sipped coffee and stared at the wall, deep in thought.

Aggie bustled into the kitchen and I shifted my attention from the wall to my housekeeper. She wore a cobalt blue kaftan edged with crimson pom-poms. Her red hair crackled with energy.

"Do you have a minute?" I asked.

"Of course."

"Mother has a problem." Those two words. Mother and problem. They were enough to send the bravest woman running.

But not Aggie. Aggie pulled out a stool and sat. "I figured something was wrong. No one calls that often without a big problem."

"Someone left a box of ashes in her hall closet."

The air around Aggie stilled. Even the bouncing pom-poms on her sleeves stilled. "You mean remains?"

"She'd like to find out who it is so she can return them to their family. Will you help? Please?" Given how far outside her job description chasing down remains fell, I held my breath.

"Of course."

Ding dong.

"Are you expecting anyone?" Aggie asked.

"No."

She stood. "I'll get it."

Max growled softly and rose from his favorite spot. Rather than follow Aggie down the hall, he came and sat next to me, leaning his head against my leg.

"What's wrong, boy?" I scratched behind his ear.

He didn't answer. Aggie did. From the doorway to the kitchen. "Detective Peters is here."

"Detective Peters?" The mere name brought on an unpleasant sick feeling in my gut. There it met another unpleasant feeling—one brought on by the sad fact that whatever brought Detective Peters to my house had not brought Detective Anarchy Jones. "What does he want?"

"No idea. He's waiting in the living room. Should I call Mr. Tafft?"

Mr. Tafft. Hunter Tafft. My lawyer. My friend. The man Mother had selected as my next husband (she was headed for disappointment).

"Let me find out what he wants first. Did you offer him coffee?"

"I did not."

"He probably wouldn't accept anyway." I rose from my stool, took a last sip from my cup, and walked the length of the front hall.

Max followed me.

I entered the living room and found Detective Peters studying a framed picture of me and Grace. He looked the same. Rumpled. Grouchy. Willing to arrest me if I sneezed. "Detective."

He put down the silver frame and looked at me with his usual expression—dislike tinged with distrust.

"What can I do for you?" I asked.

He patted his pockets, finally finding and removing a Polaroid photo. "Do you know this young woman?" He handed me the photo.

I looked down at a picture. "Her name is Leslie Smith. I met her yesterday. Why?"

"She's dead."

I sat. It was a good thing there was a couch behind me. I covered my mouth with my hand. Closed my eyes. Counted to ten. "Dead?"

"How did you know her?"

"I didn't." I shook my head. "Not really."

Detective Peters crossed his arms and tried to look intimidating. It worked.

Max growled and took up a defensive position near my left knee.

"You did know her. You just identified her."

"I didn't know her. I only met her yesterday."

"She had your name and address in her coat pocket."

"That was my coat. She had my name and address so she could return it."

"Why did she have your coat?"

"Because she was cold."

"Because she was cold? Are you in the habit of giving coats to strangers?"

"No."

"But you gave yours to Miss Smith?"

"I did."

"What was it about Miss Smith that made you hand over your coat?"

"She seemed...desperate." I looked down at my lap. "I don't think Smith was her real last name."

"You don't say?" Sarcasm positively dripped from his voice. Giant drips.

"I hit her."

"You hit her?"

"With my car."

Detective Peters stared at me with his pale blue eyes.

"It was an accident. She ran out between two parked cars." I sounded defensive. There was no reason to be defensive. I'd done nothing wrong. "I stopped the car. We talked. She said she was fine."

"You didn't report the accident?" Hanging judges sounded friendlier.

"She insisted she was fine. She got up. She danced a jig."

"And you gave her your coat?"

"I offered to take her home. When she refused to get in the car with me, I gave her my coat."

"Where was her coat?"

"I assume she forgot it at her boyfriend's house."

"Her boyfriend's?"

"She said she skipped school to spend the day with him but they had a fight and she ran out of the house without her coat."

"Do you know her boyfriend's name?"

"No."

"Do you know where he lives?"

"No."

"Which school?"

"I assumed a public one."

His lip curled. "She wasn't ritzy enough for a private one?"

"No. That's not it at all." Although her hair had been a little stringy. "I know all the kids that age at Suncrest and she wasn't wearing a uniform—" the Catholic high school girls wore plaid "—so I assumed public." It was my turn to ask a question. "What happened to her?"

"She was shot. Her body was found in an alley downtown."

"Downtown?" I cocked my head to the side. "I got the impression she was going home. What was she doing downtown?"

Detective Peters ignored my questions. "What time did you hit Miss Smith?"

"Around eleven."

"Where were you?"

"Prairie Village. Near 68th and Roe."

"What were you doing there?"

There was no way was I telling Detective Peters that I'd visited a psychic. He might interview said psychic. Madame Reyna might tell him about the One. His partner. Anarchy Jones. I shifted on the couch. "Why is that relevant?"

"I'll decide what's relevant."

And I'd decide what I'd tell him. I gave him my best, most polite smile. "Errands."

"What kinds of errands?"

None of his damned business errands. "I have nothing more to add."

"Perhaps you'd like to answer questions down at the station?"

What was it about Detective Peters that put my back up? I was easy to get along with. Ask anyone. Ask almost anyone. But there was something about Peters that put me on edge, that made me argumentative and prickly. "Do you have a warrant?"

Detective Peters scowled at me.

"I thought not. I'm not going to the station."

"There's a dead girl."

An unexpected wave of sadness filled my eyes with tears. "I'm truly sorry about that but I've told you everything I know."

"Where were you last night between six and ten?"

He couldn't possibly think—of course he could. Detective Peters always thought I was guilty.

"I was here."

"Can anyone corroborate?"

"Yes." I'd make him fight for every bit of information. On principle.

"Who?

"My friend Jinx stayed for dinner after a committee meeting. Her husband was out of town and she didn't want to be alone. He called at around ten to let her know he was home."

"How did he know she was at your house?"

"I assume she left a note."

"Why didn't she want to be alone?"

Because she was fresh out of rehab and the demons talked loudest when she was by herself. "How is that relevant to your investigation?"

Detective Peters scowled again. Deeper this time. With more feeling.

"Coffee?" Aggie stood in the doorway to the living room with a tray. Given that I hadn't heard her approaching, she'd probably been standing in the hallway for a while.

Detective Peters expanded his scowl to include her.

Aggie nodded politely, as if he were offering her a welcoming smile.

"Thank you, Aggie. Please put it on the coffee table."

Aggie deposited a tray filled with two mugs of coffee, cream, sugar, and some of the cookies left over from yesterday's committee meeting then retreated (probably not to the kitchen).

I helped myself to a mug of coffee and topped it with cream. "Please, Detective Peters, help yourself."

He eyed Aggie's cookies.

"They're homemade." Maybe they'd sweeten his disposition.

"I shouldn't."

"One won't hurt." Except no one could eat just one. They were addictive.

He selected a lemon cookie dusted with powdered sugar and took a small bite. A second later the cookie was gone except for the dusting of powdered sugar on his mustache. He reached for a second cookie—chocolate chip this time.

I thought about Leslie Smith. "I don't suppose you'd leave the Polaroid?"

His eyes narrowed. "Why?"

"I thought I'd ask Grace if she knew her."

"You said you figured her for a public school kid." He spoke around a mouthful of cookie.

"I did. I do. But Grace knows plenty of girls who go to public school." Desegregation had meant a massive flight from Missouri to Kansas. Yes, the taxes were higher but scads of people had moved across the state line to Kansas so their kids could attend the top-rated Shawnee Mission schools.

Detective Peters patted the pocket where he'd stashed the photo. "I'm not leaving it."

"I just thought—"

"Jones might tolerate your interfering in his cases. I won't. You fool with my case, I'll see you charged with obstruction of justice."

I flinched and touched my cheek as if he'd slapped me. "I was just trying to be helpful."

Detective Peters grunted.

I pulled the plate of cookies out of his reach. No I didn't. I wanted to.

When Detective Peters left, I hurried upstairs to my third floor studio and grabbed a sketch pad and mason jar full of colored pencils off the refectory table that stood in the center of the room. I settled into one of the cushy armchairs near the window and drew.

I didn't need Detective Peters' photo. I could draw Leslie's portrait.

The pencils skated across the paper. Clean lines. Pure color. Not just a drawing, but a way for me to handle grief. Heart-shaped face. Wide mouth. That poor girl. Hazel eyes. Dark hair. What a horrible place to die. Within thirty minutes I had a portrait that looked more like Leslie than the Polaroid.

I tore the sheet out of the pad and descended the stairs to the kitchen where Aggie sat at the counter making a list.

"Grocery list?" I asked. "I think we're running low on cream." The only thing worse that running out of cream would be running out coffee.

"No." She shook her sproingy curls. "It's a to-do list for identifying your mother's ashes." She looked at the paper in my hands. "Is that the dead girl?"

I nodded and handed over the picture of Leslie. "How much

did you hear?"

"Most of it." She studied the drawing. "Pretty girl."

"Yes."

"I wonder who killed her."

"Me, too." I glanced at Mr. Coffee. His pot was full as if he knew I'd need comforting. I poured myself a cup and added a jot of cream. "To be left in a downtown alley. It's tragic."

"No teenage boy did that." Her voice was hard-edged and sure.

"No."

"Detective Jones didn't come." Her voice was soft-edged and sympathetic.

"No." I took another sip of coffee and changed the subject. "What's on your list?"

"I thought I'd start with reading the obituaries."

"Mother hasn't cleaned that closet in four months. That's a lot of obituaries."

"I'll have to go downtown and use the library."

"Do you want some help?" Reading four months' worth of obituaries seemed a daunting and depressing task. "Two sets of eyes are better than one."

We left Leslie's picture on the kitchen counter, bundled up, and drove downtown.

The library lot was half-empty and I parked near the building. Even so close, the short walk to the door included blowing trash and smells I didn't care to identify.

We paused just inside the door. "Brrr."

My voice was too loud for a library. A bespectacled librarian wearing a sour-pickle expression looked up from her desk and glowered at me.

We walked toward her and I realized I was wearing noisy boots. Each hit of my heel against the floor sounded like a hammer.

"Excuse me," said Aggie. "We need to review microfilm of obituaries."

The librarian's mouth twisted as if she didn't approve of talking—or obits. "Second floor."

The heels of my boots sounded like gunshots on the granite stairs that led to the second floor. I ascended the last ten steps on my tiptoes.

Aggie marched up to a second librarian—one who made the woman downstairs look like a congeniality winner in a beauty contest. The librarian on the second floor looked like the woman in American Gothic by Grant Wood: close-set eyes, marionette lines that dragged the corners of her lips into a frown, and a long, thin neck. The expression in those close-set eyes could have scared General Westmoreland into immediate surrender. I made a silent vow not to utter a single word.

"We'd like to look at microfilm for obituaries for the past four months," Aggie whispered.

"Is there a specific obituary?" The librarian's rusty voice had a martyred quality. "Do you have a date?"

"No," said Aggie. "We're just browsing."

Barely-there brows rose. Browsing obituaries? Then, with a scowl that might have given even Mother pause, the librarian pointed us in the right direction.

Aggie threaded my film and showed me how to move the viewer forward and backward and how to make the print bigger.

"Look for members of country clubs, garden clubs, the Junior League, Society of Fellows members, and people who attended church at—"

"Shhh!" The furious sound came from the terrifying librarian at the desk. I couldn't see her or her furious scowl but I was certain it was firmly fixed on her furious face.

I sealed my lips, wrote the names of two Episcopal and two Presbyterian churches on a slip of paper I found in my purse, and handed it to Aggie.

The first half-hour was passably entertaining. I figured out how to control speed and type size. But after the mechanics were mastered, I was left with scanning back issues of the newspaper for people who'd died.

The ashes who used to be a person did not appear in the first reel. Nor the second. Nor the third.

By the fourth reel, the words ran together in a sepia soup. There! Patrick Conover. He'd belonged to a country club. Not our country club, but a country club. Apparently he'd been a scratch golfer. He'd attended Princeton and started his own law firm specializing in real estate and contracts. He was survived by his adoring wife of thirty years, Susan, two grown children, a grandchild, and his mother, Gertrude Conover. Dollars to donuts Mother knew Gertrude. Was it him? I read on. Patrick Conover had attended one of the churches I'd written down for Aggie. His funeral service was held there with an interment immediately following. An interment. Patrick Conover was not the man in Mother's closet.

I paused. I should have heard about Patrick Conover's death. A tidbit over the bridge table. A quick rumor over cocktails. I hadn't. I checked the date. October. Last October I'd been more concerned with dead clowns than dead lawyers. I made a mental note to find out his story and spooled on.

Betty Daniels had belonged to the right country club, the right garden club, and the Junior League but she was buried at Forest Hills Cemetery.

Evan Holmes was one of Daddy's cronies. He dropped dead on a golf course in Palm Desert. Of his death, Daddy had said something along the lines of, "We should all be so lucky." There had been a memorial service followed by a reception at the club. Had Evan Holmes somehow ended up in Mother's front closet? I dug in my purse, found a small notepad, and wrote his name down as a possibility.

I kept going. Kept spooling. The smell of hot film and the gentle whir of the machines didn't help my focus. Quite the opposite. Keeping my eyes open was a struggle. And my vision was getting worse. The edges of the film looked black.

I lifted my head and blinked. Three times. Then I returned my gaze to Myra Ollinger's obit. A member at one of the right clubs. A member at one of the right churches. No mention of an interment. I jotted down her name.

"You're on fire," Aggie whispered.

My list was longer than hers.

"Fire," she repeated.

I glanced her way. "Pardon me?"

"You're on fire!" Now her voice was almost loud enough to attract the librarian.

And she didn't mean my growing list of names. She meant fire. Smoke wafted up from my machine. A cigarette-break's worth. An oh-dear-Lord-I've-melted-the-reel's worth.

I waved my hands as if their flapping might cool the overheated celluloid. "Fire!"

"Shhh!" The librarian's shushing traveled the stacks.

"No," I called, louder this time. "Fire!" I turned off the machine but the smoke still rose. Acrid and unwelcome.

The librarian arrived silently and quickly and out of nowhere. Elizabeth-Montgomery-wiggling-her-nose out of nowhere. "What have you done?" she sounded massively put out—using the same tone Mother did whenever I found a body.

"I don't know what I did."

She looked over the rims of her glasses and the corner of her lip curled into a sneer.

"I'm so sorry," I murmured.

Her long, narrow face tightened and she crossed narrow arms over her narrow chest. "Didn't you smell the film getting hot?"

"Yes. But I had no idea it would spontaneously combust."

A few library patrons looked our way then quickly averted their gazes. The librarian with steam rising from her ears was that scary.

"If melting the reel is a possibility, there ought to be a warning of some kind." Aggie made an excellent point.

The librarian paled. Her cheeks went white. Her lips went white. The knuckles on her hands went white. I'd seen corpses with better color. "A five-year-old could use these machines without mishap."

"Why would a five-year-old want to use this machine? Can five-year-olds read?" Legitimate questions. Questions best left unspoken. Especially to an indignant librarian who stood a good foot taller than me in her stocking feet.

"Move," the librarian said, her voice an irate whisper.

I pushed away from the machine and the librarian stepped forward and removed the reel.

"It will have to be spliced." She shook the damaged film in my general direction.

"I am sorry."

"Shhh!"

She got to talk about five-year-old savants spooling through reels and I didn't get to apologize? "It was an accident. You can't think I came in here intending to melt the film."

"Shhh!"

"If you spent less time shushing and more time showing people how to properly use the machinery this wouldn't happen."

Which is how I got kicked out of the public library. Mother must never know.

FOUR

The next morning, Aggie returned to the library without me. I lounged on the family room couch with my feet on the coffee table. I sipped coffee, half-reviewed Anne Smith's logistics report, and half-watched *The Today Show*. Barbara Walters ought not wear beige against the beige background of the set. It washed her out terribly.

"Ellison?" Mother's voice carried from somewhere in my house.

Oh dear Lord. What necessitated a trip to my house? Mother usually called.

Max whined softly.

"Some guard dog, you are," I whispered before I sat up straight, put my feet on the floor, and called, "In here!"

A few seconds later, Mother appeared. She'd fully recovered from finding the ashes in her closet. Her hair was its usual perfect helmet and she wore her favorite pearl pin on the collar of a navy wool dress. A mink coat was folded over her arm.

"You look nice." More polite than *what are you doing here?* I stood. "Would you like some coffee?"

"Please."

I led her into the kitchen, poured her a cup of Mr. Coffee's perfect brew, and refilled my own cup. "Cream?

"How fresh is it?"

"Aggie bought it yesterday morning," I lied.

With a regal nod, she assented to the addition of cream to her coffee. "Where is Aggie?"

"At the library, looking at obituaries."

Mother looked less pleased with this news than she should

have. "Why?"

"To see if she can identify the ashes."

"I can tell you who's died."

"Suppose you don't know the person in the closet?"

"You mean a stranger? In my house?" She sounded horrified.

"Maybe. Or it could be Evan Holmes."

Mother tilted her head as if I'd given her something new to consider.

"Perhaps it's Myra Ollinger."

Mother's expression clouded. "I certainly hope not. I never liked her. I'd hate to think she's was freeloading at my house."

"Freeloading?" If it was Myra, she'd hardly been taking advantage of the meal plan.

"Taking up valuable shelf space."

"Ah."

"Don't be smart, Ellison. It doesn't suit you."

I wiped all expression off my face. "Aggie may come home with some additional possibilities."

Mother sniffed. The sniff said quite clearly that she hoped for better options than Myra Ollinger.

"I have a question for you."

Mother took a small sip of coffee. "Oh?"

"How did Patrick Conover die?"

She muttered something into her coffee mug. Mother never muttered.

"Pardon me?

She looked up and her eyes narrowed, daring me to argue. "I said there's one body you didn't find."

"What? He was murdered?"

"Patrick Conover was shot. You were so busy interfering in the Harney murder investigation, you missed it."

"Who killed him?"

"The murderer was never caught." Her eyes narrowed to slits. "Don't be getting any ideas about investigating. Patrick Conover's death is none of your business."

"Agreed."

There was a time when I capitulated to all of Mother's demands. That time had passed and she'd become accustomed to arguments. She looked almost surprised that I'd agreed without a single objection.

"What's on your agenda for the day?" Mother eyed my jeans and turtleneck with distaste. Mother did not own a pair of jeans.

"I'm reviewing all the committee reports for the grand opening."

She gifted me a small smile. Chairing grand opening galas was on her list of approved activities. "You inherited quite a committee."

Because I'd come late to the game, the committee chairmen had already been in place. "They're trying hard. Except for Joyce Petteway. If that woman doesn't make a decision about the food soon, we may be eating Chinese take-out."

Mother rubbed her chin. This was her milieu—difficult committee members and the need to create an event so memorable that people talked about it for years. "You decide the menu and tell her what it is."

"I don't want to step on toes."

"Joyce will dither until she's given you gray hair. That woman can't make a decision to save her life. If you don't choose something, we'll be eating egg rolls."

I nodded. "I'll call the caterer and have him send over the proposed menus."

Mother looked properly gratified. I'd agreed with her twice in one morning.

"Where are you off to today?" I asked.

"Bridge." She put her coffee cup down on the counter and looked at her watch. "I ought to be going."

That was it? She hadn't driven out of her way just to ask about ashes. She could have called for that. Mother's unannounced trips to my house usually meant the sky was falling. "Is everything all right?"

"Fine," she said quickly. "Everything is fine. Aside from the ashes, I mean."

I didn't believe her. "You're sure?"

"Of course I'm sure," she snapped. "Everything is fine. I have to go." With that she swung her coat around her shoulders and marched down the front hall. A few seconds later I heard the front door open and close.

I looked over at Mr. Coffee. He sat on the counter—reliable, dependable, perfect in every way. He had no comment on Mother's strange behavior.

"Whatever it is," I told him, "everything is not fine."

Brnnng, brnnng.

Aggie was at the library and Grace was at school. That left me to answer the phone. "Hello."

"Ellison! You know that favor you owe me?"

Did I owe Libba a favor? "What do you want?"

"Are you free on Friday night?"

I didn't need Madame Reyna to see where this was going. "No."

"Of course, you are."

"I just said I wasn't."

"You only said that because you're worried I'm asking you to join Bill and me on a double date." Bill was the latest man in Libba's life. On the surface, he seemed almost perfect. A transplant from Charleston, South Carolina, he had courtly manners, gainful employment, and no wife. But Libba's track record with picking men suggested there was a problem—a big one—somewhere.

"So you're not calling to ask me on a double date?"

"What if I am? You're not seeing anyone. You need to get out there."

"I have plans."

"*The Rockford Files* and *Police Story* don't count as plans, Ellison."

As if I'd watch *Police Story*. I needed no reminders of Anarchy Jones. "You're wrong."

"Fine. You're watching the ABC Friday night movie. Sitting in front of a television is not the same thing as having plans."

"Bad things happen when we double date."

"You're exaggerating."

I wasn't.

"Bill's friend will be staying in the Presidential Suite at the Alameda. He's invited us up for drinks then dinner at the rooftop restaurant."

It sounded safe enough, but I knew better. "No."

"Don't say no. Think about it and call me later."

"Hmph."

"Also, Madame Reyna called me. I know you think she's a terrible fraud but she insists someone named Leslie wants to talk to you."

There's a ride at Worlds of Fun, the local amusement park, called the Finnish Fling. One stepped inside a barrel and the barrel spun. Spun so fast that when the floor dropped, the riders stayed plastered to the wall. I rode it one time. Grace insisted. My stomach dropped with the floor and the sensation of being out of step with time and space and gravity left me ill for hours. I felt that way now. "She what?"

"I know, I know. I'm sorry I dragged you over there. I told her you didn't know anyone named Leslie." Libba paused. "You don't, do you?"

I opened and closed my mouth but no words came out. No breath came out. There was a strange buzzing in my head—like a swarm of bees only louder.

Ding dong.

I managed a breath. "Libba, someone's at the door. I'll have to call you back."

"Promise me you'll think about Friday night?"

"I promise." Anything to get her off the phone. I waited for the buzzing to subside then made my way to the front door with Max at my heels.

Ding dong.

Sheesh. "Coming," I called.

I opened the door and found Detective Anarchy Jones on the other side.

The sudden drop of my stomach made my experience on the Finnish Fling feel like a cakewalk. I stood there, gaping, silent, stunned.

Max, the traitor, pushed past me and rubbed his head against Anarchy's corduroy pants.

I didn't move.

"May I come in?" Anarchy asked.

Still mute, I stepped away from the door, allowing him into my home. I took a deep breath and my stomach returned to the general area of my midriff where it fluttered with nerves. I closed the door behind him.

We stood in the foyer. Saying nothing. Looking at anything but each other. I cheated a peek and saw his gaze fixed on the painting hung above the bombe chest. I quickly (before-I-was-caught quickly) returned my gaze to the Oriental beneath my feet. Was that medallion a true Wedgwood blue or was there too much cobalt? Careful study was required.

Anarchy cleared his throat. "I'm here about the girl." He sounded cop-like. Professional.

Of course he did. It wasn't as if the problem between us would simply disappear. Especially when we hadn't spoken in months.

"We identified her," he continued.

"Oh?" One word—all I could manage.

"Her name wasn't Leslie Smith."

I looked up from the carpet and sought his face.

"Her name was Leesa Lisowski."

"Lisowski?"

The corner of his mouth quirked for a half-second—no more—then his lips settled back into that unforgiving hard line. "Lisowski. I'd like to hear exactly what you told Detective Peters."

Looking at the distant expression on Anarchy's lean face—all harsh planes and remote valleys—and the coldness in his eyes cured the flutters in my stomach. Instead of fluttering, the flutters drooped in a dejected, hang-dog manner. "Let's sit in the kitchen." At least there, I'd be close to Mr. Coffee.

Anarchy followed me into the kitchen.

Max followed Anarchy.

And Max's stubby tail wagged ten miles a minute. As if he'd missed Anarchy. As if he was happy to see him. As if now was a chance to set things right.

"Coffee?" I asked.

"No, thank you."

I poured myself the biggest cup I could find, added cream, sat on one of the stools at the island, and told him everything I'd told Detective Peters.

"Was Leesa on drugs when you saw her?" he asked.

Drugs? I closed my eyes and thought. For the life of me, I couldn't remember if her pupils had been tiny pinpricks or dilated or normal. "I didn't notice anything off." I stared into my coffee mug. My problems suddenly seemed much smaller. "Have you found her family?" Her poor parents. What they must be going through.

"She was a runaway from Chicago."

"Chicago? What was she doing in Kansas City?"

Anarchy glanced at Mr. Coffee. "I've changed my mind. May I have a cup?"

I took a mug out of the cupboard and filled it. "Black?"

He nodded. "Thanks."

I handed him the mug and our fingers brushed against each other. Electricity jolted through me. I know he felt it too because he jerked backward. Away. From me. Sloshed coffee on the counter.

"I'll get a towel." I turned my back on him and wiped away an unexpected and unwelcome tear.

"Ellison—" his voice sounded less cop-like. More human.

I couldn't do this. Could not. If Anarchy, the man not the cop, walked out the door again, I might break. I yanked an unsuspecting tea towel off the oven handle and mopped up the small puddle of coffee without looking at him. "What was she doing in Kansas City?"

For a moment I didn't think he'd answer.

"She worked as a prostitute. We identified her from the prints we have on file.

A prostitute? My mind rejected the idea. I dared a glance his way. "That can't be right. She was too young."

He was back in cop-mode. The thin line of his lips hardened.

"How does that happen? How does a child end up working the streets?"

His gaze shifted away from me. "The usual way."

"I'm not familiar with the usual way."

"You don't want to be familiar." His voice sounded bleak.

"I do."

Somehow, the thin line of his lips thinned even more.

"I want to know," I insisted.

"Think about a girl with an unhappy home-life. For whatever reason, she feels isolated or alone. Along comes a man who says he cares about her. The life he tells her about is happy and filled with love. She goes with him and she's caught. Or perhaps things are so bad at home, she runs away. She's alone and she meets a man who says he'll take care of her." He glanced down at the floor. "In cities like New York and Los Angeles, men hang out at bus stops, waiting for runaways."

I waited for more.

"The girl has no one but him. He gives her drugs and liquor and the illusion that someone cares. Then he puts her to work."

"Why doesn't she leave? Run away?"

"Usually, she's hooked on drugs. And if she's not, she's been told her family will be hurt if she runs."

"So the girls are prisoners?" I'd never heard anything so awful. "That's what happened to Leslie—Leesa? Exactly how old was she?"

"Fifteen."

I closed my eyes. The coffee in my stomach churned. Fifteen. A year younger than Grace. That child had been in terrible trouble and I'd failed to guess. Failed to help. I lowered my head to my hands. "Leesa wasn't visiting her boyfriend."

"No." Anarchy sounded almost sympathetic.

"A client?"

"Most likely. He did something that scared her and she ran."

"And I hit her." Hit her and failed her.

The weight of Anarchy's hand rested on my shoulder. "You gave her the coat off your back."

"I should have insisted on taking her home."

"Leesa didn't have a home. Not in the way you understand the word. She'd been on the streets for two years."

Two years. Since she was thirteen. Tears leaked through the trap of my eyelids. "I could have helped."

"No."

I lifted my head. Opened my eyes. "If I can't help, who can?"

"These are dangerous people."

I shrugged.

"The girls—" he looked away from me. Shifted his gaze to Mr. Coffee. "They need more than a warm meal and a cup of coffee.

In my experience, there are few situations not improved by the addition of a perfectly brewed cup of coffee. "So what happens to them? They're written off?"

He removed his hand. "There are programs."

I turned and looked at him. "Programs?" The word had a ladies-doing-good sound to it. But in Kansas City, ladies supported the arts and the children's hospital. They joined the Junior League. They gave tours at the museum. They hosted garden tours and teas and galas to raise money for worthy causes. Programs for child prostitutes never crossed their minds.

"I can get you some information."

"Please do."

Max nudged Anarchy with his nose.

"What does he want?"

"He wants you to scratch behind his ears."

Max nudged again.

"He won't stop till you do what he wants."

Anarchy crouched on the floor and used both hands to scratch behind the gray silk of Max's ears. "Will you take me to exactly where you hit her?"

"Of course. Now?"

"Please."

Max groaned and leaned his head into Anarchy's right hand.

"I'll get my coat." The words stopped me. The coat I'd normally wear over jeans I'd given to Leslie—Leesa—and she'd died wearing it.

Anarchy gave Max a final scratch and stood. "Not everyone would do this."

"Do what?"

"Help with the investigation of a prostitute's death."

"Don't call her that." My voice was sharp. "She was a girl. A child. I have no idea what awful choices landed her in the mess she was in, but she didn't deserve the life she had." I paused for breath. "Or the death."

"I've missed you." Anarchy's words were so out of context I wasn't sure I'd heard him right. I stared at him. My jaw might have dropped. Just a little.

He looked the same. Same coffee-brown eyes—now with a hint of warmth in their depths. Same lips—no longer pressed into a thin line.

Warmth trickled from my head to my toes. Oh dear Lord. What kind of person was I? Not a good one. No good person could be so easily distracted by a thaw in Anarchy's chilliness.

He stepped closer to me. Close enough for the scent of his aftershave to tickle my nose.

"You care about people." He brushed my cheek with the back of his hand. Barely. Just enough to send every nerve ending in my body into a tizzy. "I care about right and wrong. The law. You care about people."

Max yawned. We were boring him.

"I—I missed you, too." There. I'd said it. Admitted it. To him.

To myself.

The air was charged with possibility—with magic. I rested my fingers against his chest. Was his heart thudding as hard as mine?

Brnng, brnng.

"You could ignore it," Anarchy suggested, his voice suddenly rough.

I could. I wanted to. But there was something extra shrill, extra insistent about the phone's ring.

Brnng, brnng.

Dammit.

I stepped away from Anarchy and picked up the receiver. "Hello."

"Ellison." Mother did not sound pleased. "What is that detective doing at your house?"

FIVE

Anarchy and I agreed he'd drive me back to Prairie Village, to the exact spot where I'd hit Leesa.

Max watched me don a fox jacket with disapproval in his amber eyes. In his opinion, Anarchy and I remaining in the kitchen and feeding him treats was the best course of action. Failing that, we could take him for a walk.

"Sorry, buddy," I told my dog. "I'll be home soon."

His ears drooped, the very picture of dejection.

Anarchy, unaccustomed to Max's tricks, opened the front door.

Max slipped through the opening and stood in the driveway laughing at us. Ha! said his doggy smile. Just try and catch me.

I might—might—have been able to lure him inside with the promise of a dog biscuit, that or a turkey club sandwich with extra bacon, but Max spotted a squirrel.

Sadly, the squirrel did not spot Max.

Max's jaws missed the squirrel's tail by less than a quarter of an inch.

The panicked animal ran and Max followed.

"Max!"

Max ignored me.

The squirrel cut across my yard and ran into my neighbor's lawn. My evil neighbor's lawn. Margaret Hamilton was a witch of the flew-a-broomstick-at-midnight, stirred-a-cauldron, had-warts-on-her-chin (not really) variety. And she did not like my dog.

"Max!"

Intent on the chase, he didn't even turn his head.

And the squirrel? Why was it ignoring a perfectly good oak tree?

It was unfortunate (but not surprising) that Margaret chose that moment to step outside. She possessed some kind of witchy internal radar that alerted her when any member of my household so much as touched a blade of her grass.

It was even more unfortunate that, having made the decision to scowl at me from her front steps, she didn't close her door behind her.

Most unfortunate of all was the squirrel dashing between her legs and into her house.

No. That's wrong. MOST unfortunate was the fact that my dog followed the squirrel—through Margaret's legs and into her home.

Margaret was in no position to chase him. Max had knocked her flat. Her heels were above her shoulders, her skirt gathered in folds around her waist, and her black girdle was on display for the whole neighborhood

"Oh dear Lord." I took off running.

Anarchy easily passed me.

He reached Margaret first and picked her up off her stoop.

From inside the house came the sound of glass shattering.

"Get. Your. Dog." If looks could kill, I'd have been dead.

I dashed into Margaret's home. "Max!"

If I'd given Margaret Hamilton's decorating style any thought, I'd have imagined something dark and foreboding with dried henbane hanging from exposed rafters, a giant iron pot filled with a foul smelling, acid green potion on the hearth, and a scarred table that held twisted roots, chicken bones, and a mortar and pestle ready to grind hemlock or snakeroot. The reality was grass cloth on the walls and a Kelly green shag carpet. The reality in the living room was circular floral couches that matched the rug and a glass coffee table the size of a small swimming pool. The more pressing reality was a squirrel re-enacting Custer's last stand behind a potted palm.

Potting soil flew across the raked green of Margaret's carpet and palm fronds fell to the floor like fallen soldiers.

"Max!"

Max turned and looked at me. Why was I interrupting the most fun he'd had in months?

The squirrel, sensing an opportunity for escape, made a break for the kitchen.

Max ran after the squirrel.

I ran after Max.

Margaret's kitchen had zinnia-red cabinets and foil wallpaper. I blinked, startled by all that shiny crimson, and my steps faltered.

The squirrel's did not. The damn beast scaled the counter then a cabinet and took shelter behind a stack of plates.

Max rested one front paw on the counter and stood on his hind legs. He swiped at the squirrel with his free paw. Swiped and missed. Missed the squirrel but caught a plate. The plate flew out of the cupboard and crashed to the floor.

I stared at the shards, my mouth hanging open. Franciscan desert rose? Not stoneware decorated with skulls and crossbones?

A second swipe. This one with more effort.

A second plate saucered out of the cabinet like a demented, rose-painted UFO.

Crash!

For the love of Pete, why hadn't Margaret closed her cabinet doors?

The homeowner stood beside me, presumably too angry to speak. Her lips moved without producing words.

"Max! Stop that!"

A third plate.

A third crash.

I lunged forward, grabbed Max's collar, and hauled him away from the cabinet.

He stepped on a piece of broken china and yelped.

The squirrel chittered.

Margaret planned the horrific hex she was going to cast upon me.

And Anarchy stood in the doorway looking as if he was trying very hard not to laugh.

Max pulled against my hold. There was still a squirrel to catch.

"Bad dog!"

The bad dog rolled his eyes.

With an enormous yank, I pulled him farther away from the squirrel and the further destruction of Margaret's everyday china.

Max tugged against me.

Anarchy pulled off his belt, looped it through Max's collar, and said, "Why don't I take this guy home?"

"Good idea." Bad idea! He was going to leave me alone with Margaret Hamilton and the squirrel Max had chased into her house? I'd never make it out alive. "Will you come back and help us deal with the squirrel?"

His lips quirked. "Close all the doors to the kitchen and open the back door." He nodded toward a Dutch door that opened onto a porte cochère and Margaret's driveway. "The squirrel will leave on its own."

He made it sound easy.

"Get that animal—" Margaret pointed at Max "—out of my house." Margaret had found her voice.

"Right away, ma'am." Anarchy pulled on the make-shift leash.

Margaret's expression softened. Anarchy is that hard to resist. Then she looked at me. Up until that moment I thought Mother had the best, most terrifying death glare in the world. In that moment, I discovered I'd been wrong.

Margaret's face was stark white. So white, her brows looked more like dark slashes than brows. The space between them was scrunched together in seething wrinkles and her lips were pursed, ready to croak the words that would turn me into a frog or make my hair fall out.

I swallowed. "Mrs. Hamilton—" Margaret and I were not on a first-name basis "—I am so sorry about this. I will pay for all the damages."

"I should have you arrested!"

Anarchy paused in his attempt to drag an unwilling Max out of the kitchen. "On what grounds?"

"Trespassing." She practically spat the word.

"Arguably, you invited her in when you told her to get her dog."

Margaret turned her death glare on Anarchy. "I'll call the pound."

"They might give her a ticket for allowing her dog out without a leash but I'll explain that Max's escape was my fault."

Margaret vibrated like a tuning fork. If she'd been a cartoon, steam would have blown from her ears.

"Get out." She lifted her arm and pointed toward the front door. With her black dress, black shoes, black tights, and black hair (too dark for a woman of her age) she looked like the grim reaper. "Get out now. Both of you."

I'd never seen anyone so angry. She was hexing me for sure.

We dragged Max home, locked him in the laundry room, and collapsed onto the kitchen stools. I collapsed. Anarchy merely sat.

"Are you up for that trip to Prairie Village?"

I'd forgotten all about our trip to the spot where I'd hit Leesa. "Let me check on Max's paw first."

I peeked into the laundry room where Max looked as bright-eyed and bushy-tailed as a squirrel. "How's your paw?"

He grinned at me.

I crouched on the floor next to him and examined his paw. A small cut marred the black pad. "Do you need to go to the vet?"

Max yawned.

"I'll take that as a no. And, don't forget, you're in big trouble, mister."

He yawned again.

Leaving the hound from hell in the laundry room, Anarchy and I walked back into the cold and climbed into his car.

We drove in silence.

I stared out the window at the sky. It was that pale shade of blue that only occurred in winter. A blue that said the weather was too cold for color and too lazy to snow. "This block."

Anarchy braked and the car slowed.

Barren oak trees stood as sentinels for the modest, well-tended ranch homes lining the street.

"I was heading the other direction."

"Oh?"

"We probably ought to turn around." I tended to see things in terms of where a tree was or the angle of an overhead line.

Anarchy drove to the end of the block, pulled into a driveway, then reversed out of it. "What were you doing over here?"

"Meeting Libba." That was all the explanation he was getting.

He looked curious but all he said was, "Ah."

"There." I pointed to the exact spot. "I remember that oak branch hanging over the street."

"And Leesa was crossing from the south?"

"Yes."

"How cold did she seem?"

"Pardon me?"

"How long do you think she'd been outside?"

"Her lips weren't blue."

"Do you think she ran out of one of these houses?"

My gaze traveled from house to house. One was painted buttercup yellow with hunter-green shutters, a second was a soft gray with a cheerful red door, a white house sported ornate concrete planters that spilled dark green ivy onto the front walk. They all looked warm and inviting. Homes for young families to start their lives. A neighborhood where kids learned to ride their bikes on the sidewalk on a summer afternoon and the Good Humor man was swamped every time he drove by. A neighborhood where people greeted each other and waved as they fetched the paper. A neighborhood where a man had hired a teenage prostitute then scared her so badly she ran away. Which house? "I have no idea."

He pulled in next to the curb. "Do you mind if I ask a few questions?"

Here?

He put the car in park. "I'll leave the heat on for you."

He didn't have questions for me. He meant to leave me in the car like some disruptive child? That was not going to happen. "I'm coming with you."

"Ellison, this is a police investigation."

"I won't say a word. I won't interfere. I'm not staying in the car."

His gaze traveled from my face to the buttercup house where a wood-paneled Country Squire sat in the drive. The skin near his left eye twitched.

"I promise. Not a word." I donned my best pleading face.

He sighed—a deep sigh, as if he was doing something he knew he'd regret. "I'm holding you to that."

We got out of the car and tromped up the front walk.

I glanced through the front window. Baby toys littered the living room carpet.

Anarchy lifted his finger as if he meant to ring the doorbell.

"Don—"

Too late. He'd pressed the button.

Nothing happened.

He pressed the button again and leaned toward the door as if listening for the bell.

"You'll have to knock," I said. "Quietly."

He gave me a questioning glance.

"Whoever lives here had the doorbell disconnected."

He raised a brow. "How do you know?"

I pointed at the toys on the living room carpet—they were multiplying like rabbits. "The doorbell would wake the children up from their naps."

When Grace was little, naps were a battleground. If I won, if she slept, I did a little happy dance. Anyone who rang the bell when she was actually asleep got an earful. After visits from everyone from a Girl Scout to the Fuller Brush man, I disengaged the doorbell. It had seemed the easiest answer.

Anarchy knocked.

A moment later, a young woman with a baby on her hip and a toddler wrapped around her leg like a monkey opened the door. She wore faded jeans, a wrinkled peasant top and a shapeless gray cardigan. Her hair was scraped back in a messy ponytail and her face was free of makeup. "Yes?"

Anarchy pulled out his badge. "I'm Detective Jones, I was wondering if we could ask you a few questions."

"About what?" she asked.

From behind her leg, the toddler peered up at us.

"May we come in?"

The woman stepped away from the door, allowing us entry. She led us into the living room. "I'm sorry it's such a mess."

"You've got your hands full." I offered her a sympathetic smile. "I'm glad we didn't disturb naptime."

Anarchy shot me a look. I was not supposed to speak.

"Please." She waved at the sofa. "Have a seat."

The baby gurgled, the toddler loosened his grip, and their mother collapsed into a chair. "What can I help you with, detectives?" She sounded as tired as her clothes.

Detectives? Plural?

As instructed, I kept my mouth closed.

"What's your name?" Anarchy twinkled at the woman. The smile. The eyes. The look.

The poor woman was too tired to respond but my heart skipped a beat for her. And the toddler, a little girl, gave Anarchy a shy smile.

"Shannon," the woman said. "Shannon Cooper. This—" she smoothed the toddler's hair "—is Avery. And this—" she dropped a small kiss on the baby's head "—is Simon."

Avery regarded us with eyes the size of Frisbees.

Simon gurgled.

Anarchy pulled the Polaroid from his jacket pocket. "Have you seen this girl?"

Shannon studied Leesa's face. "Does she babysit?"

"Not that I'm aware of."

"Then, no."

Anarchy crossed his left ankle over his right knee and leaned forward. "Can you tell me a little bit about the neighborhood? Who's home during the day?"

Shannon sat a bit straighter. "What's wrong?"

"The girl was involved in accident. We're looking for witnesses."

Shannon's back relaxed. "There are a handful of us who stay home with kids. Abby Harris, who lives just to the left, stays home with twins. Sandra Moore, to the right, is at home with a new baby."

"What about other people on the block?" Anarchy asked. For some reason, unknown to me, he seemed reluctant to ask about men who were home on weekdays.

Shannon didn't answer. She was busy extracting a strand of her hair from Simon's little fist.

"Mommy, I'm hungry," declared Avery. "I want a sammich."

We were losing our audience.

"Are their any widows on the block?" I asked.

Anarchy shot me a you-promised-to-keep-your-mouth-shut scowl.

"Mrs. Gillespie. Across the street and down three. She lives in the pistachio colored house with the elm tree in the front yard.

"We won't take any more of your time." I stood.

Shannon saw us to the door.

"What was that?" Anarchy asked when the door closed behind us.

"That woman has two children in diapers. She's barely keeping her head above water." Surely he'd noticed the gray circles beneath her eyes? "If you want to know what's happening on this block, talk to someone who has time to look out the window." I pointed to a light green house with cream trim. "Mrs. Gillespie."

Anarchy walked toward the car.

"Where are you going?" I asked.

"I'm taking you home."

"Because I took pity on that poor woman?"

Anarchy pressed his lips together and opened my car door.

"You're angry."

"No." The look on his face said different.

Whatever had happened in my kitchen—that moment when we'd both softened—was too new, too delicate, too easily trampled for me to start an argument.

"Please," he said. "Get in the car."

I got in the car.

He closed my door and circled to his own, but rather than get in, he stood in the street and practiced deep breathing techniques.

I waited, pulling my coat more closely around me.

Finally, he opened the door and sat behind the wheel. He put the key in the ignition and turned on the engine but did not shift the car into drive.

We sat there.

Silent.

"I'm sorry. I promised I wouldn't say a word then I did. I don't blame you for being angry."

"I'm not angry." He sounded angry and his fingers tightened around the steering wheel even though the car remained in park. "You cannot involve yourself in this investigation."

"I won't. That poor girl had a terrible death and a worse life but I didn't know her. It's not like I'm going to hear gossip over the bridge table. It's not like some man is going to show up at my house to stop me from asking questions. I don't know the questions. And if I did, I'd have no idea who to ask."

Anarchy's face was like thunder.

"And I wouldn't ask those questions anyway. Because I'm not getting involved in your investigation."

He loosened his grip on the wheel and turned toward me. "The world is a brighter place with you in it. I don't want you hurt." He still looked angry but his voice held a plaintive note.

"I don't want me hurt either."

"Please—" he reached across the distance between us and took my hand.

I wished I hadn't put my gloves on.

He squeezed. Gently. A slow steady pressure. "I've missed you."

Maybe he wouldn't notice the tears that pooled on the rims of my eyes. "I missed you, too." My voice was barely a whisper.

Anarchy leaned over and brushed his lips across my cheek. And I'd thought his touch sent my nerves into a tizzy.

"Dinner?" he whispered into my ear. "Tonight?"

How could I say no?

SIX

Anarchy took me home where I shook my finger at a not-remotely-remorseful Max, grabbed a sammich, and changed my clothes. I had to. The club did not allow denim.

I donned a pantsuit I'd recently bought at Swanson's. Dove gray and cream houndstooth, the suit came with a matching gray coat also trimmed with houndstooth. Gray heels, gray gloves—I looked pulled together. At least on the outside. What was happening inside was a study in chaos.

Nerves had set my insides churning. Me? Anarchy? Dinner?

I put those thoughts out of my mind (stuffed them into the deepest, darkest corner of my brain—a place where Libba wouldn't spot them). Then I transferred my billfold, lipstick and powder, and keys to a gray handbag that matched my shoes, gave Max one last baleful look, and drove to the club.

"You're late." Libba frowned at me from her seat at the bridge table. "Is everything all right?"

We were playing in the small card room—the one with the best view of the golf course. Although, the course, dotted as it was with half-melted snow, looked as if it had a bad case of untreated dandruff. Not remotely attractive. I hung my purse over the back of my chair and sat. "I'm sorry. Busy morning."

"Don't worry about it," said Daisy with an easy smile. "I just got here."

That might be true, but we expected Daisy to be late.

"I am sorry. I lost track of time."

"You never lose track of time." Libba regarded me with

narrowed eyes. "Were you painting?" Already she was poking around.

"No."

"Then what?"

I shifted in my seat, unwilling to talk about spending my morning with Anarchy or about my upcoming date. Definitely unwilling to talk about a dead teenage girl who'd sold her body to strangers.

"Give her a break, Libba. You've been late before." Jinx took a drag on her cigarette and blew the smoke in Libba's direction. "Let's play cards."

Jinx had gone to rehab, given up drugs and alcohol, and taken up smoking. None of us complained about her ever-present cigarettes. At least not while she was around. She pushed one of the two decks on the table my way.

I cut.

Daisy shuffled the second deck.

Jinx rested her cigarette on the edge of an ashtray and dealt. "Did you hear Joyce and Bruce Petteway are getting a divorce?"

No wonder Joyce had dropped the menu ball for the gala.

The thirteenth card landed and Libba picked up her stack. "What happened? I thought they were happy."

"There's another woman."

"Oh?" Libba looked up from arranging her cards. "Who?"

"No one knows." Jinx pursed her lips. "Who would sleep with Bruce Petteway?"

She made an excellent point. Middle age had hit Bruce hard. His hair had thinned, his waist had widened, and he'd taken to calling women of his wife's acquaintance "kiddo." What she didn't say was that Joyce still looked fabulous. The Petteways' marriage seemed like one where money met beauty. Except—I thought back to our youth—Bruce hadn't been rich when Joyce married him. Bruce with his thick glasses and scrawny neck had been lucky to land Joyce. And now he'd cheated on her.

"How did Joyce find out?" I asked.

Daisy chested her cards and leaned forward. "I heard she came home early from a meeting and he was..." her voice trailed off and her eyebrows waggled wildly.

"No!" Even Libba sounded scandalized. "In their bed?"

Daisy sat back and her brows calmed. "Exactly. Apparently the woman looked all of fifteen."

"What an idiot," I said.

Libba smiled. "Don't hold back, Ellison."

"I mean it." I tapped the edge of my cards against the table. "Joyce is a lovely woman."

"She's a scatterbrain," said Daisy.

The three of us stared at her.

"What? You think I'm a scatterbrain?"

"If the shoe fits, dear." The new, smoking Jinx sounded kinder saying it than the old, drinking, pill-popping Jinx would have. "Pass."

"We love you just the way you are, Daisy." Libba patted her hand. "One club. And I, for one, think Joyce is better off without him. She'll be fine."

"I'm not so sure," said Daisy. "By all accounts, she's devastated. Pass."

I glanced at my cards. "One heart." My late husband had cheated on me with reckless abandon. I knew exactly how betrayed and wounded Joyce felt. "I'm going to call her later."

"I'm sure she'd appreciate that." Jinx wrinkled her nose. "Pass."

"One spade," said Libba.

"Pass." Daisy shook her head. "Don't they still have children at home?"

"Their youngest is in college back east. In Boston I think."

We all stared at Libba. She, who had no children, actively avoided chatting about them.

"What?" Libba's glare encompassed all three of us. "Joyce caught me at the grocery store after the holidays and talked about how hard it was to put him on a plane back to school."

I looked down at my hand. I held four hearts, three spades, three diamonds, three clubs and fifteen points. "One no trump."

"Pass," said Jinx.

Libba regarded the cards fanned in her hand. "Three no trump."

Daisy passed.

So did I.

Jinx tossed the six of diamonds onto the table (she carefully adhered to the fourth from your longest and strongest rule when defending no trump).

Starting with four nice spades, Libba laid down her cards.

Making three no trump was not a problem, not even with Daisy recounting her son's latest exploits. Apparently he'd worked for a year, cut back on tennis and given up golf, mowed lawns in the summer, shoveled driveways in the winter, and saved up enough money for flying lessons. All he needed was his parents' permission.

Jinx dealt the next hand, I shuffled the second deck, and Daisy said, "He just doesn't appreciate how much I'll worry."

"You don't want him in a small airplane," said Jinx, sounding sympathetic.

Daisy looked at the ceiling. "It just sounds so dangerous." She closed her eyes. "But he did work so hard."

"Let him fly," said Libba. "He set himself a goal, he gave up things he liked to do, he worked hard, and now the only thing that stands in his way is you. Don't be that mother."

"He's fifteen," said Daisy.

The same age as Leesa. What different lives they'd lived. "Do you ever feel guilty?" The question popped out of my mouth, unconsidered and ill-advised.

Libba raised a lazy brow. "About what?"

"We have so much," I mumbled.

Three sets of eyes stared at me as if I'd suddenly grown horns.

"We worked for it," said Daisy. "Or our husbands did." She shook her head. "No, we worked for it too. Running a home, raising kids, it's not easy."

"It's not," agreed Jinx.

Libba, who'd inherited every penny she ever spent and had never been married said not a word.

"We do plenty," added Jinx. "You're chairing that gala for the gallery, Daisy practically lives at her kids' schools, and Libba contributes generously to the economy."

Libba wrinkled her nose and stuck out her tongue. "And Jinx keeps tennis pros employed."

"Someone has to."

"What makes you ask about guilt?" Libba's hands moved evenly, dealing cards to each of us.

"Nothing." My nose itched. My nose always itched when I lied.

My best friend stared at me from across the table, sensing the lie, inviting me to say more.

I sealed me lips.

Libba picked up her cards. "This is way too serious a topic. Guess who I took to see the psychic."

"The psychic in Prairie Village?" asked Daisy. "I went to see her but I can't go back."

"Why not?" Not going back did not sound like a hardship.

"I was wearing that charm bracelet the kids gave me and one of the charms snagged on the table cloth. When I stood up, I accidently yanked the cloth and the crystal ball went crashing to the floor."

Jinx lit a fresh cigarette. "The woman's a psychic. You'd think she'd see that coming."

"She didn't and she was mad." Daisy looked up from her cards. "She said I'd have another baby." Daisy was nearly forty and already had more children than the old woman who lived in the shoe. "Can you imagine?"

"So are you?" asked Jinx.

"Am I what?" Daisy pretended not to understand.

"Pregnant?"

"Of course not."

I couldn't help but notice Daisy scratched her nose.

* * *

"What about this?" I emerged from my closet holding a perfectly lovely silk Yves Saint Laurent blouse.

Grace, who sat cross-legged in the center of my bed, rolled her eyes. "You're going on a date not to a committee meeting."

"What's wrong with it?" The silk was a fabulous shade of jade green.

"Um, the bow at the neck. It's a date, Mom."

Maybe she had a point. Maybe she sounded too much like Libba.

"What about that cream Saint Laurent?" she asked.

"The charmeuse blouse? I haven't had time to add a snap." The neck-line was too low-cut.

"I know." Definitely she sounded too much like Libba.

I returned the conservative jade blouse to the closet and grabbed the one Grace suggested. The fabric was rich, the cut was flattering, if only—

"Wear it." Grace's voice carried into the closet. "That and jeans and those Gucci boots."

I'd been thinking camel slacks and loafers.

"You've been moping around here for months," she continued. "Now you have a chance to make things right. Don't blow it by dressing like a middle-aged widow."

"I am a middle-aged widow."

"But you don't have to dress like one." She sounded exactly like Libba. At sixteen, Grace could transition from child to angst-ridden teenager to too-worldly woman in minutes. In seconds. I blamed Libba for the too-worldly part. "Trust me. Wear the cream blouse."

I emerged from the closet wearing the blouse.

"See? It's perfect." And just like that, she transitioned to a smug too-worldly woman.

"Hmph." I reached into a chest of drawers and my fingers closed around a square of silk twill. Hermes' official name for the pattern was Eperon d'Or. Grace called it bits and spurs.

She regarded the scarf in my hand with tangible distaste. "No! No, no, no. No bits and spurs tonight. You look foxy without it."

Foxy? Was she too old for me to restrict her television and radio? And what did she and Libba talk about when I wasn't around? Foxy?

I returned the scarf to the drawer but fiddled with the deep V of the blouse's collar.

Ding dong.

"Would you get that?" Maybe I could pin the collar.

"Not on your life." She sat unmoving, surrounded by pillows like some omniscient teenage sultan. "Leave that blouse alone. It's perfect the way it is. Now go."

My nerves jittered wildly and I gripped the railing as I descended the stairs.

Max, the evil beast, stood by the front door just waiting to make a break for it.

I closed my fingers around his collar, drew breath deep into my lungs, and opened the door.

Anarchy stood on the other side.

My mouth went dry. "Come in," I croaked. Somehow I refrained from adjusting the neckline of my blouse. Probably because I could feel Grace's judgmental stare boring through my back.

He stepped into my home and fixed his gaze upon me. His coffee-brown eyes didn't warm. They glowed. "You look amazing."

I didn't have to glance up at the landing to know Grace was smirking. "Thank you."

"I have reservations at Baby Doe's."

This did not come as a surprise. The last time Anarchy had taken me to dinner, he'd chosen a steakhouse. "I've never been."

"You'll love it." He sounded hopeful rather than certain.

"I'm sure I will. Let me grab a coat."

I stepped away from him—away from the scent of good leather and cold air, away from temptation in human form—and reached into the front hall closet.

I pulled out the first coat I touched—my second-best mink.

"Let me help you with that." He took the coat from my shaking hands and held it open.

The silk of my blouse slid seamlessly through the coat's satin-lined sleeves.

With a final don't-you-dare-get-into-trouble glare at Max (one for Grace, too—the last time I went out with Anarchy, she hosted a party), I walked out into the cold.

Anarchy opened the car door for me and my jangly nerves then circled round to the driver's side.

I searched for something to say. "I'm surprised you could get away for dinner during an investigation."

He inserted the ignition key and turned on the car. "No one authorized overtime."

"What do you mean?"

He zipped down the driveway. "When someone you know dies, there's pressure to catch the killer quickly."

"And there's not for Leesa?"

"She was a prostitute. No one is calling the mayor, or—" his lips twisted into a sardonic smile "—your 'Uncle' James."

Uncle James wasn't really my uncle. He was one of Daddy's golf cronies. He was also a police commissioner. I'd invoked his name a time or two.

"So what does that mean? You're not trying to catch her killer?"

"No. We'll catch the killer. But we'll do it during regular business hours."

I thought about that for a mile or two. "Aren't the people you need to question more accessible at night?"

"We do the best with the system we've got." The answer was pure Anarchy. He didn't like the rules, but he'd follow them. He didn't like the rules, but wouldn't criticize them in front of a civilian.

"I could call Uncle James."

His lips twitched.

"I could tell him I met the girl and that I'm simply traumatized." I slid my gaze toward Anarchy's eyes, toward the set of his mouth and got my answer. "I'll call in the morning."

"Thank you." His voice was so soft it was almost as if I'd imagined it.

"You're welcome."

We drove the rest of the way in silence and pulled into a nearly full parking lot.

Anarchy led me to a doorway that looked like the entrance to a mine shaft. "Normally, there's a mule out front. Her name is Clementine."

The air was frigid and the sky dark. Hopefully Clementine was tucked safely into a warm stable eating oats rather than scrubby grass.

He led me inside to tunnels—one leading up, the other down. "Our reservations are for eight. Shall we get a drink before dinner?"

"Sure."

He chose the tunnel that headed down to a crowded bar. Floor to ceiling windows offered a spectacular view of downtown. At a distance, with lights twinkling in the skyscrapers, it looked magical. A place where exciting, wonderful things happened.

The truth was ugly. Downtown was a dirty, dying group of buildings where bums shuffled along the sidewalks, women danced topless, and teenage girls died in filthy alleys.

I knew all that but I didn't look away. The magic entranced, promising glittering, seductive moments wrapped in a golden hue. It was so much nicer to believe in magic, to forget the ugliness.

"What would you like?" asked Anarchy as he angled us spots at the bar.

I tore my gaze away from the view. "White wine."

"Anarchy!" The bartender had spotted us.

She was pretty. Very pretty.

He grinned. "Fancy Nancy!"

She ignored a man waving a twenty at her, walked over to us, and sent a thousand-watt smile in Anarchy's direction. "What'll it be?"

"The usual and a white wine." He turned his gaze my direction. "Ellison, this is Fancy Nancy, the best bartender in town. Fancy Nancy, this is my friend, Ellison."

Fancy Nancy and I regarded each other across the bar. Very, very pretty.

"Nice to meet you," I murmured through stiff lips.

"Same. What kind of white wine?"

Everyone drank Liebfraumilch. I drank Liebfraumilch. And suddenly, inexplicably, I needed to be different. "Chardonnay."

"You got it." She turned her back on me and reached for a bottle of Old Forester.

Bourbon. Anarchy drank bourbon. Fancy Nancy knew Anarchy drank bourbon. I hadn't. That bothered me. Immensely.

"What's good to eat here?" It was a better question than what have you been doing the past two months?

"Prime rib. And save room for dessert."

"Dessert?" Did women eat desserts on dates? I doubted it.

He nodded. "Upside down apple walnut pie with ice cream."

"It sounds decadent." It sounded like five extra laps around the park.

"It is." His lips twitched as if he was fighting a smile. "You won't regret it for a moment."

Were we still talking about dessert? A flush warmed my cheeks.

Fancy Nancy cleared her throat and put our drinks on the bar.

Anarchy turned his smile (the one meant for me) toward her and paid the tab.

We picked up our glasses and clinked the rims.

"Cheers," I said.

"To us."

To us? The heat returned to my cheeks.

A frown wrinkled his brow and he glanced down. A second later, he had a pager in his hand. "I've got to take this."

"I thought you were off tonight."

"I thought so too." He used his cop tone but when he stood he brushed a kiss across my cheek. Then disappeared in search of the payphone.

I nursed my wine and watched Fancy Nancy mix grasshoppers and Manhattans and—I shuddered—scotch and milk.

Anarchy returned wearing his cop expression. "I'm sorry, Ellison, we're going to have to call this short." He looked down at his shoes—or maybe my boots—and added, "May I put you in a cab?"

"What's happened?"

"There's been another murder."

There were murders all the time. That was why there was a homicide squad. Why call Anarchy? The answer dawned on me. "Another murder like Leesa's?"

He nodded grimly.

"Another girl shot in an alley." I glanced out the windows at that magical view of downtown. "What can I do?"

"Go home. Stay safe. Have dinner with me after we've caught this guy."

How could I argue?

SEVEN

Grace went to school.

Aggie went to the library to do more research for Mother.

Max circled three times and plunked onto his favorite sunny spot in the family room.

I, with a cup of coffee near at hand, sat at my desk and stared at the phone.

There were women of my acquaintance who could spend their whole morning on the phone. I was not one of them. On the phone, I couldn't read faces or body language, couldn't judge reactions, couldn't determine if I was hearing truth or lies.

Nonetheless, I pulled the telephone closer to me, took a bracing sip of coffee, and called Joyce Petteway.

She answered after three rings. "Hello."

"Joyce, it's Ellison Russell calling."

"Ellison—" my name came out in a rush of air "—I am the worst committee member in the history of committee members. I apologize."

"Don't apologize. We have plenty of time." We didn't. "Besides, I hear you've been facing some challenges."

"Did you call to ask me to resign?"

"Of course not!" No matter how far behind she was, I wouldn't kick a woman when she was down.

"I wouldn't blame you." As if I could find a replacement at this late date.

"Don't be silly. I heard you and Bruce were having some problems and I just wanted you to know I was thinking of you."

This was answered with silence.

Oh dear. I took a sip of coffee and waited.

"Thank you," Joyce's voice was small. "So it's out. Everyone knows?"

"I don't know about everyone."

"It's just so..."

Humiliating. The word she wanted was humiliating.

"Humiliating." She found the word, naming the stomach-churning sensation.

"I know. Believe me, I know. I'm here for you if you need me."

"That's right. I forgot Henry cheated."

"He did." Henry cheated was an understatement of epic proportions. Sort of. When Henry and I decided our marriage was over, we also decided to stay together until Grace finished high school. To me, that meant polite cohabitation. To Henry, that meant he was free to sleep with every woman who struck his not-terribly-discriminating fancy. Because our marriage was over, he didn't see his exploits as cheating.

He didn't face the pitying looks in the mirror of the ladies' lounge or the sudden silences when I walked into a room.

"I never thought Bruce would cheat. He promised to love and cherish me and I thought he meant it."

I made a soft, comforting sound in my throat.

"At first I couldn't believe it."

"And now you're angry."

"How did you know?"

"Been there. Done that."

"Ellison—" she lowered her voice to a whisper "—I want to punch him in the face."

"He deserves it."

"And after I punch him, I want to kick him so hard he's a soprano till Christmas."

"I understand completely."

"Last night I dreamed I took an axe and whacked it off."

No need to ask what *it* was. "I wouldn't do that."

Joyce laughed—a short, brittle sound. "Of course not. But it was fun to think about."

I took another sip of coffee.

Max lifted his head and stared at me.

"I could kill him. I really could."

A sense of foreboding chilled me and I took another quick sip of coffee. "Don't say that out loud, Joyce."

"It would be easier to tell the children their father was dead than explain he has the morals of a tomcat."

"For you. Not for them. No matter what he's done, he's their father and they love him." I spoke from experience. "Besides, your youngest is in college. They'll be able to handle this."

"What am I going to tell them?"

I didn't know. That was a conversation I never had. "Tell them you love them and that everything will be okay."

"Will it?"

"Eventually."

"I can't do this."

She didn't have much choice. "Of course, you can," I told her.

"He took his clothes. He moved out. He's staying in a suite at the Alameda until he finds an apartment."

"What does he say?"

"He says he never meant to hurt me." The bitterness in her voice told me how badly Bruce had wounded her. "If he didn't want to hurt me, he shouldn't have—" her voice broke.

"Have you hired a lawyer?"

"Sally Broome."

Sally was the only female divorce attorney in town and she was tough as nails. She had to be. "Good choice."

"She seems to think, given the circumstances, I can get a huge settlement. I told her I wanted to take him for every penny."

"Good for you." Dreams of leaving Bruce broke were healthier than dreams of whacking his thing off.

"You were so nice to call. To listen. Not everyone understands what I'm going through."

We both paused and considered lucky women whose husbands didn't roam, less lucky women who remained blissfully ignorant of their husband's roaming, and women like us—women who'd caught their husbands cheating.

"It's my pleasure." Not really. But what else was I going to say? Calm down? If someone had suggested I let go of my early anger and calm down, I would have told them to go straight where the sun didn't shine.

"About the gala..."

"Yes?" That chilling sense of foreboding was back.

"I think I'd better resign."

Dammit. "Are you sure? Don't you want something to keep you occupied?"

"I'm sure. And I'm sorry. I just can't think right now. You'll find someone who can do a much better job."

The gala was six weeks away. It wasn't as if there were spare committee members just sitting around, twiddling their thumbs, waiting for the phone to ring.

"Listen, Ellison, thanks for understanding and thanks for the call, but I've got to go. I need to get ready for an appointment with Sally."

"Call me if you need me." My voice was faint.

"I will. Thank you." Joyce hung up the phone.

I stared at the receiver in my hand. The call had not ended as I hoped. Where was I going to find a committee chairman?

I dropped the receiver in the cradle and drained my coffee cup.

Brnng, brnng.

Maybe Joyce had reconsidered. I grabbed the receiver. "Hello."

"Ellison, it's Mother."

I leaned back against my chair and stared at my empty coffee cup. "How are you?"

"Fine, thank you. Any news on the ashes?"

"Aggie's at the library researching as we speak."

I took Mother's answering silence for approval.

I wrapped the phone cord around my finger. "I'm sure she'll figure it out."

"I suppose. I spoke with Kay Starnes this morning."

"Oh?"

"She says her daughter saw you at Baby Doe's last night."

"I was there." Be honest but volunteer nothing. It was the best policy.

"She said you looked as if you were on a date."

"I was."

"With whom?"

"Anarchy Jones."

There was no mistaking the ensuing silence for approval. Mother's displeasure washed over me in waves. Finally, she said, "Did you find another body?"

What? "No. Why?"

"I'm just wondering what circumstance returned that man to your life."

That man. We were on a path that could only lead to acrimony. "Let's find something else to talk about."

"Margaret Hamilton called me."

Oh dear Lord.

"She says your dog destroyed her house."

"Not exactly."

"She said he was vicious. She said he was mean."

Mother and Margaret, they had one thing in common, they disliked Max.

"He broke a few dishes."

Again with the silence.

"Everyday dishes," I added. "He didn't touch her good china."

"Given how often there's trouble at your house, you ought to make a better effort to get along with your neighbors."

"First off, I offered to pay for all the damages. Secondly, Margaret Hamilton is a witch."

"There's no need for name calling."

"I'm not. She's a witch. She flies a broomstick when there's a full moon."

"Ellison!"

Perhaps I was embellishing. A bit. Time for a new topic. Again. "I have a problem, Mother." Mother loved solving problems.

"Oh?"

"Joyce Petteway just resigned from the gala committee."

"I heard about what happened to her. She walked into her bedroom and found her husband in bed with—"

"I just got off the phone with her. She's terribly upset."

"Well, of course she is. Any woman would be." Mother paused long enough to remind me she was a lucky woman and that my father would never cheat. "Wasn't she chairing the food and beverage committee?"

"She was."

"Ask Libba to step in."

"Libba?"

"She'll come up with a signature drink in no time. Perhaps a Singapore Sling?"

It was my turn to answer with silence.

"Well. Given the amount that Libba drinks, I'm sure she can create something marvelous without even trying. As for the menu, either one of you could plan that in your sleep."

Mother was right. Libba would have the bar and the menu sorted in an hour.

And I'd be in her debt.

"Can you think of anyone else?"

"Not off the top of my head. Why don't you want to ask Libba?"

"She'll ask me to go on a double date." I regretted the words as soon as they left my lips.

"Oh? With whom?"

"A friend of Bill Ledbetter's."

"Bill Ledbetter?"

"You've met him, Mother." Mother had trouble keeping track of people who weren't from Kansas City. "He's from South Carolina.

He came to Kansas City and took that job at Bodwin Myer Commercial."

"Now I remember. We met him at the club dance. Libba's dating him?"

"You sound surprised."

"He seems like such a nice man."

"Perhaps that's why Libba is dating him." My voice was sharper than it should have been.

"Don't get on your high horse with me, Ellison Russell. We both know Libba has terrible taste in men."

"Perhaps she's changed."

"Oh, please. Leopards don't change their spots."

"You just suggested that I ask her to chair a committee for the gala."

"Which has absolutely nothing to do with her execrable taste in men."

"If I ask her, I'll have to go on this double date."

Mother muttered...something.

"Pardon me?"

"I said, I don't suppose he can be any worse than that police detective." This time Mother enunciated clearly.

The nerves along my spine jumped to attention and I straightened in my chair. "Did you call me with the express purpose of picking a fight?"

"Don't be ridiculous. I called to find out about progress on identifying the ashes."

Mother was lying. She called because she'd heard I'd gone out with Anarchy.

"Mother, I have a million calls to make this morning. I'm going to let you go. I'll phone if Aggie comes up with any good possibilities."

"Ellison—"

"I have to go. Good-bye." Gently, I placed the receiver into the cradle.

I pushed away from the desk. Grabbing my coffee mug, I

headed into the kitchen where Mr. Coffee, strong, silent, and dependable, waited with a nearly full pot of coffee. All for me.

"I swear," I told him. "Mother finds my buttons and pushes them just for the fun of it."

Wisely, he remained mum on the subject.

I refilled my cup. "Who should I call first, Libba or Uncle James?"

Mr. Coffee had no opinion.

"I think Libba."

Rather than return to my desk, I picked up the extension in the kitchen. Grace had long since stretched the phone's cord to capacity and, if needed, I could pace as I talked.

Libba answered on the fifth ring. "Hello." She sounded groggy.

"Did I wake you? It's nearly ten o'clock."

"Not all of us get up at the crack of dawn to get our progeny off to school."

"Ten o'clock, Libba."

She groaned.

"I've been thinking."

"Oh? About what?"

"Friday night."

"Hold on a moment." Her voice brightened. "Let me make some coffee."

I listened to the sounds of Libba scooping coffee and filling her Mr. Coffee's reservoir and winked at my own Mr. Coffee, already full of coffee-goodness.

She came back on the line. "What have you been thinking about Friday night?"

"That I'll go on that double date with you."

"There's an if there. I can sense it." She sounded cautious.

"I'll go if you step in for Joyce Petteway and chair the food and beverage committee for the museum gala."

"Me? Chairing a committee? Really?" She made it sound like a terrific amount of work.

"What else do you want?"

"Go to the club party with me on Saturday night."

I considered. "Okay, but we meet there." Libba had a tendency to stay (and stay) when all I wanted was to go home.

"We have a deal. You're going to love Bill's friend."

"Have you met him?" It would be nice to know what I was getting myself into.

"Not yet. But the whole night will be fabulous. I'm sure of it."

There was an example of wishful thinking. In all our many years of friendship, Libba and I had never been on a decent double date much less a fabulous one.

"I can't wait to call Bill and let him know."

"About the gala."

"Yes?"

"We need a menu by next Tuesday."

"No problem. I'm at loose ends this afternoon. I'll call the caterer and get it worked out."

"And a signature drink."

"How about a lychee martini?"

Mother had been right. Libba had all my problems solved in a New York minute.

"Sounds perfect."

"We'll pick you up at six on Friday."

How could I object? "Fine."

"And, Ellison..."

"Yes?"

"Don't dress like a middle-aged widow."

She and Grace had compared notes. There was no other explanation.

"Fine."

"Now that I think about it, count on me at five. I'll have Bill pick both of us up at your house."

I thought about that lychee martini and kept my mouth shut. Barely.

"Toodles." Libba hung up the phone.

I hung up too. "That went about as well as I expected."

Mr. Coffee looked sympathetic.

"I didn't count on the club party."

Mr. Coffee never got his arm twisted into attending club parties but I swear he offered me an empathetic sigh. Maybe not empathetic. Maybe not a real sigh. But if he could have, he would have. Mr. Coffee is the empathetic type.

"One call left," I told him. I returned to my desk and the phone book. There I looked up the number for my Uncle James's law firm and dialed.

"Law office."

"Good morning," I said. "May I please speak with James Graham."

"Who's calling, please?"

"Ellison Russell."

"One moment please, Mrs. Russell."

It was exactly one moment before Uncle James picked up the phone. "Ellison, how nice to hear from you." Uncle James' voice rumbled like a freight train.

"How are you?"

"Fine, fine. And, you?"

"Fine." We'd established we were fine.

"How are your parents?"

"Fine. Aunt Sarah?"

"Just fine."

We'd run out of fines.

"What can I do for you, Ellison?"

"I hit a teenage girl a few days ago."

"With your car?"

"Yes." I told him the whole story—from Leslie's refusal to get in my car to my giving her my coat to the police showing up at my door. Then I told him that Leslie was Leesa and what she did for a living. Finally, I said, "The police haven't authorized any overtime to solve her murder."

"You know, Ellison, I try not to interfere in police business."

Damn. "Of course you don't. I just wanted to make you aware

of this."

"I can call and ask for an update on the case. That usually lights a few fires."

"Would you? Oh, Uncle James, thank you!"

"Tell your father to spot me two strokes the next time we play."

"Of course."

"Consider it done. I'll make the call right now."

"Thank you."

"Remember. Two strokes."

We hung up and I sat back in my desk chair and stared at the family room. I sipped my coffee. I considered my morning on the phone. Joyce Petteway and her grief. Mother and her determination to run my life. Libba and her planned double date. And finally, Uncle James and his willingness to do me a favor. Moments passed. My cup emptied.

I heard Aggie in the kitchen. Apparently she'd had enough of the library. She was talking to Max. Slowly I pushed out of my chair.

Brnng, brnng.

There was a real possibility it was Mother calling for round two.

I made my way to the kitchen where Aggie had the receiver pressed against her ear. "One moment, Mr. Graham, I'll see if she's available."

I nodded.

Aggie held out the phone.

I took the receiver from her. "Uncle James?"

"Ellison, I talked to the police chief and I want you to stay away from this case."

"I'm not involved in the case."

"You're involved enough to call me."

I couldn't argue that.

Uncle James continued, "The chief says that there have been three prostitutes murdered."

Three? Three murders. The police couldn't ignore three

murders. I'd wasted a favor from Uncle James.

"All those women were shot and left in alleys." He sounded deadly serious. "I want you as far away from this case as you can get."

"Of course."

"Do I have your promise?" he insisted. "If I don't get it, I'll call your mother."

What was I, five? "I promise, Uncle James."

We hung up and I sat down on a kitchen stool. Three girls dead? Shot? Left in alleys? And I'd promised not to interfere.

EIGHT

I shifted on the kitchen stool and watched Aggie put away groceries. Who ate Life cereal? Besides Mikey. Mikey didn't live at my house. Had Grace developed a taste for it?

"I was wondering—" Aggie's head was still in the refrigerator and her voice was slightly muffled "—if you and Grace could fend for yourselves this evening."

"Of course." I didn't ask why. I desperately wanted to. Aggie has been dating a new man. One I liked. Immensely. Did she have a date?

Aggie emerged with flushed cheeks. "There's soup you can warm up."

She'd made a wonderful vegetable noodle just the other day. The leftovers were in the fridge.

"And I bought that French bread you like." She tilted her chin toward a baguette.

"We'll manage."

"I wouldn't ask but—" the flush on her cheeks deepened "—I have a date."

Aha! Just as I suspected. "Where's Mac taking you?"

"A basketball game."

"Do you like basketball?"

"I don't know. I've never really watched a game."

How had she managed that? We were less than an hour from Lawrence, Kansas where James Naismith who'd invented the game had taught and coached. And then there was Coach Phog Allen, a name that loomed large in my childhood. My father, who adored basketball, had put me in the car and driven me to Lawrence more times than I could count. I'd watched Coach Allen pace the sidelines as his players ran up and down the court. I'd napped on the drive home, laid out on the backseat with a blanket thrown over me. When we arrived at the house, Daddy would carry me upstairs and tuck me in bed. Those warm, sleep-fuzzed moments in my father's arms made sitting through basketball games worthwhile.

"Two teams, two hoops, one ball, five team members on the court at a time. And they can't dribble with two hands."

"Dribble?"

"Bounce the ball up and down. The players have to dribble the ball between the hoops. They can't just carry it."

"Why not?"

I shrugged. "Those are the rules. Oh, some shots are worth three points but most are worth two."

"Why?"

"It depends on how far from the basket the player is when he shoots."

Aggie nodded as if my explanation of the game made actual sense. "We're seeing the Kings."

"That's the professional team."

"As opposed to?"

"College teams."

"Are the rules different?"

"I don't know. I think dribbling with one hand is universal. I'm sure you'll have fun." I wasn't sure of that at all. The highlight of my basketball game attendance had always been the trip home and snuggling into my father's arms.

Aggie nodded. Slowly. "Mac says he loves basketball. He wants to share it with me."

"He's a nice man."

Aggie nodded and produced unexpected tears. She looked at the ceiling and patted the skin beneath her eyes. "He is."

"Why are you crying?"

She shook her head and her red curls sproinged this way and

that. "Al. Every so often I think of Al."

"Al would want you to be happy."

"He would. He absolutely would."

I'd never met Al, Aggie's late husband, but everything I'd ever heard about him told me that Al wouldn't want Aggie to spend the rest of her life alone.

She'd been lucky.

If my late husband had given me any thought—and I doubted he did—he wouldn't have thought about my happiness.

Al Delucci wasn't like that. He'd want Aggie to live. And laugh. And be her wonderful self, not a woman diminished by sadness.

I climbed off my stool and wrapped my arms around her. "You loved Al. You always will. And he loved you. He would want you to grab life."

Aggie sniffled. "You're right. I know you're right." She pulled away from my embrace and wiped her eyes.

I returned to my stool and wrapped my fingers around my coffee mug.

Aggie bustled. She folded the grocery bags. She emptied a bag of grapes into a colander and washed them. She wiped a pristine counter.

"Any luck identifying the ashes?" I asked.

"I spent an hour at the library before I went to the market," she replied. "More than an hour and the words start to run together."

"I understand." She didn't need to explain the perils of microfilm to me.

She dug into her purse. "Here are a few more names."

I took the list from her outstretched hand and scanned the names she'd jotted down. "Who is Spencer Marks?"

"He sounded like someone your mother would know."

I couldn't argue that.

"Does she?" Aggie asked.

"I don't know. I doubt it. I don't."

"He was killed downtown."

"What does that have to do with the ashes?"

"Nothing. But there was that other man. The one who was shot."

"Patrick Conover?"

"That's the one."

"What about him?"

"He was shot downtown too."

"People get shot downtown all the time."

"Not your sort of people."

I opened my mouth, ready to argue, but closed my lips before I said a word. Aggie was right. The people who died downtown were drunks knifed outside strip clubs. A few, those with mob ties, were shot and stuffed in car trunks. I read about those deaths in the paper. And then there were the girls. Those poor girls—they were shot and abandoned in alleys.

"What can you tell me about Spencer Marks?"

"He was killed five months ago. That's the most interesting thing about him. He was divorced. He lived in Prairie Village. He worked for a bank."

"Which bank?"

"First National."

"How old was he?"

"Forty-seven."

"What else?"

"Nothing really. The obituary was short. It was his name that caught my eye. I looked up the newspaper articles about his death."

"His murder is unsolved?"

She nodded.

"Where was he shot?"

"In the head."

Ew. "I mean where was he when he was shot?"

"In front of a place on the 12th Street strip."

Brnng, brnng.

I glanced at the phone. "Mother's on the war path. I'm not home."

Aggie nodded, crossed the kitchen, and picked up the receiver. "Russell residence." She tilted her head and listened, an odd expression on her face. "Let me see if Mrs. Russell is available."

"Who is it?" I whispered.

Aggie covered the mouthpiece with the palm of her hand. "She says her name is Madame Reyna and that it is imperative she talks with you."

No. I shook my head. No, no, no.

"I'm sorry, Mrs. Russell can't come to the phone right now. May I take a message?" Again, an odd expression flitted across Aggie's face. "Would you repeat that, please?" She listened then rolled her eyes. "And the number?" She jotted a string of numbers down on the pad next to the phone. "I'll tell her you called."

She made a move to hang up the phone but the voice on the other end was still speaking. Even I could hear the high-pitched buzz of Madame Reyna's voice.

"No, I'm afraid I don't know when Mrs. Russell will call you back. I'll give her the message." Aggie dropped the receiver into the cradle. Not dropped. Deposited with force.

"What did she want?"

Rather than answer me, Aggie asked a question of her own, "A medium?" Disbelief colored her voice.

"Libba made me go. You know how she is. She's like water wearing down a stone. Sometimes it's easier to give in than argue."

Aggie closed her eyes. "They're charlatans. They prey upon people who are grieving or hopeless."

Something told me Aggie had visited a medium. Probably after Al had died. I didn't need to be a psychic to know her experience had not been positive.

"What did she say?"

Aggie pursed her lips as if she'd tasted something unpleasant. "She says Leesa or Leslie, she wasn't exactly clear on the name, will not leave her alone. She is begging you to call her or come see her."

The world around me—the hum of the refrigerator, the gentle buzz of Max's snores, the sway of Aggie's floral kaftan—suddenly seemed very far away. The room spun.

"Mrs. Russell!" Aggie was at my elbow. "You look as if you're going to faint. You ought to sit down."

She glanced at the kitchen stools, rejected them, and led me into the family room where I collapsed onto the couch.

I stared at my hands and searched for one rational thought in the tangle of my brain. Rational thought had decamped. Not a one remained.

Aggie wrung her hands. "Let me get you some coffee." The magical cure-all elixir.

When she returned and handed me the cup, I wrapped my fingers around its warmth.

"Did she say anything else?" I asked.

"Let's talk about this later, when you feel better."

I looked up at Aggie. Her cheeks were pale and her brows wrinkled with worry.

"What else did she say?" I hardly recognized my own voice.

Aggie glanced at the floor, the walls, the ceiling. Her gaze snagged on the needlepoint pillow Mother had made for me. Love is concerned with giving. Abundantly and lavishly. Navy background, white words. Sure, the expression sounded benign but it was one of Mother's not-so-subtle bits of advice, offered as a birthday gift when Henry was still alive. If I just gave more (as in giving up painting), my marriage would be happy.

"The woman said it was a matter of life and death."

Aggie insisted on going to Madame Reyna's with me.

I didn't argue. On the contrary, I was glad of her disapproving presence in the passenger seat and grateful for her level head.

We drove in silence until I parked at the curb in front of Madame Reyna's house.

"This is the place?" Aggie regarded the small ranch home with narrowed eyes. "You're sure?"

She'd been expecting a Romany caravan?

"I'm sure."

"Libba brought you here?" Aggie twisted Libba's name into a curse.

"She did."

Aggie snorted. "That woman needs more to do. A hobby. A job."

We both chuckled at that then together we walked up the front walk.

The front door flew open before we reached the stoop.

Maybe Madame Reyna was psychic. More likely she'd been watching for me. I had called and let her know I was coming.

"You wanted to see me?" My breath rose in the cold air.

"Yes," she replied, her coke-bottle gaze fixed on Aggie's wild curls.

"This is my friend, Aggie DeLucci."

The medium nodded once—a curt bob of her chin. "Come in." She ushered us into her home. "Leslie—Leesa—has been driving me crazy."

"What does she want?" Probably for me to hand over the crisp fifty in my billfold to Madame Reyna.

"She wants you to help her friend."

I blinked.

"Is Leslie, or Leesa, here now?" Aggie glanced around the gold brocade living room, her gaze taking in the plastic slip covers and the freshly raked shag.

"Yes!" Madame Reyna glared at a row of macramé owls. "She won't leave me alone."

"I don't suppose she'd like to tell you who killed her?" I could save Anarchy a lot of work.

Madame Reyna paled. "No. She wouldn't."

Aggie stared at the macramé owls—closely—as if she looked hard enough she too could see Leesa. "What I don't understand is this. If a murdered girl is really talking to you, why won't she just tell you who killed her? She'd get justice. She could rest in peace."

Madame Reyna pursed her lips and clasped her hands

together. "It doesn't work that way. The departed don't want the same things we do."

Aggie tilted her head and talked to the owls. "If someone murdered me, and I had the chance to finger the killer, I'd do it. Wouldn't you?" The question she directed to me.

"Of course." I too was staring at the owls. There was no spirit. No ghostly wisp. I saw only owls. They stared back at me with beady eyes.

"Leesa's life is over. She understands that. She's more concerned with the living."

"Her friend?" I murmured.

"Exactly." Madame Reyna nodded with enthusiasm as if I'd just solved the mysteries of the universe.

"Presumably her friend is in danger from the same person who killed Leesa. Wouldn't it be easier for her to reveal the killer?" Aggie, who wore a this-is-a-ridiculous-sham expression, turned and addressed the owls directly. "Leesa, why don't you tell Madame Reyna who killed you? It's the best way to protect your friend."

Madame Reyna ignored Aggie and sank onto a chair. "Her friend's name is Starry."

"Starry?" What a name. "Is Starry in the same line of work as Leesa?"

Madame Reyna winced. "Leesa says Starry works for a club on 12th Street. She says Starry has been marked for death. She says you can help her."

I closed my eyes and pictured myself walking into a downtown strip club. I wore a twin set and sensible boots. My nose twitched at the imagined stench of rotgut whiskey and watered-down beer. My eyes burned from the imagined sting of smoke-fouled air. I doubted the audience would appreciate my interruption (or my twin set). I doubted a young woman named Starry would throw on an overcoat and leave with me just because I asked.

"I can't help you. Now, if you'll excuse me—" I took a step toward the front door.

"Wait!" Madame Reyna held her hands out toward me.

Beseeching. "Please, wait! She won't leave me alone. She says to tell you Starry is just seventeen. She says you'll understand because you're a mother."

Aggie rolled her eyes so hard her dangly earrings bounced.

Tears glimmered behind Madame Reyna's thick, rhinestone-encrusted glasses. "She says if it was your daughter in that place, you'd want someone to help her."

"Why me?"

"Leesa says you're powerful."

"Leesa's wrong. I'm not. Whatever small amount of influence I might have, wouldn't mean a thing to the type of people who run clubs on 12th Street."

"Leesa says you are kind."

Oh dear Lord. No good deed went unpunished. "Look, I stopped to help Leesa at zero risk to myself or my family. If I'd seen gun-toting thugs chasing her, I would have called the police, not gotten involved." Not exactly true but Madame Reyna and Leesa didn't need to know that.

Madame Reyna's chin quivered like molded Jell-O. "Leesa can't move on until you agree to help."

Surely Anarchy could get a seventeen-year-old girl removed from a strip club. "I have a friend who's a police detective. I'll ask him to help Starry."

"No!" Madame Reyna shot out of her chair. "Leesa says no police."

"Of course she does." Aggie crossed her arms and shook her head.

Madame Reyna ignored Aggie. She leveled her teary gaze at me. "Please, help Leesa. Help Starry." She glanced at the macramé owls and her eyes narrowed. "Help me."

Coming here had been a mistake. "What's Starry's last name?"

"Knight."

Of course it was.

"I'm not going to a strip club." The sinking feeling in my stomach belied that statement.

"But you'll help?" There was so much hope in Madame Reyna's voice. Too much hope. It cut through my defenses.

"I don't know what I can do." No way was I going to a strip club.

"Convince Starry to leave. Tell her Leesa sent you. You can save her."

Aggie sighed. It was a sigh that said she knew there was a strip club in her future. "What's Starry's real name?"

Madame Reyna closed her eyes as if communing with a spirit. "Jane." She pressed her left hand against her brow. "Her name is Jane Nichols."

"What else can you tell us about her?" I asked "Is Jane from Chicago?"

"Chicago?" Madame Reyna opened her eyes. "No. Jane is from Kansas City."

"What else?" What had I got myself into? "What can I tell her to get her to leave?"

"Tell her there are people who love her."

"Why don't you go?" Aggie demanded. "You seem to know a lot about this girl."

Madame Reyna shook her head as if she regretted not marching straight down to 12th Street and whisking Starry—or Jane—to safety. "Leesa says it must be you."

I was getting tired of Leesa.

Aggie turned to me. "Assuming you're successful, what are you going to do with her?"

I blinked. "Do with her? What do you mean?"

"I mean, are you going to install her in the blue room and enroll her at Suncrest?"

"Of course not."

"Then what? She's a minor. She'll be put into the foster system."

"Maybe she has family here," I suggested.

"If she did, would she be dancing at a strip club?"

Aggie made an excellent point. I swallowed. "There must be

some program or half-way house or—"

"There isn't."

"So we just leave her there?"

Madame Reyna followed our exchange with her hands clasped and pressed against her lips.

"What if Madame Reyna really is talking to Leesa? What if this girl is in danger?"

"I'm not saying we don't help. I'm saying we need a plan."

"Just help her." Madame Reyna pleaded. "You can worry about next steps after she's safe."

Aggie shook her head. "It's not like we're going to traipse into Ronny's Playpen and grab her tonight."

Well of course we weren't. Aggie had a date.

Aggie shot a Mother-like look Madame Reyna's direction. "An operation like this takes some thought."

"But Leesa says—"

"Given that I can neither hear nor see Leesa, you'll understand that I want to make my own arrangements."

"But—"

"We'll do our best." I edged toward the door. I'd had enough of Madame Reyna and Leesa and Starry (and I hadn't even met her yet).

"You'll help this girl?" The medium's eyes were full of tears. Again. "You promise?"

"We'll try," I replied.

Aggie took hold of my elbow and pulled me toward the door. "Let's get out if here before you agree to work a pole."

"A pole?"

Aggie rolled her eyes. The second time since we'd arrived. It was quite possible she was spending too much time with Grace. "Never mind about the pole. We should go. Now."

"You'll let me know what happens?" asked Madame Reyna.

"Fine," said Aggie. Then, as soon as were out the door, she said, "What have you gotten us into?"

NINE

That night, Mac picked up Aggie at six. The man was the approximate size of a rhinoceros with the disposition of a Labrador puppy. I'd like him just for those reasons. Throw in the fact that he adored Aggie and Mac was fast becoming one of my favorite men. He had nothing but admiration for Aggie's royal blue and red kaftan with the orange flowers. "You look amazing." He leaned forward and kissed her cheek.

She smiled up at him with enough warmth to heat the whole block. "Thank you." She pulled on the bright blue ruana I gave her for Christmas and picked up her handbag. "I'm ready to go."

Mac waved at me and the twosome disappeared into the night.

I called up the stairs. "Grace, shall I warm up some soup?"

"I'd rather have a hamburger," she called back.

"Winstead's?"

Max's ears perked.

"Don't think I'm bringing you a burger," I told him. "I'm sure Margaret Hamilton is going to sue me for emotional distress."

He grinned.

Grace thundered down the stairs, the wooden soles of her clogs making a racket heretofore unachievable without setting off explosives. "I'm ready."

We drove to the Plaza, parked, and waited in line to be seated.

Our turn came quickly. "Ruby's section, please," said Grace.

The hostess looked over at a group of full tables. "It'll be a few minutes."

"We'll wait," my daughter declared.

We sat down on an avocado green Naugahyde bench and watched other groups be seated.

"It has to be Ruby?" Ruby had dark brown skin, sparkling brown eyes, and a beehive that defied gravity. She'd been Grace's favorite waitress since she was old enough to order her own meal.

"Of course."

When Grace was in first grade and able to read nametags, she asked me if everyone who worked at Winstead's had to be named after something precious.

I had no idea what she meant.

"There's Ruby and Opal and Pearl. And the lady behind the cash register is Goldy."

Neither Henry nor I had noticed the names. Henry was so impressed with Grace's observation he'd ordered her a Skyscraper Sundae (two vertical feet of ice cream, fudge, and whipped cream).

She was sick for two days.

"Your table is ready."

We followed the hostess to a table for two, where glasses of water, a stainless napkin dispenser, bottles of ketchup and mustard, and laminated menus awaited our arrival.

Neither of us bothered with a menu.

A moment later, Ruby arrived. She smiled down at Grace (their admiration society was mutual). "Hey, Sugar. What'll it be?"

"A limeade, please."

"Large?"

"Of course."

"And for you, ma'am?"

"A large—" I thought of my waistline "—make that a small frosty malt."

Ruby made a notation on her pad. "You ladies know what you want to eat?"

"Double cheese with everything. Hold the pickles. And a side of fries." Grace ordered the same thing every time we came.

Winstead's didn't sell hamburgers; it sold steakburgers. The burgers were cooked to a deep shade of brown and flavored with salt and grease. They arrived at the table wrapped in wax paper sleeves and the first bite could change a life. "A single cheese with grilled onions and a side of rings."

When the food arrived, Grace and I would negotiate the trade of rings for fries.

Ruby jotted down our orders. "It'll be right out."

I sat back and took a sip of water. "How was school?"

"Boring. What did you do today?"

I visited a medium who claimed a dead girl wants me to go to a strip club and rescue her friend. "My day was pretty boring too. Aggie's still researching the ashes in your grandmother's closet."

"Ashes!"

I'd forgotten Grace didn't know. I glanced around the nearby tables. For once, thank heavens, I didn't spot anyone we knew. Although those two little old ladies with cotton ball hair, creped necks, and bright lipstick looked vaguely familiar. Not so the man with the long sideburns and a leather coat. He was staring at Grace as if she was a slice of chocolate cake and he was starving. He wasn't starving. A burger sat in front of him and a fry dripping ketchup was frozen half way to his mouth.

I shifted my expression from polite interest to don't-you-dare-think-it.

The man caught my gaze (his eyes were icy gray and slightly bloodshot) but his expression didn't change. A mother's disapproval meant nothing to him.

Grace tossed her hair over her shoulder.

I wished she wouldn't. The man two tables away needed no encouragement.

Ruby delivered Grace's limeade and my frosty. She glanced at me then followed my line of sight. "Oh." She positioned herself between the man and Grace, blocking his view, and added, "Do you want me to call the manager?"

"No. But, thank you."

When Ruby moved, the man had looked away.

I watched him for a while longer but his gaze was now fixed on the newspaper folded on his table.

"Tell me about the ashes," said Grace

I spooned into the frosty and explained.

She tilted her head. "So Granna found these ashes in her front closet and she has no idea who it is?"

"Exactly."

"She must have had kittens."

An understatement. "She'll definitely have kittens if this becomes public knowledge." I donned a severe expression. "This goes no farther. Get it?"

"Got it."

"Good."

"Grace!" A young voice carried across the restaurant.

Three girls paused just inside the entrance then headed our way.

I glanced at the man. He was staring at Grace again and now he knew her name.

I didn't have time to worry. Grace's friends swarmed our table.

"We tried to call you but we got your machine," Peggy said to Grace. "We went to a matinee."

"I was at the library working on that essay that's due on Monday."

Peggy groaned then turned her attention to me. "How are you, Mrs. Russell?"

And just like that the creepy man—Sideburns—knew our last name. I had the sudden urge to bundle my daughter into the car and drive hell for leather. Instead, I smiled at Grace's friends. "Fine, thank you. Would you like to join us?"

I never expected them to accept.

Peggy and Debbie slid in next to Grace. Kimberly sat next to me.

None of them looked at the menus.

"Have you seen The Stepford Wives, Mrs. Russell?" asked Kimberly.

"I read the book." At the time, the idea that perfection was a mask hiding terrible, sordid secrets had seemed ludicrous. I knew better now.

"We just saw the movie. It's super scary," Kimberly added.

"So is the book," I replied

"Men aren't really like that," declared Peggy. "They can't be."

"Like what?" asked Grace.

"Like—" Peggy paused and ordered a single cheese from Ruby. She waited until Kimberly and Debbie had ordered then said, "Like...jerks. More interested in having a perfect woman than a real one. That isn't true, is it?" She looked at me for an answer.

I glanced at the man—the jerk—with the sideburns. He was now staring with an avid expression at all four girls. For heaven's sake, they were sixteen. He had to be in his thirties.

I averted my gaze. "There are good guys out there, Peggy."

The girls were so young, so sure their lives were going to be grand adventures, so untouched by the ugliness best swept under the museum-quality Sarouks in their future living rooms. Except for Grace. Grace's father had been murdered. Grace had faced men determined to kill us. Grace had seen the ugliness.

And, the ugliness had made her stronger. Grace already knew no one led a charmed life.

Except possibly Mother. True, Mother spent the bulk of her energy beating back anything that remotely resembled chaos. True, something as simple as unidentified ashes wobbled her carefully stacked apple cart. But Frances Walford would prevail. And if she couldn't prevail, she would ignore. Ultimately, her charmed life would not be affected.

Grace, who never ignored anything, glanced sideways at Sideburns. Could she feel the weight of his stare?

Maybe she could. She rolled her eyes. With one teenage expression, she reduced his obvious desire into something less, something pathetic, not worth the worry. She leaned forward and whispered, "That perv is staring at us."

Three additional gazes landed on Sideburns then shifted away. The message was clear—he was beneath their consideration. Debbie tittered.

Why were the girls asking me questions about life? They'd just demonstrated that I had plenty to learn from them.

I too should have looked away. But I didn't. I watched. Sideburns dug inside the pocket of his coat, removed a handful of horribly crumpled bills, and threw them on the table. He stood, glared at the girls who'd dismissed him so easily, then stalked out.

I breathed easier when he was gone. The way he'd looked at Grace might have meant less than an eye roll to her, but the raw desire I'd seen in his gaze—on his face—had unsettled me.

We finished our suppers and drove home but thoughts of Sideburns lingered and I checked my rearview mirror at least ten times.

"Relax, Mom." Grace had noticed my anxious glances. "We'll never see him again."

I hoped she was right.

Grace left for school and I sat at the kitchen counter with the morning paper and an almost full cup of coffee (my cups never stayed full—or almost full—for long). I scanned the editorial page. In Britain, a woman had become the leader of the Conservative party and men—and a few women—wrote letters foretelling the end of the world. On the sports page, President Ford was playing golf. Hardly news. Except he was playing in a PGA tournament. I scanned the article. His foursome also included Jack Nicklaus, Bob Hope, and Jackie Gleason.

Aggie bustled in. "Good morning."

"Good morning," I replied.

She pulled Mr. Coffee's pot off his warmer and poured herself a cup. "Refill?"

A rhetorical question. I pushed my cup across the counter and she topped off the level of coffee.

"Anything interesting in the paper?"

"The Wall Street Journal says the Social Security System is

going to go broke."

"Hmph."

"There are still plans to raze a block of 12th Street and build a hotel."

"A whole block?"

I nodded.

"Where will those businesses go?" Unlike the city leaders, Aggie was not so foolish as to believe that erasing a building would erase the strip club inside.

"I don't know." I took a sip of coffee. "How was the basketball game?"

"Couples don't have to like the same things."

"Ah."

"I told Mac about Starry." Aggie fixed her gaze on a half-asleep Max and fidgeted with the sleeve of her burnt sienna kaftan. There was more she wasn't telling me.

"Oh?"

"He said he'd go look for her." She did not sound happy.

"Go? To the strip clubs?"

What an excuse. I'm sorry, honey, I had to go to the strip clubs. You were looking for that girl and I thought I'd find her for you.

Except Mac was so wild about Aggie that the excuse wasn't an excuse. It was true.

"Did he locate her?"

Ding dong.

"I guess we'll find out."

"Mac?" He's here? I wore white flannel pajamas, a camel-hued cashmere bathrobe, and slippers that had seen better days. My hair hadn't been combed. I rubbed my tongue over my teeth. Had I brushed them? I had. Still, I wasn't anywhere near ready to welcome a guest into my home.

"I'll get that," Aggie trilled before she floated down the front hallway.

A moment later, Aggie's Mac stood in my kitchen with his

hand swallowing a mug of fresh coffee.

If Mac noticed I was still in pajamas, he gave no hint. His gaze remained fixed on Aggie. "You look pretty this morning."

Aggie flushed. "Thank you. Who's at the shop?"

"Shorty."

"Shorty?" I asked.

"Mac's brother," Aggie explained.

Mac, who ducked when he walked through doorways, had a brother named Shorty?

"He's an inch shorter than me. Kinda like Tiny Archibald."

Who was Tiny Archibald? "Tiny is an inch shorter than you, too?"

"Nah, Tiny is eight inches shorter than me."

"Tiny is Mac's favorite Kings player," Aggie explained. She tilted her head back and beamed at the man taking up half of my kitchen. "He's not tiny, but he's not as tall as everyone else."

They smiled at each other. The sort of smile that belongs to people in love. Their features softened. Their eyes sparkled. Their lips parted.

My mind, suddenly nimbler than Olga Korbut, double-flipped away from an unbidden image of Anarchy Jones.

I needed more coffee. Stat. I climbed off my stool, made my way to my One True Love, stroked the side of Mr. Coffee's reservoir, and refilled my cup. "More coffee?" Where had that bedroom voice come from?

Mac and Aggie tore their gazes away from each other and looked at me.

"No, thank you." Mac looked bemused. I bet he didn't usually spend his mornings with women in their nightclothes who were seduced by a mere wink from their coffee makers.

Aggie, who was accustomed to my relationship with Mr. Coffee, simply shook her head and recommenced gazing at Mac.

I resumed my seat and asked, "Did you find Starry Knight?"

"Those places." He put his cup down on the counter and his features firmed into a deeply disapproving expression. "If you really think there's a minor working in one of those places, we should call the cops."

"I don't disagree. The problem is a medium told us about Starry." I could just imagine that conversation. No, Officer, I've never met Starry. No, I don't know her family. How do I know she's working there? A medium told me. She got the information from a dead girl.

"The worst of the worst is Ronny's Playpen. I gotta wonder who the owner is paying off to keep the place open."

"What was so awful about it?" asked Aggie.

"The girls looked stoned. My drink cost five dollars and came in a dirty glass. And my shoes stuck to the floor."

Who knew Mac was so fastidious about cleanliness? An admirable trait in a man who ran a deli.

"What did drinks cost in the places where your feet didn't stick to the floor?" asked Aggie.

"Seven. Eight."

"Well, there you have it. Ronny's is the bargain basement of strip clubs. And—" she shifted her gaze from Mac to me "—they're all paying someone off. That's what the mob does."

The mob? I swallowed past a sudden tightness in my throat. "Did you find her?"

"No," said Mac. "Are you sure this girl exists?" Exactly what I'd been thinking.

Aggie and I exchanged a glance. Madame Reyna had convinced us. Then. But in my kitchen without the wild pleadings of the medium ringing in our ears, Starry Knight's existence was easily discounted.

"I've got a friend at the police station," said Aggie. "I'll see if they have a record for Starry Knight or Jane Nichols."

I too had a friend at the police station. But, if I asked Anarchy to look into a stripper for me, his head would explode. If he learned Aggie was asking on my behalf, his head might still explode. "Please keep my name out of it." I turned to Mac. "Thanks for going to those places." Then, because I was too curious for my own good, I asked, "What's the inside of a strip club like?"

Mac's lips pulled back and his jaw tightened as if I'd shown him something disgusting. "Sleazy. Seamy. Seedy."

Apparently Mac was fond of S-words. Or alliteration. "But what does it look like?" I insisted. "The interior?" I was unlikely to ever see a strip club myself.

His face wrinkled with concern and he stared at me as if divining my reason for asking. "The nicest place has mirrored walls and an island a little bit bigger than this one—" he patted my kitchen island "—right in the middle of the club where the girls dance on poles. The island has a lip where men can set their drinks on it. There's also a stage with half-naked girls shaking everything they've got. It's dark. It's smoky. It's no place for a lady."

"I won't ever see it."

His face remained clouded.

"Aggie won't ever see it."

His face cleared. "Like I said, it's no place for a lady."

As if I'd ever ask Aggie to go to a strip club.

I wouldn't have to ask.

Mac glanced at his watch. "I should be getting to the deli."

"Already?"

Easy for Aggie to say. She was dressed in actual street clothes. I pinched the collar of my robe together. "Thanks for coming, Mac. And thanks for going to those places."

"Sure thing, Mrs. Russell. It was my—" he stopped. It was my pleasure didn't sound right when talking about going to strip clubs. Especially not with Aggie hanging on his every word. "I'm glad I could help."

His gaze returned to Aggie. "If that girl exists, this is a job for the police. You two should stay out of it."

Was it my imagination or had the smile curving Aggie's lips tightened?

She stepped closer to him and patted his arm. "I'll see you to the door."

Aggie walked down the front hall with Mac and I stared at Mr.

Coffee. "You'd never tell a woman what to do, would you?"

He didn't reply. He didn't have to. I knew his answer was no.

Aggie blew back into the kitchen like a stiff breeze. "Okay then. I'll call Sadie and find out if there is such a person as Jane Nichols."

"And if there is a record? What then? Mac just told you to stay out of this."

"He did, didn't he?" Aggie wore an expression usually reserved for watching a baby's first steps.

"He did."

"It's early days. He hasn't figured it out yet."

"Figured what out?"

"I don't respond well to men who tell me what to do."

I lifted my coffee mug and toasted her.

TEN

Click.

I hung up the phone with more force than was strictly necessary. But Mother's calls about the ashes were growing tiresome. I'd fielded at least five. And poor Aggie—if she answered the phone, Mother harangued her for not being at the library.

Apparently Mother expected Aggie to move in with the pickle-face librarians.

But Aggie, usually so good at finding things, was striking out entirely. No leads on the ashes and her source at the police station hadn't found any information about Starry Knight or Jane Nichols. If the girl did exist, she didn't have a police record.

The only thing that had worked the way it was supposed to this week was my call to Uncle James. And that had worked too well. Anarchy was now so busy investigating murders we'd only managed a brief conversation.

Grace wandered into the kitchen, opened the refrigerator door, and peered inside.

"Are you looking for something?" I asked.

"No. I'm hungry."

She was in the right place.

"I thought you were going out for pizza."

"I am." She emerged from the depths of the fridge with a container of yogurt. "Don't you have a date?"

I did but I'd rather review a week's worth of microfilm with a disapproving librarian standing over my shoulder than spend the next few hours with Libba, Bill, and Bill's friend. "Yes."

"You should probably change." Grace pulled out a spoon out of the drawer, opened her yogurt, and stirred.

"I'll be home early."

The spoon slowed.

"No parties, Grace. No one in this house but you and Max."

"Okay." She sounded put upon.

"I mean it. Margaret Hamilton is ready to hex me. If we cross her again she may make my hair fall out."

"Okay." Annoyed but not convincing. I needed to be convinced.

"Grace." My voice was a warning.

"I got it." The hint of put-upon in her voice gave way to unfairly-accused. "No one comes over. Sheesh!"

"It's going to take a while for you to win back my trust."

That got an eye roll. "I've been an angel for three months."

But before she transformed into an angel (debatable) she had a huge, unsupervised, unsanctioned party. I tilted my head to the side, lowered my chin, and narrowed my eyes.

"You've got to start trusting me sometime."

"You're sixteen. You're going to make mistakes. My job is to help you learn from them."

"You don't think I learned my lesson?"

"The jury's still out."

With an epic eye roll she tossed her not-yet-empty yogurt in the trash and stomped out of the kitchen.

Mother-not-friend, mother-not-friend, mother-not-friend. A mantra. Maybe, when Grace was older, that would change.

Max stood.

"Don't even think about getting that out of the trash," I told him.

He tried to look innocent.

I didn't believe him for a second. "You need to earn back my trust, too." With a small sigh, I pulled the yogurt container out of the trash and rinsed it.

With a regular sigh, Max returned to his spot.

With a big sigh, I trudged upstairs and donned a black wrap dress, a king's ransom in gold chains, and high-heeled boots purchased from the most charming boot-maker in Milan (at the time, I'd hesitated at the cost of custom boots but Grace had talked me into them. For which, with the buttery soft leather hugging my calves, I was grateful).

I put on makeup, combed my hair, checked my purse for bail money (double dates with Libba never went well), and called myself ready.

Libba was late. No surprise.

I flipped on the television, watched *Sanford and Sons* (not my favorite but ABC and CBS were showing movies), and sipped on half a glass of Blue Nun.

Maybe Libba would cancel and I could spend my evening curled up on the couch watching *The Rockford Files*.

Ding dong.

With the biggest sigh yet, I left the couch, made my way to the front hall, and opened the door.

Bill stood on the other side. "Ellison, you look lovely." He glanced back at the idling car. "Libba sent me to fetch you." Libba's date had the kind of craggy face that improved with age, a hank of hair that defied his attempts to tame it, and a ready, infectious smile.

"Let me grab my coat."

Bill offered me his arm, escorted me to the car, tucked me into the back, and settled behind the wheel.

"Nice boots," said Libba.

She was dying to know what I wore beneath my mink. Was it on-a-date Ellison or middle-aged-widow Ellison? "Thank you."

"We're having dinner at the Alameda's rooftop restaurant."

The hotel's restaurant had replaced the venerable Putsch's 210 as the best restaurant on the Plaza.

Mother was still mourning Putsch's. "Ellison—" her voice shook like a leaf in a storm just thinking about the void its departure had made in her life "—we had every birthday dinner I can remember there. Louis Cina would play 'Happy Birthday' on his violin. You girls always ordered Lobster Newberg." And then the dessert cart would appear—serving crêpes Suzette, Cherries Jubilee, and Bananas Foster (flaming desserts were a specialty of the house). Marjorie and I gorged on sweets until our stomachs ached.

The new hotel and its new restaurant had wonderful food and a view (even Mother had to admit the view was better than Putsch's) but it wasn't venerable. "Sounds marvelous." I was missing *Rockford* but at least I'd be served a delicious meal.

"Wright's looking forward to meeting you," said Bill. "Thanks for joining us."

"It's my pleasure. Why is he in town?"

"Business," Bill replied. "He's buying a shopping center."

"Which one?"

"No idea. Wright never talks about his deals until the ink is dry."

Libba twisted in her seat and looked back at me. "After dinner, we're invited to the Presidential suite for drinks. I'm dying to see it." Translation—I was not to beg off early.

I smiled at her (bared my teeth). "How fabulous."

A moment later, we pulled into the circle in front of the hotel entrance and a man in a dark suit bounded to the car.

Bill jumped out and the two men gave each other that odd claspy hug that men have—bodies apart, shoulders touching, solid pats on the back, and a quick release.

Their voices wafted into the car.

"How long has it been?"

"Too long."

"I saw you in California when you were buying that vineyard."

"But that was three years ago."

The door to the backseat opened and Wright thrust his hand toward me. "Ellison? Wright Halstrom, pleased to meet you."

I took his hand and climbed out of the car. "A pleasure."

"And you must be Libba. Bill said you were pretty. He didn't do you justice."

"Pretty? He told you I was pretty? I'm going to talk to that man about improving his adjectives." Libba was charmed. I could tell. And Wright Halstrom had managed it with only a few words.

Bill handed over the keys to the valet attendant and we stepped into the lobby's warmth.

Libba loosened the buttons on her coat. "Well?" she whispered.

"He seems like a nice man to have dinner with," I whispered back.

"He seems like a nice man period. And handsome."

"Really? I hadn't noticed." I'd have to be blind not to notice. He was that good-looking. And I didn't care.

"Pfft." Libba handed over her mink to the coat check attendant. "You can't keep comparing every man you meet to Anarchy Jones."

My jaw dropped and I handed over my coat. If the girl who took it thought me mentally deficient (mouth hanging open and "bu, bu, but"—the closest I could come to actual words), she hid it well.

Finally, I managed a coherent sentence. "I have no idea what you're talking about."

Libba smirked.

The attendant handed me a chit for my coat.

"Thank you." I dropped the chit into my purse.

"Drinks before dinner?" suggested Wright.

"That would be lovely," said Libba.

The four of us rode a glass elevator to the hotel's rooftop restaurant. The lighting was dim, the conversations were genteel, and a pianist seated at a baby grand played a quiet version of a Burt Bacharach song. A maître d' seated us at a table with a view of the Plaza and we ordered cocktails. Scotch for the men, a stinger for Libba, wine for me.

"You know," said Libba. "He's from Kansas City."

"Who?" asked Bill

Libba waved a lazy hand toward the pianist. "Burt Bacharach."

"Really?" Wright glanced at the pianist who was wrapping up "Do You Know the Way to San Jose."

"Isn't he married to Angie Dickinson?" asked Bill.

The pianist transitioned to "I'll Never Fall in Love Again."

"Pepper Anderson." A naughty grin played across Wright's lips. "Thanks, honey." This he said to the waitress who delivered our drinks. He turned to his friend. "Say Bill, do you know anything about escrow laws in Missouri?"

Bill and Wright launched into a technical discussion about commercial real estate. The boring topic and Wright's hard-to-follow-rapid-fire delivery glazed my eyes in no time.

Libba yawned, leaned closer to me, and said, "I've been meaning to tell you, I ran into Mark Kittering."

"Oh?"

"He asked me about the top sponsorship level for the gala." She smirked. "You can thank me later."

"Qing Dynasty?" I squeaked. It had not been my idea to name the sponsorship levels after Chinese dynasties—Qing, Ming, Tang, Han, and Zhou. I'd inherited the levels with the chairman's job.

"Yes." She looked inordinately please. "He said he'd have his banker send a check."

"But Cole Cantwell is Ming."

Mark Kittering and Cole Cantwell were charming, urbane, and rich. Each man was in possession of a hollow leg (seriously, they could drink anyone but each other under the table). Each man lived in a home filled with gorgeous antiques and drool-worthy art (Mark went for impressionist and Cole collected pop art). Each man was philanthropic.

It was too bad they hated each other with a passion that rivaled the Hatfields and McCoys (more like Bette Davis and Joan Crawford—they were that catty).

Cole Cantwell was going to be madder than a wet hen when he saw Mark's name above his in the program. But, if I called Cole and warned him, Mark would be furious.

Libba had positioned me between a rock and a hard place.

Her lips formed a small, distressed circle. "I'm sorry. I didn't know."

At least she hadn't hung me out to dry on purpose.

"What are you girls whispering about?" asked Bill.

"Ellison is chairing a gala for the museum." Libba smiled as if being called a girl didn't bother her. Maybe it didn't. It bothered me. "We're just talking details."

"I think it's great you keep yourself busy with parties." He patted the back of Libba's hand.

Was it me, or did Libba's smile look a bit strained? I, for one, wanted to stab one of those little cocktail swords into his thigh. He'd called us girls and made the gala sound like a party planned on the fly.

"It's a lot of work," Libba insisted. "It will raise a lot of money for the museum."

"Of course it will. I bet you're great at soliciting donations." Bill combined being patronizing and salacious in just two sentences. It had to be some kind of record.

Libba's smile faltered.

I clenched my fingers together. It was a good thing we weren't at the table where I'd have access to flatware. Bill deserved a fork in his thigh.

Wright directed his gaze toward the Plaza which twinkled below us like an enchanted fairyland. "This is some view. You know, Nichols, the developer, invented the percentage lease. It started there." Wright didn't see magic; he saw dollar signs.

The conversation turned toward the weather, the Kansas City Kings (I dropped Tiny Archibald's name as if I actually knew who he was), and dinner.

We were led into the dining room.

We sat.

We perused the menu.

Lemon Sole Caprice for Libba, Chicken Almandine for Bill, a filet for Wright, and the South Pacific Salad for me.

"You need more than a salad," said Bill. "You girls diet down to nothing but men like girls with some meat on their bones."

"Ellison likes salad." Libba's tone carried too much intensity for the banality of her words.

"Especially this one." Keeping my voice light and polite required effort. "There's crabmeat and scallops and artichoke hearts. And water chestnuts. I love water chestnuts."

"I only like 'em when they're wrapped in chicken liver and bacon." Bill grinned at Wright.

The men returned to talk of real estate. Again.

The girls (this girl) stared out the window at the home of the percentage lease.

Libba (the other girl) called the waitress over and ordered a third stinger.

We made it through dinner on the back of a convoluted story about a real estate investor who'd gamed the system.

We made it through dessert talking about basketball.

"You girls like hoops?" If Bill called me a girl one more time...

"Ellison knows more about it than I do," said Libba

"And I know next to nothing."

"The tournament's coming up." Bill rubbed his hands together.

"UCLA will probably win."

He looked at me as if I'd just sprouted a second head. "Pardon?"

"They always do."

Wright chuckled. "Ellison knows more than she's telling."

I didn't.

The men ordered desserts. A mocha torte for Bill, a slice of Black Forest cake for Wright. Libba and I opted for coffee.

"Wright, where are you from?" I asked.

"You can't tell? Most people peg my accent. New York."

I had pegged his accent, I was just tired of talking about real estate and sports. "Really? What part of the city?"

"Brooklyn born but I live in Manhattan now."

"Ellison was just there for an art opening," said Libba.

"Oh?" So much boredom in one word.

"Her art. She sold everything."

Wright looked like he was stifling a yawn.

"I think it's great the way you girls find ways to keep busy," said Bill.

When I declined dessert, the waiter had taken my fork. Too bad. I knew exactly where I'd sink the tines.

Wright scraped the last morsel of chocolate and cherry off his plate and glanced at his watch. "I'm afraid I'm going to have to call it a night. I've got a call."

A crestfallen expression settled on Libba's face. "On a Friday night?"

"It's to Hawaii."

"Hawaii?" Libba sounded like a child denied a promised treat—the treat being a private tour of the presidential suite.

"I'm thinking of buying a hotel."

Libba shot Bill an I-want-to-see-that-suite-and-you-promised look.

Bill pulled at the collar of his shirt.

Wright called the waitress over. "Charge this to my room." He stood.

I stood.

Libba remained seated, looking as if she'd like to cross her arms and pout.

Bill helped her from her chair, pausing to whisper in her ear.

Her expression softened and she regarded him with a sparkle in her eyes.

"Thank you for dinner, Wright." I smiled at my host. If Bill drove quickly, I might make it home in time for *Police Story*.

"My pleasure." He glanced at his watch a second time. "Would it be awful if I didn't ride down to the lobby with you?"

"Not at all." We'd be able to leave with less fuss. "Thank you again."

We parted at the elevator bank. Wright took a regular elevator down to his suite. Libba, Bill, and I rode the glass elevator to the lobby.

They held hands and admired the hundred-eighty-degree view.

I dug in my purse for the coat check. The damned thing had to be in there somewhere.

We stepped into the lobby and I saw him right away—the sideburns, the leather coat, the man from Winstead's who'd stared at Grace. My feet slowed. Was he following me? No. That wasn't possible. Still, a shiver skated across my shoulders.

There was a girl with him. She was thin and blonde and the hard-edge of her gaze couldn't hide the fear in her eyes. I guessed her age at seventeen.

The girl noticed my staring and, in a bit of admirable bravado, rolled her eyes.

I adjusted my guess. She was sixteen.

Definitely too young to be with the man. Definitely too old to be wearing a school-girl uniform (a school-girl uniform except for the shoes. Real school girls didn't wear stilettos with their knee-socks).

I walked toward them and the man scowled at me. That I could live with. But the smell of stale cigarette smoke?

I wrinkled my nose in distaste.

The girl looked away.

The man's eyes narrowed.

My steps slowed. Self-preservation. The look on his face (predatory and mean) was too alarming to continue.

"Ellison, what are you doing?" Libba grabbed my elbow. "Let's go."

"Just a minute." I freed my arm, pretended I didn't notice the man's death-glare, and approached the girl. "Are you all right?"

"I'm fine." Her voice was small and miserable.

"Ellison, get your coat. The valet is bringing the car around."

I hated to leave the girl. "You're sure you're all right?"

"She's sure." The man's voice turned the words into a snarl.

"I didn't ask you."

His eyes narrowed to slits, and predatory and mean morphed into downright scary.

"I'm fine." The girl rubbed her arms.

"Where's your coat?" I asked. The man had one. Where was the girl's? She wore only a white blouse unbuttoned low enough to reveal the lace of her bra.

"Ellison!" Libba was getting impatient.

"One minute." With Libba trailing behind me, I marched over to the front desk. "May I please speak with the manager?"

A young man with diminutive stature and neat hair (he was barely out of high school) looked up from a register (maybe he was twenty-five—probably he was twenty-five). "I'm a manager."

"Is that man a guest in your hotel?"

"Which man?"

I pointed at the man with his sneer, and sideburns, and leather coat.

"No."

"I think he's—" I searched for the right word "—pandering. And I'm sure she's a minor."

The young man, not much more than a minor himself, paled. "I'll take care of it, ma'am."

"Thank you." I turned and walked back toward the girl, ignoring Libba who was actively tapping her foot.

"What's your name?" I asked the girl.

She glanced at the man and shook her head.

"I'm not leaving until you tell me."

"Tell her," said Libba, who'd followed me from the front desk. "She's as stubborn as a mule."

The girl's gaze traveled from me to Libba and back again. Then she tilted her head and looked up at the Sideburns.

He answered with a tiny shake of his head (and another death-stare for me).

"My name is Starry. Starry Knight."

ELEVEN

"Starry Knight!" Libba's voice was loud enough to turn every head in the the lobby. She clapped a hand over her mouth and mumbled, "You made that up."

Of course she had.

"You're Starry Knight?" My voice was pitched lower than Libba's but it communicated the same level of surprise. We'd found Starry Knight at the Alameda?

"So what if I am?" The girl might be miserable, maybe even terrified, but she had teenage attitude in spades.

"Keep your nose out of this." Side-burns paired this bit of advice with his most menacing glare yet.

Libba waved away his sorry (to her) attempt at a glare (three stingers and two glasses of wine with dinner can render the deadliest of glares banal). "Pish."

Side-burns' eyes narrowed to a point where his vision was probably impaired.

Libba hiccupped and her lips parted. She looked as if she meant to tell him if he wasn't careful his face might get stuck that way. A sentiment Side-burns might not appreciate.

"Do you want to be here, Starry?" My words came out in a rush.

The girl lifted her chin. "Listen, lady. Do yourself a favor. Leave me alone."

I'd walked away from one girl in trouble. I wasn't about to walk away from a second one.

"What's going on here?" Bill appeared at Libba's elbow with

her mink draped over his arm.

"We're just chatting with these lovely people," said Libba.

Since Side-burns was as far from being a lovely person as New York was from Hong Kong, Bill's brows rose. "Is there a problem?"

The manager joined our little party. "I called the police."

Side-burns' furious gaze encompassed us all. "I told you to mind your own damned business." His fingers wrapped around Starry's upper arm. "Come on. We're leaving."

The manager looked relieved.

Bill looked confused.

Libba and I looked at each other. I took a deep breath and said, "You're not taking that child anywhere."

"Lady, if you know what's good for you, you'll stay out of this."

"Are you threatening her?" asked Bill.

"I don't make threats."

"That's supposed to be a promise?" Bill puffed up his chest and scowled. He might have achieved menacing himself were it not for his plaid sport coat and Libba's draped mink.

The manager whispered something that sounded suspiciously like a four-letter word.

Frankly, he looked too young to whisper those kinds of words.

I held up my hands. Palms out. Fingers spread. "Let's all calm down."

Libba and Starry rolled their eyes, Side-burns settled his glare on me, Bill snorted, and the manager looked as if bursting into tears might happen—soon.

I swallowed. "I mean it. If this young woman is your daughter, you have nothing to worry about. If she's not, I'm sure you won't mind explaining to the authorities why you're at a hotel with a minor dressed this way."

With her-arm-is-on-fire speed, Side-burns released his hold on Starry.

She smoothed her too-short plaid skirt and stared at the carpet. I couldn't see her face but the frantic tension radiating from her told me she was out of her depth.

"Erp." The hotel manager was definitely out his depth.

"Did the police say when they'd be arriving?" I asked.

"Erp."

I presented the manager with an encouraging smile. "Perhaps a time frame?"

"Five minutes." The manager was deathly pale. Poor man. Having someone arrested for pandering in the lobby wasn't likely to attract the kind of guests the hotel wanted and a manager who looked older than nineteen would probably blame him.

I kept the smile in place—more difficult when it was directed at Side-burns. "You could leave," I suggested. "Before the police get here."

He considered my excellent suggestion and reached for Starry's arm. "Come on, Starry."

My smile disappeared. "Like I said, the girl stays." With Mother for a mother, I'd learned how to sound implacable at an early age.

Or not. The corner of Side-burns' lip curled into a sneer. "Starry." He sounded impatient. He expected her to leave with him.

"She stays," I repeated.

The girl looked up from her study of the carpet, her face unreadable. Did she want to go with him? Did she want to stay? Impossible to tell.

Libba cocked her head. "Do I hear sirens?"

Side-burns' jaw worked. Hard. Chewing-an-enormous-wad-of-gum hard. He cast a vicious death-glare my way. "I know who you are. I'll find out where you live."

"Are you threatening her?" Bill needed some new material (and a different sports coat—one with a bit of gravitas—but that was Libba's problem not mine).

"I don't make threats." Side-burns needed a new response. And a new death-glare. The one he had was wearing thin with repeated use.

"Erp." The manager needed a new word. Or maybe a string of them.

Side-burns shared one last death-glare with all of us, stalked through the lobby, and paused at the entry. His gaze sought Starry's and he waited.

Seconds passed.

The girl didn't move a muscle.

With a shake of his head, he pushed through the revolving doors. We watched through the plate glass window as he jumped into a cab and drove away.

"Ellison—" Libba was practicing her own death-glare "—who was that awful man?"

"No idea," I replied.

Starry shook her head as if she couldn't believe she'd landed herself in the midst of meddling socialites. "That was Ray. His name is Ray."

"What now?" asked the manager.

"You might want to call the police and tell them not to come."

"They're not coming." He shrugged his narrow shoulders. "I lied about that."

"Erp." It was the only answer I could think of.

Libba, with multiple stingers and two glasses of wine to her credit, shook her finger in the young man's face. "You lied?"

"I figured if he thought the police were coming, he'd leave." The manager glanced at Starry and a bubble appeared over his head. Inside the bubble floated the words, I thought he'd take you with him. "May I call you a cab?"

"No," I replied. "We're going to sit down in the lounge and talk."

"We are?" Bill didn't sound remotely pleased by my plan.

To be fair, the manager didn't look remotely pleased by my plan either.

"You and Libba go on, Bill. I'll catch a cab."

Bill nodded. Once. A short, decisive jerk of his chin. Then he handed the manager his valet ticket. "Would you please have them bring the car around?"

The manager smiled, delighted to be rid of at least part of his problem.

"We can't leave Ellison," said Libba.

"Of course you can," I told her. "You and Bill go somewhere fabulous and grab a nightcap." Libba needed another drink like she needed a hole in the head. "We'll catch a cab in a little while."

"We?" Libba grabbed my arm and pulled me a few feet away from Bill and Starry. "We don't know this girl."

"No," I agreed. "We don't." We knew she was in trouble.

"She looks like an exotic dancer."

I made no comment.

"Or worse." It was hard to argue Libba's point when Starry was dressed like a sexy school girl.

"I'm not leaving her." I'd left Leesa and she'd ended up dead.

"What are you going to do with her?" Libba's eyes widened. "You're not planning on taking her home?"

That was exactly what I was planning. "No, of course not."

"Good, because if your mother found out you brought home a stripper, her head would spin in full three-hundred-and-sixty-degree circles. Multiple times."

Libba was right. Mother's reaction would make Linda Blair's performance in *The Exorcist* look like a young lady taking tea. When her head was done spinning, she'd lecture me (deservedly) on exposing Grace to unseemly elements. But if I didn't take Starry home, if I left her, she'd be on her own. I couldn't do that. I just had to make sure Mother never found out what I'd done.

"Libba." Bill jerked his chin toward the drive where his car waited in front of the door. "The car is here."

Libba cast a quick glance at the car then focused on me. "What are you going to do?"

"I have no idea." It was the absolute truth. Sort of. "I'm going to help her."

Libba leaned closer to me. "You can't save everyone."

Maybe not, but I could at least try.

Bill held up Libba's mink. "Are you ready?"

Libba walked over to Bill, slid her arms into the coat's sleeves, and gave me a last penetrating stare.

Bill rubbed his chin. "Ellison, you're sure I can't take you home."

"I'm sure. Thanks for offering." I shooed them toward the door. "Be careful on the roads."

They walked toward the door—at least ten feet before Libba glanced over her shoulder. "Call me."

"I will."

And then they were gone.

I looked at Starry. Pigtails, a smattering of freckles, cherry red lip gloss, lace bra, short skirt, stilettos.

She looked at me. "Those people that just left, who were they?"

"My friend, Libba, and her date."

Starry rubbed her arms and looked worried.

"They're good people. I promise."

She fixed her gaze on the revolving door to the outside. The wrinkle in her brow suggested she suspected them of being undercover vice cops.

"Really, you don't need to worry. Are you hungry?"

She shrugged. "I could eat."

"I skipped dessert."

She snorted.

"Do you like pie?"

"Everyone likes pie." She paired this pronouncement with an eye roll.

"Not everyone. There are cake people out there who won't touch pie."

"I like cake."

"But you like pie better?"

She nodded.

"Wonderful. We can be friends." I glanced at my watch. "The Pam Pam Room is still open. Let's get some pie." For Starry, we'd add a side of dinner.

We walked down the hall toward the restaurant. I could feel the manager's gaze between my shoulder blades. I didn't have be a psychic like Madame Reyna to know he wanted us out of his hotel. Well, he'd get his wish. After Starry ate.

I glanced over my shoulder.

Sure enough, the manager was watching us.

And Wright Halstrom was striding out the front door.

Starry and I sat at a corner table in the Pam-Pam Room and ate pie. She ate pie. I pushed bits of lemon meringue around my plate.

Starry put down her fork and took a sip of water. "Why did you help me?"

If some stranger told me she'd interfered in my life at the behest of a spirit, I'd run away. Far away. "The man you were with didn't look very nice."

"Ray? Ray's all right. Better than most."

That didn't say much for most.

"Why were you here?" I asked.

"You mean why was a girl like me at a swanky hotel?" The bitterness in her voice curdled the milk in my coffee.

Actually I'd been looking for a client name. Soliciting prostitution was against the law. I was sure of it.

Starry picked up her fork and downed another bite of pie. "Ray was supposed to meet with some guy."

Who would designate the Alameda as a meeting place with Ray?

"What's Ray's last name?"

Starry looked me in the eye. "Smith."

And her real name was Rapunzel.

"Who was Ray meeting?"

Her shoulders rose and fell. If she knew, she wasn't telling. "Ray brought you to the hotel dressed like that?"

She looked down at her blouse and buttoned two buttons. She didn't blush, didn't seem overly concerned that everyone in the lobby had seen her bra. "He's worried. Someone's been asking around the clubs for me."

Oh dear. I picked up my coffee cup and let it warm my hands. "How did you meet Ray?"

Her lips twisted. "You mean how did I end up like this?"

That was exactly what I meant. "I suppose."

"Why do you care?" she demanded.

"I have a daughter about your age." That and I should have helped your friend. "I'd like to help."

The skin around her eyes tightened and she looked away. "Take care of your daughter. It's too late for me."

That was maudlin. I sat up a little straighter and gave Starry a Mother look. "Don't be ridiculous and stop feeling sorry for yourself. Your life is just beginning. You can make of it whatever you want."

She stared back at me. Suddenly tough as nails. "Easy for you to say."

"It is," I allowed. "Life isn't about easy or difficult. Right now, for you, life is about being smart enough to accept my help."

She dropped her gaze and lifted another bite of cherry pie to her lips.

I waited.

"My dad died when I was five. For a few years, it was just me and my mom. Then she married Gary." Starry scraped the edge of her fork across her plate, picking up lingering bits of crust and melted ice cream.

I waited.

"At first, Gary was nice. Things were better. Mom didn't have to work so hard." She put down her fork and studied her plate. "Then she got sick. Cancer. And Gary—" she turned her head away from me, staring at the view of the Plaza. Her lips thinned. A single tear welled over the rim of her eye. She swiped at it. Viciously. "After she died, I figured the streets couldn't be any worse than Gary."

"There wasn't anyone else?"

"My mom's mom. But she didn't believe me."

"So you ran away and met Ray."

"No. I met Leesa. I'd been on the streets for a while and she said she'd get me a job." She sent her version of a death-glare across the table, daring me to pity her. "I knew what the job was but I was desperate. Besides, it couldn't be any worse than Gary." She laughed softly. It was the kind of laugh reserved for three-time divorcees or women who caught their husbands in bed with their best friends. It was a laugh that belonged to those who'd seen pain and heartache and the horrible things people do to each other. It was laugh that acknowledged life was solitary, poor, nasty, brutish, and short. It was the laugh of a girl who'd been wrong. Gary was not the worst thing in the world.

I clenched my hands to keep them from reaching across the table. I pressed my lips together to keep them from uttering something sympathetic and trite. The girl staring at me knew better than to trust such easy expressions of concern.

She put the fork down on the edge of her empty plate. "Leesa had it worse than I did."

"Oh?"

"I can dance. I'm good at it. Dancing's better than—" she looked at her empty plate as if she couldn't imagine where the pie had gone.

"Do you want more to eat? A hamburger? A steak?"

"No. I'm good." She took a drink of water. "Also, Leesa looked too young to work at the club. Getting busted for minors is bad for business."

"What happened to Leesa?"

Starry shook her head. "She went out to the suburbs. I told her I'd go. The guy, he's—twisted. But she went. And she came back with this coat. Said a lady had given it to her. I told her she should sell it. But she said she was going to return it."

My throat swelled and I nodded, unable to reply. Now I took a sip of water. "What about the other girls who were shot?"

Starry's eyes widened. She pushed her chair away from the table and stood, sending the chair crashing to the floor. "I didn't tell you Leesa was shot."

She hadn't. I was an idiot. Any trust we'd established was gone. I held out my hands, pleading. "I'm the woman who gave her the coat."

Starry pinched the bridge of her nose. Was she considering her choices? At least she hadn't walked away. Yet.

A waiter appeared next to her and righted the chair. "Are you all right, miss?"

"Navy blue with brass buttons. A pea coat." I told her. Then I shifted my gaze to the waiter. "She's fine, thank you."

"What to do you want?" Starry's hand reached for the back of the chair. She gripped the wood so hard her knuckles turned white.

"To help. Like I should have helped Leesa."

"You have no clue what my life is like. But, because you're feeling charitable today, you decided you'd swoop in and help me? How did you know my name? I know you and your friend recognized it. Tell me."

"We went to a psychic. She said Leesa wanted us to find you."

"A psychic?"

"Yes."

Her lips pulled back from her teeth. "Let me guess. Shag rug and plastic slipcovers."

I nodded.

"Madame Reyna." And I thought her voice was bitter before.

"How did you know?"

Her gaze slid away from me. "Leesa talked about her." Her hand loosened its grip on the chair. "I'm out of here." She turned and marched toward the lobby.

Dammit. I dug in my purse for a five, found a twenty, threw the bill on the table, and rushed after her.

I caught up with her before she pushed through the revolving door. "Where are you going?"

She turned and looked at me. "Stay away from me. Stay out of my life. I'm not your problem, lady."

"Ellison."

"What?"

"My name, it's Ellison. And yours is Jane."

The girl shook her head. "I don't use that name anymore."

"Maybe you should."

"Maybe you should mind your own business."

"I think that ship has sailed."

She laughed then. A laugh that got caught in her throat and turned into a sob.

Starry Knight, stripper, prostitute, and all-around tough girl stood in the hallway of the Alameda and cried. The kind of cry that melted mascara, swelled eyes, and left skin blotchy for hours. The kind of cry best cried alone.

I took her by the arm. "Come on, let's go home."

TWELVE

We drove home in silence. To be more accurate, we drove home without talking.

Even the cabby was quiet. His sole comments were, "Where to?" and "Radio's broken."

Starry sniffled and hiccupped.

I swallowed trite expressions of sympathy.

No, I didn't understand what she was feeling.

No, I couldn't promise her problems would look smaller in the morning.

No, every little thing was not going to be all right.

Poor kid. She'd only left the hotel with me because she had no place else to go.

We pulled into the drive.

Starry looked at the house and shot me a you-didn't-tell-me-you're-loaded look. "You live here?"

I glanced at my house. "Yes."

She crossed her arms and slouched lower in the seat. Why was she upset? The size of the house meant I had the means to help her.

"It's just a house." A big house. "Come on." I handed the cab driver the fare and a tip and opened the car door. "We'll get you settled."

I climbed the front steps and slid the key into the lock.

Starry shuffled behind me.

I pushed open the front door and looked over my shoulder. Starry lingered at the bottom of the stoop. The cab's tail lights glowed red at the bottom of the drive. By the curb, the streetlight illuminated a car I didn't recognize as it cruised slowly by.

I'd never seen an El Camino within two miles of my neighborhood before. It was as out of place on my street as...as a teenage stripper. My heart skipped a beat. "Come on in. Hurry." We stepped into the foyer and I closed the door and locked it. "Grace? Are you home?" My voice sounded too loud.

"Family room."

I exhaled.

Max trotted into the front hall and stopped when he saw a stranger.

"What a pretty dog." Starry crouched and held out her hands. "What kind is she?"

"He's a Weimaraner. His name is Max."

Max trotted up to Starry, stuck his face up her skirt, sniffed, and let her scratch behind his ears.

"You've made a friend for life."

"I love dogs."

"Mom—" Grace stopped in her tracks and stared at the stranger petting her dog.

"Grace, this is St—Jane. Jane, this is my daughter, Grace."

"Hi." Grace wore a who-the-hell-is-this expression. "Nice to meet you."

Jane stood. "Hi."

"Jane's going to be spending the night. Would you please loan her a nightgown?"

"Sure. Of course. No problem." Grace tore her gaze away from Jane's outfit. "I'm glad you're home. Someone's been calling and hanging up. Like a million times."

And there was an El Camino cruising my street.

Ice trickled through my veins. "I've got to make a call. St—Jane, would you like some hot chocolate?"

"No, thank you."

"How about you and Grace go watch some TV? I'll be in shortly."

Both girls gave me what could be charitably called baleful

looks.

Brngg, brngg.

They'd have to figure things out on their own. I had bigger problems.

I hurried into the study and reached for the phone.

What had Ray said? "I know who you are. I'll find out where you live."

I picked up the receiver. "Hello."

Nothing. Not even breathing.

"Hello."

Still nothing. Well, no sound. Menace traveled the phone line loud and clear. Menace and something darker, something twisted and rotten.

I slammed the receiver into the cradle and jerked my hand away as if the molded plastic had been infected with evil.

My heart raced.

My mouth was suddenly dry.

Deep breaths. One, then another, then a third. Breathe. If only the air could reach my lungs.

The phone couldn't be blamed for the caller on the other end of the line.

The phone wasn't actually touched by evil.

Such an idea was ludicrous.

Ludicrous.

But I had to force myself to reach for the receiver.

I dialed. Please let him answer.

Three rings. "Jones."

"Anarchy." His name was a plea.

"What is it, Ellison? What's wrong?"

"I think we're in trouble."

"Where are you?"

"At home."

"I'm on my way."

And just like that my lungs inflated. "Thank you." I was talking to a dead line. When Anarchy said he was on his way, he meant it.

I hung up the phone, climbed the front stairs, slipped into my bedroom, and opened the drawer to my night stand. My gun, a .22, waited for me. Looking at the glint of metal calmed my heart beat. Holding the pearl handle in my palm returned saliva to my mouth.

I tucked the gun into my pocket and descended the stairs.

Grace and Jane were in the family room. They sat on opposite ends of the couch and watched the late news as if their lives depended on it.

Grace held a mug of hot chocolate.

Jane held an old-fashioned.

I frowned. "What are you drinking?"

"Vodka and soda." Her voice was matter-of-fact.

"You're not old enough to drink."

She looked at me as if I'd taken leave of my senses. "It's just a drink."

"You're underage."

Defiance flared in her eyes. "Really?" She packed the soul-killing hopelessness of stripping for a room of drunk men, the skin-crawling horror of prostitution, and the terror of living on the streets into that one word.

"Really. Minors don't drink in my house." I took the drink from Jane's hand and felt like a hypocrite. It wasn't as if Grace abstained. I was sure she had the occasional drink. But she cared enough about my good opinion to hide it from me. "Besides, Anarchy's on his way over."

"Who's Anarchy?" asked Jane.

"Mom's detective." Grace shifted her gaze to the bulge in my pocket and paled.

"Your detective? Jane's voice rose. "You're busting me?"

"He's a homicide detective," I explained. "You're not in any trouble."

Grace's brows rose but her gaze remained fixed on the way the gun pulled at the fabric of my dress. "Was it the phone calls?" Her gaze shifted to Jane. "Or something else?"

"The phone calls and the El Camino in front of the house.

Anarchy's on his way."

"The cop's name is Anarchy? And he's coming here? Now?" She looked ready to run.

"He looks out for us," said Grace. "He has a thing for Mom."

That last comment was totally unnecessary (even if it did warm the cold knot of anxiety in my stomach).

"What time did the calls start?" I asked.

"I don't know for sure." Grace glanced at her watch. "An hour ago. Maybe two."

Brnng, brnng.

Grace shuddered.

Enough was enough. I marched over to the phone and grabbed the receiver. "I don't know who this is, but I called the police, they're on their way." Righteous anger lit my veins.

"Ellison?" Mother's voice was like a fire hose on the flame of my anger. "What have you done now?"

"Nothing," I told her. "I've done nothing." Except rescue a teenage stripper. I took a sip of the teenage stripper's vodka soda which was somehow, fortuitously, still clutched in my hand. "Someone's been crank calling the house."

"Hmph." Which was better than her asking why the police were coming to the house for crank calls.

"What do you need, Mother?" Ten o'clock on a Friday night, she had to have a good reason for calling.

"We need to talk."

Uh-oh. "About what?"

"Your father."

"Has something happened to him?" Everything slowed. My heart. My breathing. The spinning of the earth.

"He's fine. For now. Those ashes in the closet—" she paused and I pictured her propped up in her bed wearing a quilted satin bed jacket in a chilly shade of blue "—they belong to your father's—"

"What?" His what? Had she lost her mind?

"They. Belong. To. The. Other. Woman." Compared to her voice, the South Pole sounded like a tropical vacation.

I swallowed. "Mother, have you been drinking?"

Grace's mouth dropped open.

"Don't be ridiculous." Mother's tone was icy. How-dare-I-suggest-such-a-thing icy. Even-Admiral-Byrd-would-shiver icy.

Ridiculous was thinking the phone might be infected by evil. Thinking Mother might be tippling—especially when she told me my steadfast, loyal father had left another (the other) woman's ashes in the hall closet—was the opposite of ridiculous. The alternatives—Mother was right or she'd gone round the bend—were too awful to contemplate

"Daddy would never—"

"I should have known you'd take his side."

"I'm not on anyone's side. I just can't imagine Daddy cheating. He's sixty." Did men still cheat at sixty?

"I never said his affair was recent."

Oh dear Lord. I sank onto the nearest chair and lowered my head. Mother had lost her mind.

Ding dong.

I lifted my gaze. "Mother, there's someone at the front door." Please let it be Anarchy. Please. "I'll call you in the morning." When she was sober. "We'll sort this out."

"You don't believe me."

"I just find it hard to believe that Daddy would cheat on you. He adores you. And if he did cheat, why in the world would he leave her ashes someplace you might find them?"

"If they're not hers, then who do the ashes belong to?"

Ding dong.

"I'll get it," said Grace.

"No!" I wanted her nowhere near a door without protection and I wasn't about to give my child a gun. "Listen, Mother, I've got a situation here. I've got to go. May I call you later tonight or first thing in the morning?"

Click.

She'd hung up on me.

Mother's ire was a problem for tomorrow. I had bigger, more

immediate problems. I reached into my pocket and closed my hand around my gun. "Come on, Max." I glanced at the two teenagers. "You two stay here."

"Bu—"

"No buts, Grace. If you hear anything odd, run to a neighbor's." I paused in the doorway to the kitchen. "Don't go to Margaret Hamilton's. She probably wouldn't let you in."

Max and I made our way to the front door, stopping briefly in the kitchen to pour what was left of Jane's drink down the sink. At the door, I peered through the glass side panels.

Anarchy waited on the stoop.

I yanked open the door and he blew into the foyer like a gust of March wind. His hands circled my arms. His eyes searched my face. "What happened?"

"I—" explaining seemed overwhelming "—let me make some coffee and I'll tell you everything."

Grace was lurking in the kitchen. The color returned to her cheeks when she saw Anarchy and she smiled. "You're here."

"I'm here." He rested his hand on the small of my back. His hand was big, and comforting, and warm. Its position on my back said he'd take over now. How easy would it be to lean into him? To let him take over? Too easy.

"Where's Jane?" I stepped away from Anarchy's hand and hurried over to Mr. Coffee. I took his pot and held it under the running faucet.

"Watching the news."

"Who's Jane?"

Grace rolled her eyes. "Mom brought her home."

"She's part of the everything I have to tell you." I turned off the faucet, poured the water into Mr. Coffee's reservoir, and settled the pot on the warmer. "I suppose we'd better drink decaf." Regular at this time of night and I wouldn't get a wink of sleep. I might not anyway. I inserted a filter and scooped out decaffeinated grounds.

Grace pulled out a stool and sat as if she planned on listening to my story.

Not.

"Grace, I think we're safe now. Why don't you and Jane go upstairs and get ready for bed? She can sleep in the blue room."

Grace crossed her arms and shifted on her stool—settling in.

"I'll tell you tomorrow. Everything. I promise."

Mr. Coffee (God love him) gurgled.

"I mean it. Tomorrow."

Grace's gaze traveled from me to Anarchy and back again. "Fine." She stood with grudging slowness, turned, and called, "Jane, are you ready to head upstairs?" Then she turned back to me and whispered, "If I were you, I'd lock up the silver."

Jane appeared in the kitchen, took one look at Anarchy, and lost her hard edges. She gazed at him like a lovestruck school girl whose middle name was Innocent.

"Anarchy, I'd like you to meet Jane Nichols. Jane, this is Detective Jones."

"Pleased to meet you, Jane."

Jane blushed. She didn't reply. She didn't extend her hand. She just stared. And blushed.

"Come on." Grace tugged on Jane's sleeve. "I'll show you to your room."

Jane shook her head as if waking from a trance and followed Grace. She paused at the bottom of the back stairs and cast one last lingering glance at Anarchy. "Nice to meet you, too." Then, if the clack of her heels was any indication, she ran up the stairs.

"Do you have that effect on every woman you meet?"

"What effect?" Anarchy's brown eyes twinkled.

"Don't play dumb with me."

"No, I don't. You seem completely immune to my charms." Boy, was he wrong.

"Coffee?" I squeaked.

"Sure." I poured us two cups and handed him one. "Cream or sugar?"

"Black."

I added a jot of cream to my mug, led Anarchy to the family

room, and sank into a club chair.

He sat on the corner of the couch nearest to me. If we'd scooched forward just a smidge, our knees would have touched.

He took a sip of his coffee. "What's happening?"

"It's a long story," I warned.

"I've got lots of time."

"Libba took me—dragged me to a medium." I shifted my gaze to my lap and told him everything.

I told him about seeing Ray at Winstead's and the way Ray had looked at Grace.

I told him about Madame Reyna and her insistence I save Starry Knight.

I told him about seeing Starry in the Alameda lobby.

I told him about Ray's threats, the hang-up phone calls, and the El Camino.

I didn't tell him about the ashes in Mother's closet, Starry's lace bra, or Wright Halstrom.

Then I drank the last sip in my mug. "Do you need more coffee?"

Anarchy stared straight ahead and tapped his fist against the thin line of his lips. He was too deep in thought to be tempted by coffee.

"I need more." I left him to his thoughts and went to the kitchen where Mr. Coffee, who would never dream of judging my actions, sat on the counter with a pot of not-quite heaven. Heaven was caffeinated, of that I was sure. "That was rough," I told him.

He looked sympathetic and offered me a refill.

I took him up on his offer, returned to the family room, and sat.

Anarchy's had crossed his ankle over his knee. He leaned toward me. "I have a few questions."

I took a too large sip of hot coffee. "Okay."

"Jane or Starry?"

"Jane."

"Jane said Ray's last name was Smith?"

"She did."

Anarchy's lips thinned. He believed in Ray Smith as much as I did. Not at all. "Any ideas as to his real name?"

"Not a one."

"Do you know where she danced?"

"I didn't think to ask."

"We can find out in the morning." He leaned back against the couch. Lines radiated from the corners of his eyes and the weight of the world seemed to push on his shoulders.

"You look tired."

He smiled. A tired smile. "You look beautiful."

I did?

"What were you doing at the Alameda tonight?"

"A favor for Libba."

He chuckled. "Another double date?"

"How—"

"I am a detective and you look particularly beautiful." A wry smile twisted his lips. "At least you didn't get injured or arrested." He closed his eyes. "This couch is comfortable."

Was he asking me to join him?

"I'll sleep here."

"You'll what?" My voice was so high Max's ears perked.

Anarchy's eyes opened and he stared at me with...with intent.

Flutters of nerves tied my stomach into knots. "You'll what?" This time I managed the question a few octaves lower.

"I'm not leaving you and Grace alone. Not until we know more about Ray Smith. Not until I know you're safe."

Lord love a duck! Did he plan on moving in?

THIRTEEN

Saturday morning dawned cold and crystalline bright.

The light was perfect for painting but instead of my paint clothes, I donned a pair of gray flannel pants and a sweater unmarred by daubs of cadmium yellow or burnt umber. The only brush I touched was dipped in blush and I swiped it across my cheeks, not a canvas.

Thus prepared for the day, I descended to the kitchen where Anarchy, stubbled, mussed, and more attractive than ever, stood next to a full pot of coffee.

"Good morning."

"Morning. Hope you don't mind that I started coffee?"

"Are you kidding? I'm grateful." I pulled two mugs out of the cabinet and handed him one. "I hope the couch wasn't too uncomfortable."

"It was fine."

"I have plenty of guest rooms."

"Which you offered last night. I wanted to be downstairs."

I took my first sip of coffee. All sips of coffee are good but the first sip of the morning is the best. I sighed. "What now?"

Anarchy took a sip of coffee and seemed unaffected by its perfection. "I'll talk to Jane and figure out who Ray Smith is."

I glanced at the clock. Seven thirty. "I didn't hear anyone stirring when I came down. It may be awhile."

A slow smile spread across Anarchy's face, and he pulled out a stool for me. "I'll make you breakfast."

"Don't be silly. You're the guest. I'll cook."

"Ellison." His voice turned serious. "I'm hungry. I'll cook."

"How do you know I can't cook you a gourmet breakfast?"

"Tales of your exploits have traveled before you." His eyes twinkled.

Someone was in trouble. Grace? Aggie? Libba? Someone. I sat on the stool and drank my coffee.

Anarchy pulled eggs and butter from the refrigerator, a whisk from a drawer, and bread from the breadbox. "Do you have any bacon?"

"I don't know," I admitted.

He went foraging in the fridge and emerged triumphant with a package wrapped in butcher's paper. "Aggie buys the good stuff."

She did. The quality of meats and cheeses in our fridge had risen markedly since Aggie started dating Mac.

"Where are your pans?"

I pointed to a cabinet below the counter and was treated to the sight of Anarchy's hiney as he bent to fetch a skillet.

The view rivaled my first sip of coffee.

"Hey, Mom."

I nearly leapt off the stool.

"Jumpy much?" Grace grinned at me as if she knew exactly what I'd been looking at.

"Anarchy is cooking breakfast," I said with as much dignity as I could muster.

"You're letting a guest cook?"

"Someone told him about my cooking skills."

She ran a hand through her messy hair and she shifted her gaze to the floor. "You don't have cooking skills."

"Which is why he's cooking."

"Morning, Grace." Anarchy was grinning as if Grace and I were part of a skit on The Carol Burnett Show. Any moment now, Harvey Korman would appear.

"Morning," she replied. "Can I help?"

"Can you cook?"

"Better than Mom."

They exchanged a look that said Max was a better cook than me. I smiled at them both despite myself.

Brnng, brnng.

Not yet eight o'clock on a Saturday morning.

"I'll get it," said Anarchy.

"No!" I held up my hands. "I can't have a man answer the phone so early in the morning."

Brnng, brnng.

We stared at each other across the counter.

"Whoever was calling and hanging up stopped once I'd told them I'd called the police."

A slight jerk of his chin was the only acknowledgment I got for my excellent point.

We had reached an impasse.

Brnng, brnng.

Grace rolled her eyes and answered the phone. "Hello." She listened for a moment then held the receiver out to me (it would reach anywhere in the kitchen because she'd stretched the cord to its limit).

"Hello."

"Ellison, it's your father."

"Hi, Daddy." My father never called. Something awful was coming. I sensed its approach. "What's wrong?"

He answered with silence.

"Daddy?"

"Is your mother at your house?"

"No. Why?" With my free hand, I clutched my coffee mug.

"She left me."

Crash!

I'd stood and knocked over the stool. How had that happened? Also, there was coffee all over the counter. Coffee dripping onto the floor. How had that happened? "She what?"

"She's gone."

"Mother would never leave you." She wouldn't. People might talk.

"She left a note."

"What does it say?"

"Harrington, I'm leaving you."

I squeezed my eyes closed and pressed a hand against my chest. "It's the ashes."

"The ashes?"

"Mother found someone's ashes in the front hall closet. She's convinced they belong to another woman."

"That's ridiculous." Finally, sanity.

"Exactly what I told Mother."

"I would never leave Sylvia's ashes where your mother might find them."

Wait, what? "Who is Sylvia?" My voice was calm but my stomach was doing the merengue with my heart beat. I collapsed onto the stool next to the one I'd knocked over. I had to. My knees felt less solid then the eggs Anarchy had broken into a mixing bowl.

"Are you all right?" Grace whispered.

No. I wasn't. I mimed drinking coffee and my angelic daughter brought me a fresh cup.

"Who is Sylvia?" I was pretty sure Daddy had heard me the first time.

"It happened a long time ago."

Oh dear Lord. "You cheated on Mother?" My father had an affair. My father.

"It's ancient history." His tone told me that history was none of my damned business. "Do you have any idea where Frances might have gone?"

"No. If it's ancient history, why would Mother think you'd put Sylvia's ashes in the hall closet?"

Daddy didn't answer.

"Daddy?"

"There are things you don't know."

Apparently.

"You've got to help me find your mother."

I did?

I did. Daddy knew next to nothing about Mother's haunts. "Maybe she's driving to Marjorie's." My sister lived in Akron.

"By herself?" Now Daddy's tone told me how far off he thought I was.

Admittedly, Mother barreling down I-70 by herself was unlikely but I couldn't think of a single friend she'd trust with the knowledge that her perfect marriage was less than perfect.

Ding dong.

"Daddy, there's someone at the door. Maybe it's Mother. I'll call you back."

I stood, dropped the receiver into its cradle and hurried toward the front of the house.

"Wait, Ellison." Anarchy edged past me and peered outside.

Satisfied that Ray Smith didn't stand on the other side, he opened the front door.

All I could see was an enormous flower arrangement.

Big enough for a buffet table. And filled with over-the-top flowers—orchids and lisianthus and Gloriosa lilies.

Definitely not Mother. Where was she?

Anarchy opened the door and the flower arrangement said, "Delivery for Ellison Russell."

"I'm Ellison Russell." I stepped out of the way, allowing the delivery man entrance into my home.

"Where do you want 'em, ma'am?"

"The living room." I pointed, realized he couldn't see me, and added, "To the right."

Anarchy and I followed the delivery man into the living room. "Please put them on the library table."

"Whew." The man, free of his load, planted his hands on his waist and twisted. "Those are heavy." Hint, hint.

"Just a moment, I'll grab my purse."

"I've got it." Anarchy pulled out his wallet and handed the man a few dollars.

The delivery man, hand pressed against his back, left us with the enormous arrangement.

"Is there a card?" I asked.

Anarchy reached, plucking a small white envelope from the center. "Here."

I took the envelope and opened it.

Ellison, thanks for a wonderful evening. Wright

I rolled my eyes. I couldn't help it.

Anarchy took the card from my hand. "Who is Wright?"

"The double date." I spoke through gritted teeth.

"That must have been some date."

"Not really." Telling Anarchy everything did not include the embarrassing truth that Wright Halstrom had been so bored with my company that he'd faked a call to Hawaii. "No one got arrested and there were no trips to the ER."

He stared at me, his eyes almost cop-like in their intensity.

"Seriously. I took Jane out for pie and we were still home in time to catch part of the ten o'clock news."

His expression didn't soften.

Was he jealous? Surely not.

Brnng, brnng.

I left him with the flowers (the living room was going to smell like a garden—or a funeral parlor, it was all in one's perspective) and hurried back to the kitchen.

Brnng, brnng.

I took a deep breath, preparing to tell Daddy that Mother was still missing. "Hello."

"Ellison," said Libba. "I hope I'm not calling too early but I've got plans today and I wanted to remind you about the club party tonight."

"About that—" someone was threatening us, Mother was missing, Daddy had a (dead) mistress (really?), and I had a teenage houseguest.

"Oh no you don't. You promised."

"Things have come up."

"You promised."

"Mom!" Grace stood at the bottom of the backstairs. Five feet away. Strictly speaking, she didn't need to yell.

"You promised and I'm holding you to it." Libba sounded adamant.

"Hold on, Libba."

"Mom!" Grace drew the word out so that it lasted ten seconds. At least.

"What is it, Grace? I'm on the phone."

Grace's cheeks were flushed and there was a wild look in her eyes. "Jane's gone."

"Gone?" I stared at her unable to process that another person was missing. "You're sure?"

"Positive."

"Libba, I'm going to have to call you back. We have—we have a situation here." I hung up the phone before Libba could argue. "Where did she go?"

Grace shook her head. "I have no idea but my car is gone. She stole it."

Brnng, brnng.

"Your car?" Sweet nine-pound Baby Jesus. "Are you sure?"

"She's gone. The car is gone." Eye roll. "I'm pretty sure."

Brnng, brnng.

"Hello!" My voice was too sharp. "Hello."

"Have you heard from your mother?"

This again? "No, Daddy."

"What are we going to do?" We?

I looked at Mr. Coffee but his only suggestion was more coffee. As suggestions went, it was a good one.

I looked at Grace. She'd crossed her arms and her expression said very clearly that the stolen car was my fault and should be my top priority.

I looked at Max—or where Max was supposed to be. He wasn't there.

"Daddy, things are—" I rubbed my eyes with the heel of my hand "—things are chaotic here."

Ding dong.

"I'll get it," said Grace.

"Wait!"

She paused in the doorway to the front hall.

"Where's the bacon?"

Our eyes scanned the counters. No bacon. And worse, no Max.

"Daddy, I have to go. I'll call you back soon. I promise." I hung up the phone. "Max!"

My dog did not come.

I raced past Grace into the front hall. "Anarchy, did you leave the bacon out? I think Max—" the words died on my lips. Mother stood in my front hall.

"Ellison Walford Russell, what is going on?" She was talking to me but her gaze was fixed on Anarchy.

What is going on? I could ask her the same question. But, if Max had taken the bacon, all other questions were moot. No one would get any answers because I'd be at the emergency veterinarian all day having the dog's stomach pumped (been there, done that).

"Anarchy, where's the bacon?" I asked. The man wasn't accustomed to a dog that counter-surfed and took what he wanted but there was an outside chance he'd put it back in the fridge.

"Max!" Grace's voice carried. "Give me that!"

Max raced out of the dining room with the still-wrapped bacon clamped between his jaws. He saw Mother and changed course.

"Max! Bad dog!"

Max was not listening to Grace.

He flew back into the dining room.

I followed him.

The dog took a ready-to-run stance at one end of the dining room table.

Grace stood ready on the other side.

Getting the bacon back required a pincer maneuver. We had to come at him from both sides. Catch him in the middle.

But he had bacon. Our usual maneuver was doomed to failure. He eluded us by dashing under the table.

"Max! Drop it." The dog rolled his eyes at me and feinted left.

Bacon!

Anarchy grabbed his collar.

Max turned his doggy head and looked up at Anarchy with liquid eyes. He had bacon. Surely no one would deprive him of such a treat.

Anarchy clasped the package and pulled the bacon from Max's teeth.

"I wouldn't have that dog." Mother posed in the arched doorway to the dining room, a tragic figure forced to deal with her daughter's craziness when her own life was falling apart. "Where did those flowers come from? The arrangement is very large." Translation: very gauche.

"I went on a double date with Libba last night. A friend of Bill's. He sent them."

"Bill?"

"No, his friend." I took the mangled package of bacon from Anarchy's outstretched hand. "Daddy's called here twice."

Mother lifted her nose. "I do not wish to talk to your father."

For the love of Pete. "Talk to him. Don't talk to him. I need coffee."

I turned on my heel and headed toward Mr. Coffee.

Mother followed me. "Your father—"

I held up a hand. "I don't want to hear it."

"But—"

"No buts. You and Daddy work this out. Or don't. It is your problem, not mine."

"But—"

I shook my head and kept walking, taking care to keep the bacon package out of Max's reach.

The six of us—me, Grace, Max, Anarchy, Mother, and Mr. Coffee—reconvened in the kitchen.

I returned the bacon package to the fridge.

Grace righted the fallen stool.

Max slunk over to his spot.

Anarchy poured me a fresh cup of coffee.

Mother glared.

And Mr. Coffee shared his sunny face with all of us.

"Grace, we'll discuss your problem later." I shifted my gaze to the not-remotely-repentant dog. "You're in big trouble, mister."

"I'm sorry about the bacon," said Anarchy. "I had no idea he'd take something off the counter."

It was a rookie mistake. As he was around more, he'd learn Max's tricks. "All's well that ends well."

As for Mother, I studied her carefully. Not a hair out of place. Perfectly dressed. A familiar put-upon expression on her face. "You're being dramatic. You're never dramatic."

"Your father—"

"I know. He told me. But he also said it was ancient history."

Mother snorted. Mother never snorted. Then, like any good general who sees a battle being lost, she changed strategies. "What is Detective Jones doing here so early in the morning?"

"Detective Jones spent the night."

Mother's mouth opened and closed. Like a goldfish. Or a woman struck dumb by her daughter's scandalous revelation.

"Ellison received a credible threat," said Anarchy. "I spent the night on the couch just to make sure she and Grace and Jane stayed safe."

Mother's eyes narrowed "Who is Jane?" She turned on me. "Why is someone threatening you?"

Oh dear. Then it hit me—two could play that change-strategies game. "Why did you leave Daddy?"

"I'd like coffee."

"Of course." I'd never deny Mother coffee, no matter how badly she annoyed me. I poured her a cup.

She took it from me, sipped, and said, "Thank you." Her tone left no doubt she was barely surviving a life-altering tragedy.

"Why leave now, Mother? You've obviously known about Sylvia for a while." I wrapped my hands tightly around my mug.

"He told you her name?"

"He did. Answer the question."

Mother's gaze shifted from Grace to Anarchy and her lip curled slightly. "You're right. I knew about Sylvia for years. Karma, too."

I swallowed a sigh—and some coffee. "Who is Karma?"

"Your half-sister."

Which is how I dropped my second cup of coffee in one morning.

I spluttered. I wiped the front of my sweater with the tea towel a pale-faced Grace forced into my hands. I clutched the edge of the counter. "My what?"

"Your half-sister." Mother's gaze shifted between Grace and Anarchy as if she regretted dropping this bombshell in front of her granddaughter and a cop.

"How old is Karma?" Grace posed an excellent question.

"Around forty."

Forty? I was almost forty. My hands clutching the counter were the only thing keeping me upright.

"Ellison, you need to sit down." Anarchy slid an arm around my waist.

I leaned into him and let him lead me into the family room—to the couch where the blankets and sheets he'd used last night were neatly folded.

"Here, Mom." Grace, God love her, handed me a fresh cup of coffee.

I stared up at Mother. "How long have you known?"

"Since she was born."

"And you're just telling me now?"

Mother donned her sour-pickles expression. Children were not supposed to question their parent's decisions. Not even when the children were staring down forty. "It's complicated."

Complicated? I put my coffee cup down on the coffee table and lowered my head to my hands. I needed to think.

The couch shifted with the weight of someone sitting next to me. An arm circled my shoulders. "Are you all right?" Anarchy's voice was gentle.

"No." I kept my head down and reviewed my morning. One missing girl, one stolen car, and one long-lost half-sister. Not long lost. She hadn't been lost. She'd been there all the time, but no one had seen fit to tell me about her.

I lifted my head and glared at Mother.

"Don't you scowl at me. She's not my mistake." Mother clasped her hands and looked regal.

"Granna—" where had had the steel in Grace's voice come from? "—I think Mom needs a break."

"Hmph."

"Grace is right. I've had enough chaos for one morning. You and Daddy need to work this out." I'd worry about this mysterious half-sister later.

Mother stood straighter. "Your father—"

"You wouldn't enjoy life as a divorcee, Mother. You wouldn't. If Daddy says the ashes don't belong to Sylvia, believe him."

"Well." She infused that one word with forty years' worth of outrage. Outrage with Daddy. Outrage with Marjorie. Outrage with me. And outrage with Sylvia and Karma. Mother outraged was a force of nature.

"Hop on a plane and go to Palm Springs for a week. Drink a few martinis. Play golf. Enjoy the weather. Calm down. But then, come back and talk to Daddy. Work things out."

She stared down her nose at me.

"Do you love him?"

Her eyes widened as if I'd surprised her with my question. "Of course."

"Then take my advice."

She sniffed. A good sign. "Palm Springs is lovely this time of year."

"It is," I agreed.

"So many of my friends are out there now."

"Go." I made a shooing gesture with my hands.

"I believe I will." She looked only slightly mollified. "You may tell your father where I've gone. Tell him I'll be back in a week." She turned to Grace, who'd been swiveling her head, watching our exchange as if we were Billie Jean King and Bobby Riggs trading volleys. "Call me a cab, dear. I'm going to California."

FOURTEEN

With what felt like fifty million problems circling my head, I spent the afternoon in my studio painting. The application of paint to canvas calmed me.

Missing girl? Pthalo blue.

Stolen car? Cadmium orange deep.

My parents' marriage? Payne's gray.

Karma? Dioxazine purple.

The whole damned mess? Napthol scarlet.

I spent hours transforming blank white into something resembling the enormous floral arrangement in my living room.

Tap, tap.

"Come in."

Grace tip-toed into my studio, concern writ large across her face. "You okay?"

I nodded. Not one of my problems had gone away but I felt better able to deal with them.

"Earlier this week, I made plans to sleep over at Donna's. Is that still okay?"

Even with the promised patrol car cruising our neighborhood, I'd feel better with her safely away. "Of course."

She gave me that look unique to teenage girls who are about to ask for something big. A combination of their five-year-old selves (and all the cuteness that went with that age) and the women they'll become (women who don't much like asking their mothers for favors). "May I take your car?"

Her car was gone. My fault. "Yes."

She shuffled her feet and shifted her gaze to the view outside the window. She wasn't done. "Libba called."

Oh, sugar. I'd forgotten about Libba. I should have definitively cancelled going to the club party before I stuck my head in the sand. "And?"

"She wants you to pick her up at seven."

I glanced at my watch. Five forty-five. Too late to cancel now.

"You're sure you don't mind driving the Mercedes?"

The Mercedes. I stretched my fingers then tightened them into fists. "No, of course not."

"This will be your first time driving the new car." Her voice was bright, as if driving a new Mercedes should be a treat.

Mother didn't approve of my Triumph and was of the opinion that I needed a sedan. When my late-husband's Cadillac was totaled, she began a campaign. I needed a four-door car. Especially if I was going to drive her around. I needed a trunk that held more than a weekend bag. I needed a car that was solid, dependable, and reflected my position in society.

For Christmas, she and Daddy gave me a 280 sedan.

I'd stared speechless at the keys in the gift box.

"Since there's no man in your life who can give you a new car, your father and I decided to splurge."

She'd expected effusive gratitude.

I tried. I did. And maybe she mistook the tears in my eyes for tears of thanks. But, the drops that wetted my cheeks were born of frustration. Mother and I would never see eye-to-eye.

Aggie drove the car to the store once a week. Other than those brief trips to the market, the sedan sat in the garage. Until tonight.

I cleaned brushes and put away paints, then went downstairs for a shower.

An hour later, I walked out the back door, opened the garage door, climbed behind the wheel of Mother's idea of what my life should be, and drove to Libba's.

"You're driving this?" she asked as she settled into the passenger seat.

"Grace has my car."

"Where's her car?"

I readied myself for an I told you so and mumbled, "Starry stole it."

"Is that all she took? Did you check the silver?"

"Very funny." I didn't mention the cash missing from my billfold—I hadn't mentioned it to Anarchy either.

"Well, your mother will be pleased you're finally driving her gift."

Mother wouldn't know. She was on a plane to Palm Springs.

Libba leaned forward and fiddled with the radio.

Don Henley sang "The Best of My Love."

Libba sang with him.

And for a few seconds, we were teenagers again—out in Mother's car, on our way to a party where any number of fabulous things might happen.

The song ended and was replaced by a Mennen Speed Stick commercial.

We pulled onto the long drive to the clubhouse.

"Bill and Wright might stop by."

Oh, goodie. I made an oh, really noise in my throat.

"Bill says Wright sent flowers. Did you get them?"

"Mixed bouquet. Very nice." I parked the car in the farthest corner of the parking lot.

Libba sighed. "Why did we bother driving?"

"Very funny. It's not that far."

"It's a country mile."

"I can drop you off at the door and you can go in by yourself."

I couldn't see Libba in the dark but I knew she rolled her eyes. "Ha ha."

"Bad things happen in this parking lot." People—bad people—lurked between parked cars. Approaching a car I couldn't see clearly was dangerous. I'd learned my lesson well. "There's nothing wrong with this spot."

We walked to the clubhouse (Libba would say we hiked),

surrendered our minks to the coat check, and paused in the entrance to the ballroom.

The room was already half full.

"Who's that talking to Jinx?" I nodded my chin toward a woman in a black wrap dress similar to the one I'd worn last night. Hers was floor length.

"Joan Conover."

"Who?" The name sounded familiar

"Joan Conover. She's a widow. Recently I think." And just like that, I remembered. Patrick Conover shot in a downtown alley.

Libba scanned the room. "Do you want a drink? I want a drink."

"Not right now, thank you."

"Okay. I'll see you later." Now that we'd walked in together, Libba was fine being on her own. She left me.

I approached Jinx.

"Ellison," she cried. "What a treat to see you!" She leaned forward, kissed the air near my cheek, and whispered, "Save me."

We stepped away from each other and I extended my hand to Joan. "Ellison Russell."

Joan's lips had thinned and her hand was limp within my clasp. Apparently she didn't appreciate being interrupted. "Joan Conover."

"A pleasure."

"Ellison and I are old friends and she's been holding out on me." Jinx's smile was Christmas lights bright—it even twinkled. "Where did you find that skirt?"

I wore a long midnight blue skirt embellished with tiny crystal stars. I'd paired it with a white silk blouse and rope of pearls. Every woman in the room wore something similar—long skirt, silk blouse—it was our uniform. "Swanson's."

"Well, it's fabulous."

"Yours is too." Jinx's long skirt was red and black striped—the black enlivened by bugle beads. Her blouse's red matched the red in her skirt. "Libba is looking for you." I scanned the quickly filling room. "She was on her way to the bar."

"Libba and I have that—that thing to talk about." That wasn't awkward. Not at all. Jinx might as well have said I'm tired of talking to you. "Joan, nice to see you. Ellison, I'll talk to you later." And she was gone.

Joan and I stared at each other.

She took a sip of what looked like straight scotch.

"How do you know Jinx?" The only question that came to mind.

"Our husbands. When my husband was alive he represented George in buying some commercial property."

"Oh?" I was impressing Joan with my scintillating conversation. No doubt about it.

"My husband was a real estate attorney."

My turn. "Mine was a banker."

"Was a banker? You're a widow?"

"I am."

She smiled. We'd found common ground. "For how long?"

"Henry died last June."

"I lost Patrick just a few months ago." She rubbed her wedding ring as if the gold band was a talisman. "I still miss him."

"If I might ask, how did your husband die?" I knew the answer but it was my turn to say something and I wasn't about to lie and say I missed Henry.

"He was murdered. Shot." Joan patted the skin beneath her eyes with the pads of her fingers.

"How awful." I meant it.

"It was. It is." She patted harder. "And your husband?"

"Also murdered."

She stopped patting and stared at me. "Why was he killed?" Why? Not how?

"He got involved in some rather unsavory things." To put it mildly.

Joan looked up at the ceiling. Her chin trembled and she waved her fingers at her eyes. "Patrick, too."

Really? That hadn't made the obit.

"You wouldn't think real estate would be unsavory but—" she covered her mouth with her hand and shook her head. Tears spilled over the rims of her eyes and coursed, unchecked, down her cheeks.

"How awful for you." What else could I say?

"Ellison!"

I shifted my gaze from Joan. Kay Starnes stood next to me looking supremely put out.

"Mrs. Starnes, good evening."

"Where is your mother?" Kay Starnes and mother had been friends for years. Not close friends. Not close enough for Mother to share travel plans. But friends nonetheless. "I've been trying to get ahold of her all day."

"Palm Springs."

Kay shifted her gaze to Joan who was clearly in distress, wiping her eyes with a lace-edged hanky. "May I steal Ellison for a few minutes? It's terribly important."

"Of course," Joan murmured, her voice thick. "It's been a pleasure." So pleasant I'd left her in tears.

Kay practically dragged me to the ladies' lounge where she ducked her head into the bathroom. "We're alone. I have a confession. I've done a terrible thing—a terrible, terrible thing."

Oh dear. Had she too had an affair with my father?

"Your mother, who is such a wonderful friend, did me a tremendous favor."

"Oh?"

"She went with me to pick up Mary."

"Who is Mary?"

"My sister."

Kay sank onto the chaise and looked at her hands—well moisturized and well manicured. "We had drinks afterwards." She looked up. "I needed one."

I made a sympathetic noise. So far this wasn't much of a confession.

"They were so delicious—Frances mixes a mean martini." She

did. She had to living with Daddy. "I had three and Frances matched me drink for drink." Kay bit her lip. "I left her."

"Left who?"

"Mary."

"Where?"

"At Frances's."

Kay shifted her gaze away from me. She also pursed her lips, clasped her hands, and straightened her shoulders. "I put her in the hall closet and forgot her."

The desire to throttle Kay was so strong my fingers curled into claws. "You what?" My voice was too loud for the ladies' lounge.

"I know it's the worst thing anyone could ever do. Unforgivable."

Oh dear Lord. I sank onto one of the lounge's uncomfortable wicker chairs. "Mother didn't know you put Mary in the closet?"

"No, she didn't. I was going to leave Mary in the car but I just couldn't. Leaving her on the floorboards of the backseat seemed so horribly callous." Abandoning her in Mother's front hall closet said I care? "I followed Frances into the house, hung up my coat, and put Mary on the shelf."

And then she got drunk.

"How long was she there?" Why in the name of all things holy hadn't Kay gone back the next day and fetched Mary's ashes?

"Months. I would have picked her up the next day but your parents went out of town." Kay studied the carpet. "We buried an empty box. I felt absolutely awful but what else was I going to do? Tell everyone I'd left my sister at a friend's as if she were a spare umbrella? By the time Frances and Harrington got back from their trip I was out of town. And when I got back—" her cheeks flushed and her forehead wrinkled. She covered her eyes with spread fingers "—I forgot. I simply forgot. Mary's been in that closet for months. I woke up this morning with the most sinking feeling in my stomach. You know that feeling, the one where you know you've forgotten something terribly important and you can't remember what."

I did know that feeling. I said nothing.

"And then I knew. I just knew. I'm the worst sister ever. And Frances—" Kay shook her head "—what will she think of me?"

"Mother will be relieved to know who the ashes belong to." I spoke through gritted teeth. Kay and Mary had caused so much trouble.

"She found them?" Kay pressed her palms flat against her cheeks. "Oh, dear."

Oh, dear was right. Finding Mary's forgotten ashes had nearly destroyed my parent's marriage. Any number of cutting remarks scrolled through my brain. "Those ashes have been a problem."

"They have?"

I made no mention of the hours Aggie spent in the library nor the secrets brought forth by that accursed box. "Mother has been going out of her mind trying to figure out where they came from."

Kay paled. The ripples across her forehead spoke of contrition but the hand pressed against her mouth and the wideness of her eyes revealed raw fear. "She has?"

"Ellison, there you are." Libba sounded accusatory as if I'd been hiding or avoiding her. "Wright and Bill are here."

I stood. "Kay, if you'll excuse me." If I stayed much longer, the tirade scrolling through my brain might reach my lips. You're thoughtless and selfish. How could you?

"Wait!" Kay leapt to her feet. She was incredibly spry for a woman approaching seventy. "Will you fetch the ashes for me? Please? I'd be incredibly grateful."

I bet she would. "I think you'd better talk to Mother."

I left Kay sinking back onto the chaise with her hands pressed against her heart and tears in her eyes.

Libba paused in the hallway outside the lounge. "What was that all about?"

"You don't want to know."

She looked as if she did want to know. She had an avid, gossip-hound look on her face. She might have pushed for more information, but she spotted Bill and called, "Here she is!"

I offered up my cheek to Bill. He kissed it then wrapped an arm around Libba's waist.

Wright stepped forward and brushed his lips across my skin. "You get prettier every time I see you."

"And you get more charming. Thank you for the flowers they're—" over-the-top, too much, ostentatious "—lovely."

"You're welcome. Say, you don't have a drink." He said this as if someone had snubbed me.

"I'm not drinking tonight."

His brow wrinkled as if the idea of not drinking at a cocktail party was foreign and confusing. "You're sure? I'm happy to get you whatever you'd like."

The four of us strolled back to the ballroom.

"I'm sure." And then because I was feeling contrary, I asked, "How did your call go?"

"We got our wires crossed. The man I needed to speak with was already gone for the day. Annoying because I would have enjoyed spending more time with you."

I didn't believe him. He'd spent the better part of dinner talking to Bill and then come up with a sudden, urgent phone call.

"Would you care to dance?" he asked.

A jazz trio with a singer had taken their places on the riser in front of the dance floor.

"I'd love to." I missed dancing. One of the few good things about being married to Henry was having a dance partner.

Wright took my hand and together we stepped onto the dance floor.

The band played the opening notes of "The Girl from Ipanema."

Wright led with a firm hand.

I followed.

"How are you enjoying Kansas City?" I asked.

"More now."

"There you go, being charming again."

He gave me an aw-shucks smile.

Wow, he was handsome.

"Kansas City is a great town." We completed a spin and he added, "The downtown revitalization is amazing. When the new convention hotel and center are completed there will be no stopping this city."

Kansas City had been on a building binge—a new airport, a new football stadium, Kemper Arena where the Republican Convention would be held next year, and the new hotel (if they ever got the strip bars torn down) and convention center. Soon, I'd hardly recognize my own city.

"I want to be a part of this city's success."

It was a good thing Mother was half a country away. If she met Wright Halstrom, if she listened to him, she'd have him in a jewelry store buying a diamond the size of Texas before he knew what hit him. I might be leery of too handsome, too charming men, but Mother had no such hang up. She would approve of Wright. Whole-heartedly.

The girl in the song walked to the sea and failed to notice the boy pining for her. The last notes ended to polite applause.

Wright looked down at me. His eyes sparkled. "You're a good dancer."

"So are you."

"I need a drink. You're sure I can't tempt you?" With his hand on the small of my back, he walked us to the edge of the dance floor.

"I'm sure."

"Don't go anywhere. I'll be right back." With a last sparkling smile, he headed toward the nearest bar.

"How do you know Wright Halstrom?" Joan Conover sounded as if she'd had a few drinks since our earlier conversation. Her words were slurry.

"A blind date."

She blinked. Several times. "Listen to me." She leaned forward and nearly overwhelmed me with the scent of scotch. "Be careful. He's not a nice man." She glanced over her shoulder as if she worried he might be listening. "Patrick said—"

"Ellison!" Jinx's hand closed around my arm and she pulled me toward her. "Do you mind, Joan? We need Ellison to settle a dispute."

When we were twenty feet clear of Joan, Jinx loosened her grip. "You've already listened to that woman once tonight. It was my turn to save you."

How was Jinx to know I'd wanted to hear what Joan had to say?

FIFTEEN

By the time I convinced Jinx I really did want to talk to Joan, she'd disappeared.

The crowd of seemingly happy, shiny people circulated, ice clinked in old-fashions, and the spice of curried chicken let me know the buffet was open. A typical party. I'd been to a thousand just like it.

Exhaustion reached out its arms and hugged me tight

I could spend more time with Libba, Bill, and Wright. I could explain sponsorship levels for the museum gala to Mark Kittering (who spotted me from across the room and waved). But both of those options required energy I didn't have. Or, I could slip out, go home, put my feet up, and doze.

I chose Option C, said a quick good-bye to Libba and company, and slipped away.

Outside, the night swirled with a heavy, cold mist. March deciding lion or lamb. The mist clung to my hair, and lashes, and coat. The click of my heels echoed on the pavement. The darkness breathed—thick and dangerous. I shivered.

I should have accepted Wright's offer to walk me to my car. I should have, but the thought of being alone in the night with a man who might want to kiss me—a man who wasn't Anarchy Jones—had sent me scurrying for the exit.

Now with odd night noises and a rising fog I wished for my gun.

I wished the parking lot lights were brighter.

I wished—just this once—I'd parked closer.

I wished for Anarchy.

Maybe Libba was right. Maybe I needed to reconsider this parking as far away from other cars as possible policy. While no one could hide between cars that weren't there, being isolated didn't feel particularly safe either.

Miraculously, I reached the lonely Mercedes without anyone bashing me on the head, shooting at me, or tackling me from behind.

I jammed the key in the lock and opened the door.

"Eeek!" I leapt backward fifteen feet. Ten feet. Maybe five feet. Possibly three feet. My heart careened around my chest like a demented pinball. My lungs emptied and refused to inflate.

"What the hell are you doing?" My voice sounded far away, as if I was in a mile-long tunnel. What my eyes had seen, my brain refused to process.

"This is your car?" A woman spoke. Oh dear Lord, was that who I thought it was?

"Get out!"

"Now, now. Calm down," said a man in a reasonable tone.

"Calm down?" I screeched. "Have you lost your mind?" He'd definitely lost his tie, and his jacket, and most of his shirt, and all of his pants. I rubbed my eyes. There were some things that could never be unseen. "Who does this?" Was having sex in a strange car the latest fad sweeping the nation?

Strange sounds were coming from the Mercedes' interior. The sounds of people separating in a small space—an elbow hit against the dash, a leg knocked against the...I covered my ears with my hands.

I kept them there until Bruce Petteway climbed out of my car.

"You?"

He looked only mildly embarrassed. "Good evening, Ellison."

No. It was not a good evening. "Wh—" what, why, who—there were so many questions my brain couldn't decide "—wh—"

"Listen, sorry about this."

"Sorry?" My screech reached new heights. Unimagined

heights. "This is my car. What's wrong with your car?" If one was going to have sex in a parked car, surely it was better to do it in one's own.

"I took a cab."

Ah. That excused everything. I tapped my clasped hands against my forehead.

Bruce spread his fingers and mimed pressing down as if patronizing me would somehow make everything better. "You're overreacting." He took a step toward me.

I took a step back. "Get any closer and I'll press charges. This has to be trespassing."

"You don't want to do that." Now his voice had an edge.

"You're right. I don't." It would be far better to call Joyce's lawyer and tell him (or her) the whole sordid story.

Bruce was pushing down on the air again. How had Joyce stayed married to him for as long as she did? "We're all friends."

We were?

A woman emerged from the car. A woman with horse teeth and a horse face. Henry had once called her a bony-assed harpy (but that was before he started sleeping with her).

Bruce was very wrong—we were not all friends.

"Ellison." Prudence Davies twisted my name into an insult.

She looked, as Mother would say, like something the cat dragged in. Her hair was a disaster and her clothes were akimbo. And, if the light were better, I knew I'd see smeared makeup.

"You know, Bruce, I heard you liked younger women."

Prudence scowled at me.

The daggers she shot my way were nothing compared to the fierce look on Bruce's face. His expression was alarming.

I took another step backward.

"What the hell is that supposed to mean?" he demanded. His hands tightened to fists and he advanced on me. "What have you heard?" His tone was alarming too. Lord, I was tired of men who took pleasure in intimidating women.

I took yet another step away from him.

"She's just insulting me," said Prudence. "Don't let her get to you."

I had heard Bruce liked younger women—girls, even—who had told me that?

Bruce stopped walking but his expression remained terrifying. "Is that true? Is that what you were doing? Insulting Prudence?"

I'd been insulting him too but I wasn't about to point that out. Starting an argument with a man who'd obviously had a few (why else would he be with Prudence?) wasn't smart. "Prudence is too old to be sleeping with other women's husbands." Not that age would stop her.

Prudence's scowl darkened to a death glare but Bruce's expression cleared and he chuckled as if he enjoyed the idea of two women fighting.

His gaze traveled between Prudence and me. "We'll all laugh about this some day."

Perhaps he believed saying something made it true. Perhaps he thought he might lighten the mood. Perhaps he was dumb as a pile of rocks. I, for one, would never laugh about this. I was going to have to trade in the damned car. Unbidden images of Prudence Davies having sex in the front seat made the vehicle undrivable.

Mother would have a fit.

I'd have to explain.

She'd blame me for not locking the car doors.

Wait.

I had locked the car doors.

"How did you get in the car?"

"The passenger door was unlocked," said Bruce.

I was going to kill Libba.

"Do you have everything out of the there?" I wanted no reminders of this night. No stray earrings, no neck ties, no—God forbid—condoms.

"Yeah." Bruce crossed his arms. The mist was cold and he had no winter coat.

I tightened my grip on my keys and willed him away from the

car.

He didn't move.

"It's cold out here." He wanted to complain about the weather? He should have checked the temperature before he snuck out of the club party and had sex in my car. "Would you give us a ride back to the clubhouse?"

My jaw dropped. The hinge that kept my teeth together just gave up—shocked into laxity by his unadulterated gall.

Prudence stepped forward. "She's not going to give us a ride, Bruce."

Prudence was right.

"But I'm cold."

Steam may have erupted from my ears. "Get out of my way."

I climbed into my irreparably soiled car, slammed the door shut, and locked the doors.

They had not removed all their belongings.

A bra remained on the passenger seat. Not a serviceable nude bra. No, Prudence's brassiere was black and lace and...oh-dear-lord-was-that-leather? Ugh.

My lips drew away from teeth and my chin receded into my neck. Ick, ick, ick. I picked up the bra by the strap—thank God I wore gloves—rolled down the window, and dropped the offending garment onto the pavement. Then, without another glance at Bruce or Prudence (my head contained too many images of the twosome already), I drove away.

I might—might—have muttered to myself the whole way home.

I might—might—have been in the worst mood of my life.

I might—might—have done a better job checking the locks on the back door.

I stepped inside and sniffed. The smell of cigarette smoke lingered in the air.

Max, who could be bribed by strangers carrying meat, lay on his bed in the kitchen. He lifted his head from his paws and stared at me.

I stared back at him. "Are we alone?" I whispered.

His answer was a yawn.

I backed out the door, cut through the side yard, stood in my front lawn, and waited for the patrol car Anarchy had promised would be circling the block. Fortunately, the ground was too cold for my heels to sink. That was about the only thing going right. I scowled at the street.

There. I waved at the cruiser.

The policemen pulled into my drive and the driver rolled down his window. "Ma'am?"

"I'm Ellison Russell. A stranger has been in my house."

"I'll call it in." He reached for the radio.

My head ached. Badly. But I held up my hand. "Wait. Will they send multiple patrol cars?"

"Probably." His hand closed on the talkie-thingy.

Margaret Hamilton would be furious. Marian Dixon, my neighbor across the street, would have the news out—police at Ellison's. Again—to all and sundry before the policemen were even out of their cars. "Please. Wait."

The officer looked at me as if his patience was running thin. I could tell him a thing or two about worn out patience.

"Could you just walk through the house with me? Please?"

The two officers exchanged keep-the-crazy-lady-happy-or-Detective-Jones-will-have-our-asses looks, then the driver—I squinted through the window and read his name tag—Officer Collins put the car in park.

The three of us searched every inch of the house. The basement, where the Christmas decorations waited for next year. The ground floor, where we opened every cabinet and looked behind every drape. The second floor, where Officer Collins got down on his hand and knees and peered under beds while his partner, Officer Pearson, searched behind my ball gowns and the unbelievable pile of clothing stuffed into Grace's closet. Even the third floor, where there was no place to hide. Max, with a mixture of boredom and disdain in his amber eyes, supervised the whole operation.

"What makes you think someone was in your house?" asked Officer Collins whose keep-the-crazy-lady-happy-or-Detective-Jones-will-have-my-ass look was sliding into one of annoyance.

"I smelled cigarette smoke," I explained. "No one smokes in my house."

He rubbed his chin. "Well, there's no one here now."

"No. I can see that. Thank you, Officers. It was kind of you to indulge me."

"Our pleasure, ma'am." His tone said something different.

It was official. I was the woman who cried wolf. I locked the door behind them, checked the windows, turned on a few extra lights, and climbed the stairs.

I read Centennial until my eyes grew heavy (Michener was a great fall-asleep author). Five minutes later (three hours according to the clock), Max's growl awakened me.

Grrrr.

I fumbled for the phone and pressed the receiver to my ear. No dial tone.

No phone?

Any nerve, any fiber of my being that wasn't fully awake jumped up and took notice.

I reached into my bedside table and closed my fingers around my gun.

Armed, I tiptoed to the window and peeked around the edge of the drape.

Grace's car sat in the drive. Was Jane back? Was she in trouble?

Grrrr. Max thought so.

Together we descended the stairs. Slowly. Max, because he was in stealth mode. Me, because my knees were wobbly.

I snuck into the living room and pulled aside the curtain for a view of the darkness outside.

Two figures were swathed in mist and shadow.

One crouched next to Grace's car. The other crept toward the croucher.

Two villains in cahoots?

A villain and a hero?

Impossible to tell.

Bang!

Max barked.

I jumped.

In the street, rubber squealed.

I moved the curtain and pressed my nose to the glass.

The croucher had collapsed on the drive.

Oh dear, Lord.

The creeper nudged the body with his toe. It was too dark to see the creeper's face but I felt his gaze. He was looking at the window where I stood.

Ice ran in my veins and I tightened my hold on my .22.

The creeper stepped into the shadows and disappeared into the night.

The croucher didn't move.

Part of me wanted to run to the croucher. Maybe I could help. What if it was Jane laying there on the pavement? The sane part of me, the part that enjoyed seeing the sun rise on Sunday mornings, turned on lights. Every light in the house. Then the sane part of me went to the kitchen, asked Mr. Coffee to work his magic, and waited for the police.

I knew they'd come. My phone might not work but I bet my last dollar Marian Dixon's or Margaret Hamilton's did and there was nothing either one of them enjoyed more than calling the police when there was trouble at my house.

Three minutes. That's how long it took for the police to arrive.

Three of the slowest minutes in history.

Three minutes I spent agonizing. What if the croucher was bleeding out? What if all the croucher needed was compression? What if the creeper was still out there?

Three minutes I spent walking between the kitchen, where Mr. Coffee made comforting sounds, and the front of the house, where

I'd be able to see patrol lights.

With the first flash of blue and red, I ran into the driveway.

Ran to Grace's car.

Light poured out of the house and illuminated the body on the ground.

The creeper had shot the croucher in the back of the head. Even if I'd run outside right away, I couldn't have helped the man at my feet.

The man.

Not Jane.

Thank heavens.

Although the man on the cold concrete probably wouldn't have agreed.

He lay on his stomach, his face hidden from me.

There was no doubt I'd be asked if I knew him. Too many bodies had appeared at my house—I knew the drill.

I nodded to a sergeant I recognized and went inside to wait for Anarchy.

Did I have time to change? Probably not. But a bathrobe over my nightgown would look better than the mink and galoshes I'd thrown on to run outside.

I climbed the stairs, put my gun back in the drawer, brushed my teeth, and ran a comb through my hair.

Ding dong.

My robe hung on a hook on the inside of my closet door. I grabbed it, jammed my arms through the sleeves, and tied the sash as I descended the stairs.

Max waited for me in the foyer.

I pulled open the door and my eyes filled with tears.

Tears I wasn't expecting.

My chin quivered.

Anarchy stepped inside and closed the door. "Are you hurt?"

I shook my head. My throat was too thick to speak.

A tear spilled over the rim of my eye and wet my cheek. I wiped it away with the back of my hand.

"Let's get you some coffee." He took my hand and led me to the kitchen where Mr. Coffee waited with his full pot.

"Sit down."

I rested on a stool while Anarchy reached into the cupboard, took out two coffee mugs (one of them my favorite), and poured. Then he opened the fridge, fetched the cream, and added the exact right amount to my mug.

He'd been watching, kept mental notes.

My heart fluttered. Of course, that might have been from the heaven-sent sensation of closing my hand around a warm mug.

He took the stool next to mine.

"Tell me."

I told him about the smell of smoke in the house, Max and his growl, about the phone that didn't work, and the return of Grace's car. I told him about the croucher, the creeper, and the squeal of tires in the street.

He stood and picked up the receiver. "This line works fine."

Of course it did.

"Are you okay for a minute?"

I tightened my grip on my mug and nodded.

"I'll be right back."

Max stayed with me.

"I don't know why I'm so emotional," I told him.

He cocked his head and stared at me with amber eyes. Their message was simple. Duh.

"It's not like it's the first time I've found a body."

Duh.

"I'm just so tired of it. Libba never finds bodies."

Duh.

"What did I do to deserve this?"

"Who are you talking to?" asked Anarchy.

"Max." At least he hadn't caught me talking to Mr. Coffee. Lots of people talked to their pets. I doubted there were many who conversed with their coffee makers.

"Your bedroom phone was unplugged."

Chills crept up my arms like spiders. The stranger had been in my bedroom. Touched my belongings.

Ding dong.

"I'll get that." Anarchy strode into the hallway.

I watched him go then scowled at Max. "Some guard dog you are."

The guard dog yawned.

I sipped my coffee and waited.

A moment later, Anarchy reappeared. "Are you up to going outside and taking a look?"

I nodded and rose from my stool. It was best to get this part over with.

I stopped at the hall closet and re-donned my coat and boots.

Together we stepped into my front yard.

There were lights, and uniformed officers, and Anarchy's partner, Detective Peters, and a tight little cluster of neighbors at the bottom of the drive.

We walked toward Grace's car and the body on the pavement.

Someone had turned the corpse over onto its back.

I saw the face and stumbled over a rock that wasn't there.

Anarchy caught my elbow. "You know him?"

I knew him. "That's Ray Smith."

SIXTEEN

Long didn't begin to describe the night I had. Interminable night. Endless night. Please-let-me-go-to-bed-if-only-for-a-few-hours night. Scare-me-half-to-death night.

Officers Collins and Pearson pulled into the driveway and climbed out of their cruiser. Their keep-the-crazy-lady-happy-or-Detective-Jones-will-have-our-asses looks had been replaced by sheepish, when-will-the-hammer-fall expressions.

When. Not if. Under their watch, someone had snuck into my home.

The sheepish officers and I led Anarchy on a second walk-through of the house. Still no one under the bed (Officer Collins got down on his hand and knees and checked). Still no one in the closets.

"Meat van's here," said Officer Pearson, who was searching behind the drapes (still no one there).

"The meat van?" I asked.

"The coroner's van," Anarchy said gently. "They're taking the body away."

I shuddered.

Anarchy gave Officer Pearson a look that would scare me into a week's worth of wakefulness. "That will be all, officers."

They practically ran for the door—especially Pearson.

When they were gone, Anarchy's expression softened. "Ellison—"

Ding dong.

I was willing to ignore the bell if he was. "What?"

Ding dong.

"We'd better answer that."

We descended the stairs and Anarchy opened the door.

Another policeman stood on the stoop. He looked at Anarchy and swallowed hard enough for his Adam's apple to bob. "Mrs. Russell, would you please come outside and look in the car? We'd like to know what belongs to you."

"Of course." I put my mink and boots back on, trekked out to the front yard, and peered into Grace's car.

Her key was in the ignition and a house key and a turquoise dyed rabbit foot hung from her keychain.

I should have thought about that house key when Jane stole the car. With it, anyone could gain entrance to my home.

The key was easily copied. Call the locksmith went to the top of my morning to-do list.

I leaned into the car. If anything, the interior looked cleaner than usual. A few eight-track cartridges littered the passenger seat floor. *Elton John's Greatest Hits*, which I'd used for stuffing Grace's Christmas stocking, peeked out from under *Band on the Run* and *Heart like a Wheel*. The tapes were joined by a Charleston Chew wrapper. "That's not Grace's." I pointed to the wrapper. "Grace doesn't like that candy. But, it could easily belong to one of her friends." I stood up. "I don't see anything that isn't Grace's."

A tow-truck pulled into the driveway.

"What's that for?" A sinking sensation in my stomach provided the answer. The police were taking Grace's car as evidence. "Please don't take this car."

Detective Peters, who'd watched me inventory the contents of Grace's car, actually smiled. Not a nice smile. Then he ignored my plea and waved the truck driver farther up the drive.

"Please don't." I wasn't too proud to beg.

Detective Peters shrugged and his lips, barely visible under his mustache, twitched a second time. Anything that caused me consternation (except for murders he had to investigate) was a good thing.

Anarchy offered me a sympathetic grimace. His hand closed around mine for a half a second. But during that second, he squeezed. "We'll get it back to you as soon as possible."

If they took Grace's car, she would drive mine. I'd be left with the defiled Mercedes. There was no other option. I wasn't about to put my daughter behind the wheel of a car in which Prudence had— had played with Bruce's gear shift.

The men stayed outside and supervised hooking Grace's car to the tow truck. Unable to watch, I trudged inside and sought comfort from Mr. Coffee.

I cozied up next to him and whispered, "You wouldn't take Grace's car away."

He quietly assured me he most definitely would not and then he gave me a fresh cup of coffee.

I could have kissed him.

Instead, I sat in the kitchen, stared into my coffee, and waited.

I sat in the living room, stared out the window at the activity in front of my house, and waited.

I sat in the family room, listlessly flipped through a magazine, and waited. Under other, better circumstances, I'd have been interested in Vogue. Margaux Hemingway was on the cover and she wore a peppy smile. Perhaps that's why the headline next to her read "the great pepper-uppers." My mind immediately went to pills, but Vogue promised two hundred and fifty different shoes, belts, bangles, and beads.

Brnng, brnng.

I looked up from my study of peppy pumps (at least according to Vogue). The clock read just after two.

Oh dear Lord.

With a trepidatious hand, I reached for the phone. "Hello."

"Ellison?" Daddy's voice was both worried and groggy. "Are you all right?"

"Are you?"

"Me?"

"You don't sound like you." He didn't. He sounded sad and

lonely and somehow diminished. He also sounded almost drugged. Mother had left him. And who knew how long her week away would stretch? His long-kept secret was a matter for family discussion (I for one hadn't had time to process how I felt about an unknown sister). And, now someone had awakened him in the middle of the night.

He cleared his throat. "I haven't been sleeping well so I took one of your mother's pills. Then Marian Dixon rang the damn phone off the hook. She's says the police are at your house."

Marian Dixon. The spy across the street. "The police are here. But I'm fine. Grace is fine."

"Thank God." I could almost see him raking a hand through his white hair. "What happened?"

"Someone was shot in my front yard."

"Who?" Did I detect a note of resignation in his voice?

"I'm not exactly sure. No one from our set."

"What were they doing at your house?"

"As far as I can tell, they were returning Grace's car."

"What?" Now he sounded like Daddy, completely awake and ready to take charge.

"It's a long story, Daddy. Perhaps—"

Beeeeep. "This is the operator. Will you accept an emergency breakthrough from Frances Walford?"

A few seconds passed while we considered the ramifications of Mother calling from California.

"You're sure you're safe?" The sad and lonely notes had returned to Daddy's voice. "You're sure you're safe?"

"Half the police force is in my front yard."

"Take your mother's call—and Ellison—"

"Yes?"

"Tell her I miss her."

"I will."

"I love you, Daddy."

"Love you too, sugar. I'll be by first thing in the morning."

I hung up but didn't bother releasing the receiver.

Brnng, brnng.

I brought the phone to my ear. "Hello, Mother."

"I can't go out of town for even a few days."

I swallowed a sigh. "Of course, you can. You did."

"Don't be smart with me, young lady."

"Who called you?"

"Marian Dixon. She says your father isn't answering his phone. You need to check on him. Right away."

"He's fine. I just got off the phone with him."

"He's fine?" Mother sounded almost disappointed.

"He misses you."

"He said that?"

"He did. He sounds sad and lonely and lost."

"He does?" Now she sounded worried.

"If you're worried about him, you could always come home."

"This trip was your idea."

There was no arguing that point.

"What is happening at your house?" she demanded.

"Someone was shot in the front yard."

Her response was a disgusted sigh. Mother had an enormous cross to bear. Having a daughter who attracted murders better than honey attracted flies wasn't easy. "Who is it?"

"I'm not sure." It was the truth. Sort of.

"So we don't know them."

"Definitely not."

"What was this person doing at your house?"

I was hoping she wouldn't ask me that. "They were skulking around Grace's car." Not exactly a lie. A sense of self-preservation prompted me to change the subject. "I found out who the ashes belong to."

"You did?" In my mind's eye, I could see Mother tilting her head. "Who?"

"Kay Starnes' sister."

"That can't be right." Now I could see her shaking her head. "Kay buried her sister. Your father and I missed the funeral to be with Sis and Marjorie."

"I saw Kay at the club party tonight. She pulled me aside and admitted everything. She buried an empty box because Mary was in your front hall closet."

"And she left her there?" Righteous indignation turned Mother's usually well-modulated voice shrill. "Why?"

Mother wasn't going to like my answer. I held the phone away from my ear and said, "She forgot."

"She forgot?" Shriller still. So shrill that Max whined and covered his ears with his paws.

"That's what she said." Talking about ashes, no matter how high Mother's pitch, was preferable to talking about the dead man I'd found next to Grace's car. Definitely preferable to explaining I'd invited a stripper for an overnight and she'd stolen the car. "Kay's going to call you."

"Hmph."

"Mother, it's late."

"I know, dear. It's even late in California."

"May we talk about this tomorrow?"

"I'm playing bridge tomorrow. Then golf. Then I'm having dinner with the Fowlers."

"It sounds like you have a busy day planned. You need your rest."

"It sounds to me like you want to get me off the phone."

"I'm exhausted, Mother. All I want to do is lock the door and go to bed."

"Fine. But you make sure someone spends the night there." She considered her statement. "And by that I mean a patrol car in the driveway not a homicide detective in your house."

"Got it." Anarchy was too busy to spend the night on my couch. "I'll talk to you tomorrow."

"Ellison."

"Yes?"

"Be careful."

Oh. Wow. My throat tightened. "I love you, too."

I hung up the phone, leaned my head back and closed my eyes.

Brnng, brnng.

What now? Did Mother want me to deliver the ashes to Kay? Did Daddy want to hear about my conversation with Mother? I sighed. "Hello."

"Stay out of this." A man's voice, rough with cigarettes and blurred by drink.

"Pardon me?"

"Stay out of this or you'll never see that pretty daughter of yours again."

My heart stopped beating. "Who is this?" More of a gasp than actual words.

"I'm the man who can make sure your daughter spends the rest of her days strung out on heroin with her legs spread for a line of johns."

I dropped the phone as if the plastic casing had burned my hand. Then I fumbled in my lap for the receiver. "Who is this?"

There was no one on the line.

I lowered the phone from my ear and stared at the receiver in my hand as if a few pieces of metal covered in harvest gold plastic could explain the evil I'd just heard.

The blood that normally flowed to my head and my heart seemed to have moved elsewhere. To some other woman's body.

The world spun.

"Ellison."

Spun out of control.

"Ellison." I heard my name from a great distance.

I raised my gaze from the phone. The simple movement required effort.

Anarchy knelt in front of me. "Ellison, what happened?"

He didn't ask if I was all right. He could tell I wasn't.

His fingers touched my cheek. "What can I get you?"

Two plane tickets to Paris.

"Someone just threatened Grace."

"What did they say?"

Repeating the threat might make it real. I shook my head and tears welled in my eyes.

He took the phone from my shaking hands. "Where is she?"

"Donna's."

"Do you know the number?"

"It's two in the morning." We couldn't call at two in the morning. We had to call at two in the morning. Donna's mother, India, would forgive me. "The number is in the book." I pointed to my desk.

Anarchy fetched my address book, found the number, dialed, and handed me the phone.

"Hello." India sounded every bit as groggy as Daddy had.

"India, this is Ellison Russell. I am terribly sorry to call so late—so early— but we've had an incident at my house. Would you please check on Grace?"

"Of course. I'll check on her now. Hold on."

I waited, my nails cutting crescents into the palms of my hands.

"Ellison, she's asleep in Donna's room. Should I wake her?"

I exhaled. "I—"

Anarchy gestured for me to hand him the phone.

"India, Detective Jones would like to speak with you." I gave the receiver to Anarchy.

"Ma'am, we'll be sending a patrol car over to your house. Don't be alarmed if you see the vehicle in your drive."

He listened for a moment then said, "No, ma'am, you're not in any danger."

He listened for a moment then said, "I'll put Mrs. Russell back on the line."

I took the phone from him, covered the mouthpiece with the palm of my hand, and said, "I should go get her." I'd feel better knowing Grace was safe in her own house. With me. With Anarchy.

"Let her sleep. Nothing will happen to her at her friend's house."

He was right. My head knew it. My heart rebelled. "But—"

"No, buts. We'll pick her up first thing in the morning."

Picking up Grace bumped calling the locksmith from the top of the to-do list. Unless—

I brought the receiver to my ear. "India, do you feel safe? Do you want me to come get her?"

"We're locked up tighter than Fort Knox and your detective is sending a squad car. Grace is fine. Donna and me, too. Don't worry."

I still wanted to feel my daughter in my arms, tactile proof that she was unharmed. Proof that the horrific threats were only threats. "I'll come get her in the morning. Thank you."

"You're welcome."

We hung up and I stared at Anarchy.

"What exactly did the person on the phone say?"

I took a deep breath. "It was a man. He said I should stay out of this or Grace would spend the rest of her days strung out on heroin with her legs spread for a line of johns." The words and the awful image they conjured were branded on my psyche.

The scowl that settled on Anarchy's face was fearsome. "What do you know that you're not telling me?"

"Nothing. I promise." I might not have the best track record when it came to sharing but this time, right now, Anarchy knew everything I did.

"Why call you?"

"I don't know. I saw that man—Ray—twice. Three times if you count identifying his body."

"Who brought the car back? Ray?"

If Ray had Grace's car, that would mean Jane had returned to him when she ran away. "I don't know. Maybe. I heard tires squeal right after the shot was fired."

"Do you think it was Jane in the other car?"

"I have no idea. Maybe. Maybe not. She had to have given him Grace's keys at some point."

I lowered my face to my hands. My neck ached with tension and the caffeine Mr. Coffee had shared with me jittered in my veins.

"Do you think—" I looked up. Looked into Anarchy's warm brown eyes "—Do you think Ray's death is related to the girls who were found shot in the alleys downtown?"

Anarchy shrugged. Sharing information was not a two-way street.

"What about Patrick Conover's death?" I glanced down at my hands clasped tightly in my lap. "His wife said he was doing business with some unsavory people."

"Who is Patrick Conover?" Anarchy's tone was frightening. I looked up at him.

"We came across his obit. He was shot and left in a downtown alley, too."

Anarchy rubbed the back of his neck as if he too held tension there.

"Who is we?"

"Me. And Aggie."

"Why were you looking at obits?"

I told him about the ashes in Mother's closet and our attempts to identify them.

"Aggie and I were looking for possibilities."

"Where and when did you talk to Conover's widow?" He made it sound as if I'd been sneaking around, conducting some sort of clandestine investigation.

"At the club party earlier this evening."

Anarchy gave up rubbing his neck and pinched the bridge of his nose.

I sat and watched him. "Do you want coffee?"

"What? Why?"

"You look as if you could use a cup."

"No. Thank you." He shifted his gaze to a point somewhere above my head. "Please tell me how you put all this together."

"I didn't put much together. Not really."

That earned me a scowl. "Ellison." There was a dangerous edge to his voice.

I gathered up my jumpy nerves and stuffed them into a closet near the back of my brain. "Leesa, who was shot in an alley, knew Jane. I'm assuming Jane knew the other girls who were shot."

Anarchy's expression was fierce.

A few nerves snuck out of the closet. "Or maybe she didn't." I swallowed and kept going. "She knew Ray. And now Ray's dead. Shot." I probably didn't need to add that part. "As for Patrick Conover—" I bit my lip and stared up at the ceiling "—this sounds awful."

"What?"

"People like us don't get shot in alleys." I spoke in a rush. And a wash of guilt warmed my skin. No one should get shot in an alley. Not Patrick. Not Leesa. Not the other girls. "It's odd. And suspicious. And I can't help but wonder if all the murders are related."

"What unsavory people?"

"Pardon me?" The escaped nerves tap-danced on my spinal cord.

"You talked to Conover's wife. She said unsavory people. Who?"

"She didn't say." I ignored the nerves' tapping and shifted my gaze from the ceiling to Anarchy's face. "She was going to tell me but Libba interrupted us."

Anarchy muttered something about Libba (it didn't sound complimentary) and went back to rubbing his neck.

I did not take this as a good sign.

Ding dong.

For once, I was glad to hear the doorbell. "I'll get that."

"We'll get that."

I wasn't about to argue. Anarchy was in a mood.

Together we walked to the front door.

Together we reached for the handle.

Our fingers brushed.

Fire.

I pulled my hand away.

Anarchy pulled open the front door.

Detective Peters stood on the other side looking more rumpled, disgruntled, and unpleasant than ever. "We're done here. Let's go."

"I'm staying."

He was?

Peters glared at me like I was someone who kicked puppies as a hobby—or stole partners. He was clearly unhappy about Anarchy spending the night.

Peters was unhappy?

Mother would be apoplectic.

SEVENTEEN

Anarchy insisted I get some sleep (like that could ever happen).

I insisted I couldn't possibly sleep (no way, no how).

Max yawned.

"Too much has happened," I explained. "My brain won't turn off." Plus, he was in my house. Again.

"Just try." He coupled his request with a look that could melt steel.

As any woman would, I melted.

I melted, handed over blankets and pillows for the couch, and climbed the stairs to my bedroom. I'd rest my head on a pillow for a few minutes and prove him wrong.

My eyes opened shortly after eight. The light sneaking past the curtains had a gray, translucent quality and the patter of rain was loud enough to breech the window's glass.

It was a day made for staying in bed. On any other Sunday, I would have done just that—lingered beneath my blankets with the paper or a book (not Michener—not in the morning) and a cup of coffee.

I swung my feet to the floor and stumbled into the bathroom.

Twenty minutes later, I was showered, dressed, and presentable (if one overlooked the dark circles beneath my eyes). I daubed on some concealer, brushed my lashes with mascara, and hurried downstairs for my morning rendezvous with Mr. Coffee.

Anarchy was already in the kitchen. "Did you sleep?"

"I did."

He smirked. Funny. Up until that moment, I'd found smirking

unattractive. Not anymore. I clutched the counter with one hand and accepted the cup of coffee he was offering with the other.

"We're supposed to pick up Grace at nine," he said.

I blinked.

"And I called a locksmith. He'll be here at ten."

I blinked again. And sipped my coffee. Words would kick in after the first cup. Hopefully.

"Do you want eggs?" he asked. "I'm making you breakfast."

Anarchy Jones was the perfect man.

I gulped my coffee. "I can cook."

He ignored my suggestion. "Scrambled?"

"I can make them."

"Just sit down, Ellison." He took the cup from my hands and refilled it.

I sat.

Anarchy took the egg carton from the fridge and cracked eggs into a bowl.

With one hand.

Show off.

I couldn't crack eggs into the bowl with two hands. Whenever I tried, half the white slithered down the outside of the bowl and made a sticky mess on the counter.

He opened a drawer and pulled out a whisk.

Ding dong.

"I'll get that."

His lips thinned.

"It's broad daylight and Max will come with me, won't you Max?"

Max yawned.

Anarchy rested the whisk against the edge of the bowl.

"Seriously, it will be fine."

Max and I walked down the hallway to the front door. I pretended I couldn't feel Anarchy's gaze fixed on my back.

Rather than opening the door, I peeked out the side panel.

My father waited on the stoop and he looked awful. Fifteen

years older than before Mother left. Gaunt. There was stubble on his chin. Stubble. Mother leaving had hit him hard. Much as I was dying to know about my mysterious half-sister, now didn't look like the best time to ask. Besides, I had more immediate problems.

I yanked open the door. "Come in."

Daddy stepped into the front hall.

I reached up on my tip-toes, kissed his cheek, and, ignoring his wet rain coat, wrapped my arms around his neck. "I'm glad you're here."

Daddy's arms wrapped around me. For half a second I was nine, with a father who could fix anything, and all was right with the world.

There were things not even Daddy could fix. I pulled away. "Let me take your coat."

I took Daddy's dripping trench and hung it over the newel post. "Are you hungry?"

"Is Aggie here?" There was note in his voice that said, quite clearly, he was hungry but didn't want breakfast if I was cooking.

"Aggie is away. Anarchy's making eggs."

"The detective? What's he doing here?"

"He spent the night on the couch."

Daddy's eyebrows rose.

"He didn't want me to be here alone after a man was murdered in the front yard."

Daddy couldn't argue with that sentiment—Mother could have. "Where's Grace?"

"She spent the night with a friend."

"What happened here last night?" He sounded more like himself, a man accustomed to running things, fixing things.

"Come on back to the kitchen, I'll get you some coffee and tell you everything."

I poured Daddy a cup while he and Anarchy exchanged tight nods.

"I understand you looked after my daughter last night." Daddy accepted his coffee. "Thank you." He was talking to Anarchy not me.

"My pleasure, Mr. Walford."

"Harrington."

Oh. Wow. Harrington.

"Harrington," said Anarchy.

Ding dong.

"I'll get that."

Both men looked at me as if I'd lost my mind.

With Anarchy, Daddy, and Max trailing behind me, I returned to the front door and pulled it open.

Bruce Petteway thrust a bouquet of flowers at me. "I wanted to apologize for last night. My niece is a florist and she says these are apology flowers." He'd dragged his niece out of bed on a Sunday morning to create a bouquet? He should be apologizing to her.

The bouquet was lovely—blue hyacinths, white roses, and pink carnations.

The hyacinths smelled like they'd been picked from a garden in heaven. I smiled—but I did not forgive. Bruce had ruined a perfectly good Mercedes. "They're lovely. Thank you."

Bruce noticed Anarchy and Daddy. I didn't realize you had guests—" he glanced around my warm, dry foyer and wiped a raindrop from the tip of his nose "—may I come in?"

Behind me, I could sense Anarchy and Daddy exchanging looks.

"I'm really quite busy."

"It will only take a moment. Please."

A gust of wind blew water through the doorway.

"Fine." I stepped aside and allowed him entrance.

"Ellison, give me those flowers." Daddy took the bouquet from my hands. "Detective Jones, she keeps the vases on the top shelf and I've got a touch of vertigo."

Liar, liar. Daddy was being kind, allowing Bruce a moment alone to say his piece without an audience. Bruce didn't deserve such kindness.

Daddy, Anarchy, and the hyacinths disappeared down the

hallway.

Bruce, Max, and I remained.

Bruce cleared his throat. "About last night—"

"I don't want to talk about last night." I didn't want to think about last night. I longed for a magic wand that would erase the memory of last night.

"So you won't tell Joyce?" He stood as stiff and straight as a nine iron.

That was what got him up on a Sunday morning, out in wretched weather? He worried I'd tell Joyce I'd caught him grinding gears with Prudence in my Mercedes?

"Telling Joyce would be cruel."

Bruce's shoulders relaxed.

"I'm going to tell her lawyer." Not the nicest thing to say to a man who'd brought me flowers but true.

The color drained from Bruce's face and his eyes narrowed. "You wouldn't."

"I would. I will."

He stepped closer to me, invading my space. He smelled of damp and last night's vodka. "I wouldn't do that if I were you."

The hair on the Max's back stood up in a neat little ridge and he growled.

Bruce's face scrunched into something mean and nasty. "I mean it, Ellison. If you know what's good for you, you won't—"

"Elli, should Jones cook the eggs? Are you almost done?" My father stood in the doorway to the kitchen.

Bruce's gaze traveled from me to my father. "I'm not kidding, Ellison."

"Are you threatening me?" Unlike Bruce, I spoke loud enough for my father to hear.

Daddy said something over his shoulder and Anarchy joined him in the doorway.

Faced with two scowling men, Bruce said, "No. Of course not. You misunderstood."

"I thought as much. Thank you for the flowers." I opened the front door.

With a final threatening glare, Bruce left.

I closed the door firmly. The house shook.

"What was that all about?" asked Daddy.

"You don't want to know." I walked back to the kitchen.

"He threatened you. Why?" Compared to Anarchy's expression, the weather outside was balmy and pleasant.

I might as well tell them. "I caught him having sex with Prudence Davies in my new car."

Daddy spit coffee across the counter.

Anarchy covered his mouth. Hiding a smile? Hiding a scowl?

"He doesn't want me to tell his wife, or her lawyer." I fiddled with the floral arrangement that was perfuming my kitchen. "Don't worry about Bruce. It's an empty threat."

Daddy wiped his sweater with a tea towel. "Ellison is right. All hat, no cattle. Always has been."

Anarchy, looking only slightly mollified, poured the eggs into a skillet.

Daddy warmed my coffee

I sat.

Ding dong.

Seriously? It was Sunday morning. What was wrong with people?

Anarchy raised his gaze from the skillet of eggs and a look passed between him and my father.

"Come on, Elli. Let's get the door."

They'd silently decided I couldn't open a door by myself? Oh dear Lord.

"Stay. Here." I stood. "Come on, Max."

With a sigh (I asked so much of him—there was food in the kitchen), Max trotted down the hallway with me.

I peeked outside.

Wright Halstrom waited on the front stoop. He'd parked an enormous, presumably undefiled, Mercedes in the drive.

I opened the door. "Wright."

He thrust a bouquet of roses at me.

It was déjà vu all over again.

"Thank you. They're lovely."

"I'd like to take you out for brunch." Wright spoke with the assurance of a man so handsome he'd never had a woman turn him down.

"I'm sorry, I can't."

A shadow passed over his features.

Who was I to disappoint Adonis in human form? "I really am sorry, Wright." Why did I apologize? I wasn't sorry. He'd appeared at my house without an invitation and expected me to drop everything and go out with him.

"I won't take no for an answer." He coupled this pronouncement with a dazzling smile.

I focused my gaze on something other than his white teeth—on the street where a blue Impala was cruising slowly by. "I'm afraid you'll have to. I can't go."

"But we didn't get much of a chance to chat last night. Libba tells me your art would be perfect for my new hotel in Chicago. We need pieces for the lobby and the rooftop restaurant. We could discuss an acquisition over Eggs Benedict."

Without so much as seeing a canvas? "As tempting as that sounds, I must pass."

"Elli, your eggs are ready." Daddy's voice carried down the hallway.

"You have company."

"My father."

"I'd love to meet him." Wright pushed past me and headed for the kitchen.

I stood in the foyer, flabbergasted. Who did that? Who barged into someone's home?

Wright Halstrom. And he'd disappeared into the kitchen.

I closed the front door and followed. Slowly. The combination of Anarchy, Daddy, and Wright struck me as combustive.

Deep breath. Deep breath. I tarried. I stopped and smelled the roses, but they had no scent. Finally, I stepped into to the kitchen.

Wright was staring at Anarchy as if a gauntlet had been thrown.

Anarchy's lips were sealed in a thin line and his eyes were as cold, and hard, and flinty as Clint Eastwood's.

Daddy looked as if he was fighting a grin.

Combustive, with a near overwhelming scent of testosterone. That I could smell.

"Your friend, Mr. Jon—"

"Detective Jones." Anarchy's voice was a blade cutting through all pretense.

"Detective Jones," Wright corrected with a twisted smile that told me he'd made the mistake on purpose. "He was telling me you had some excitement here last night."

"That's one way to put it." Excitement wasn't the word I'd use to describe seeing a man gunned down in my driveway.

"A man was murdered?"

"Yes." I searched the counter for my coffee mug, my free hand reflexively clutching an imaginary handle. My other hand held Wright's bouquet. The roses were wrapped in crinkly plastic—most likely purchased from the hotel gift shop.

"You saw the murder happen?" There was sympathy in Wright's voice.

"Yes." Where the heck was my mug?

Anarchy poured a fresh cup of coffee, brought it to me, and took the flowers from my hand.

"Thank you." Two words completely inadequate for the depth of my gratitude.

Now Wright's eyes narrowed. He smoothed his red cashmere scarf over the lapel of his camel hair coat, sprinkling raindrops onto the kitchen floor, and jerked his chin toward Bruce's bouquet. "Pretty. Where are the flowers I sent you?"

"The living room. Thank you, again. They really are lovely."

"Not nearly as lovely as the woman I sent them to."

What was that sound? Was Anarchy grinding his teeth?

I painted on the brightest smile I could muster. "Wright and I met on Friday night. We had dinner with Bill and Libba at the Alameda."

"Yes," said Anarchy. "He told me."

"Best blind date I've ever been on." Wright beamed at the room at large.

The sound again. Anarchy was definitely grinding his teeth.

It hadn't been a date. Not really. Except for the part about drinks. And dinner. And two couples.

"I learned so much about commercial real estate." Surely Anarchy would understand how incredibly bored I'd been.

"You're a developer?" asked Daddy.

"I am."

"What are you in town for?" Daddy was being polite. That or he was trying to defuse the tension that pulsed in my kitchen like the beat of a kettle drum.

"Downtown development." Again Wright smoothed his lapels.

"The new convention hotel?"

Wright answered with a nod and a satisfied smile. "Exactly."

"Are they going to get that thing up before the Republican convention next year?"

Wright's smile faltered. "We're trying." He glanced around my kitchen—at the copper pots hanging from a rack in the ceiling, at cooling plates of eggs, at the paintings on the wall. "Are those your paintings, Ellison?"

"They are."

"You're talented. Very." He sounded almost surprised.

"Thank you." My voice might have been a tad dry. The man had offered to buy paintings sight unseen. One would think he would have at least asked if they were any good before saying he'd cover the walls of his new hotel with them. I shifted my gaze to the three plates of food. "And thank you for stopping by."

Not a subtle hint.

"Libba said you have a daughter. I'd love to meet her."

"She's not here." And, for a half-second, much as I wanted her home, I was glad she was away.

"Oh?"

"She spent the night with a friend."

"So she missed all the excitement." There was that word again. "It's hard to keep track of teenagers these days."

"Do you have children?" Daddy asked.

"No." Wright shook his head as if his lack of children was the single biggest regret of his life. "I just think it must be hard being a parent. Especially to a teenager. There are so many temptations out there. So many ways to fall off the straight and narrow."

Anarchy's brows, which had been drawn together rose slightly. "Grace is a great kid. She's got her head on straight."

"Do you know her well?" There was a challenge in Wright's question.

"Yes."

Wright's face tightened. Anarchy's one-word answer hadn't pleased him. "She can't be as pretty as her mother."

"Prettier," I said. And smarter. And braver.

"Not possible." Wright's dazzling smile was back in force. He looked around the kitchen as if he was just realizing Anarchy was cooking breakfast. "I won't keep you."

"Thank you for the flowers." I nodded toward the bouquet Anarchy had abandoned on the counter. "All of them."

"You're welcome. I don't suppose you'd like to have dinner with me tonight?"

There was that grinding noise again.

I didn't dare look at Anarchy. "I'm sorry. I can't."

"Another time." Wright's devil-may-care tone made it sound as if I'd be willing to go out with him on a different night. "I can see myself out." With one last dazzling smile, he leaned forward, brushed an unexpected kiss across my cheek, and pushed through the kitchen door.

A charged silence followed him. A silence that lasted an eternity (fifteen seconds).

Finally, I whispered, "Is he gone?"

"I'll check." Daddy pushed through the kitchen door. Either my father had adopted a significantly more helpful attitude than he'd ever exhibited before, or he wanted to escape the arcs of electricity zapping from Anarchy's narrowed eyes.

I clutched my coffee cup. Tightly. I swallowed.

Brnng, brnng.

Saved by the bell.

I grabbed the receiver. "Hello."

"Mrs. Russell? This is Donna calling. Would you please let Grace know she forgot her sweater?"

Grace forgot her sweater? That couldn't be right. Grace was still at Donna's house. "Grace isn't there?"

"No, she left a little while ago."

The cold rain pelting the windows was warmer than the blood in my veins. "She left?"

"Yes, ma'am. With a friend named Jane."

EIGHTEEN

Walls were made for sliding—down, down, down to a heap on the floor. I took full advantage and did just that. I blame my knees. They'd disappeared and left me with Jell-O.

"Ellison?" Anarchy's voice was insistent. "Ellison?"

I clutched the phone and stared at my non-working knees. Donna was wrong. She had to be wrong.

Anarchy pried the phone from my stiff fingers. "Hello, this is Detective Jones, with whom am I speaking?"

He listened for a few seconds, the expression on his face as cold as the blood in my veins. "May I please speak with your mother?" Another pause. "Thank you."

He crouched next to me, somehow inserted his arm between my back and the wall, and hauled me off the floor.

With Anarchy supporting me, I staggered to the island, and collapsed on a stool.

He spoke into the phone. "Mrs. Hess, Detective Jones on the line. Am I to understand that Grace Russell left your house?"

Again he listened.

"We'll be there in ten minutes."

Daddy walked into the kitchen as Anarchy hung up the phone. He took one look at my face and asked, "What's happened? Are you all right?"

"Grace—" my throat closed, tightened by unspeakable fear.

"Grace left the Hess's house and we don't know where she is," Anarchy explained.

"She'll be home soon," said Daddy.

Tears spilled over the rims of my eyes. "There were—" telling Daddy about the threats was an impossibility.

"There were threats." Good thing Anarchy could finish my sentence.

Daddy's brows drew together. "What kind of threats?"

A sob escaped my throat. When I'd thought Grace was safe, facing the myriad problems in front of me seemed doable—especially with Anarchy beside me. Now that she was missing, fear and horror and panic clawed for supremacy in my chest. I could think of nothing but her. I shook my head unable to speak.

"Things no parent wants to hear," said Anarchy.

I bit the knuckle of my thumb. Hard enough to hurt. Hard enough to draw blood.

Now Daddy looked worried. "What can I do?" He was letting Anarchy take charge?

"Stay here in case Grace shows up," said Anarchy. "Ellison and I are going to the Hess's."

Somehow I made it from the kitchen to the passenger seat of Anarchy's car (hard to do with knees made of Jell-O).

Anarchy turned the key in the ignition. "Address?"

"What?"

"What's the address? Where are we going?"

Coming up with an actual address was an impossibility. My brain, filled as it was with awful images and numbing fear, refused to fetch details. "Turn left at the corner."

Anarchy drove as if the streets were dry. Houses and trees and sodden leaves blurred past the windows.

"Right at the stop sign."

He turned without coming to a full stop and the rear of the car fishtailed. "We'll find her." His tone left no room for doubt. "I promise, Ellison. We'll find Grace."

We had to.

Despite the heat blasting from the vents, I shivered. And shivered.

Anarchy reached across the seat and took my hand. "We'll find her."

If he said it often enough, it had to be true. I nodded, again unable to speak, my voice held hostage by horrific what-ifs. I wanted to scream and rail and beat against the windows of the car. Not my daughter. Not heroin. Not men. Not that. Had Leesa's mother felt this way? Had Jane's? Of course they had. In that moment, I understood desperation. There was nothing—nothing—I wouldn't do to get Grace back.

More houses whizzed by.

Anarchy slowed for another stop sign.

"Straight through here then the third house on the left." My voice didn't belong to me. It quavered like an old woman's—one beaten down by hardship and sadness and unrelenting terror.

Anarchy pulled into the drive and together we ran to the front door.

India was waiting for us.

She hugged me. "Ellison, I'm so sorry. I had no idea Grace left. Not until I spoke with Detective Jones." She ushered us inside. "Coffee. Do you need coffee?"

Like I needed my heart and lungs. Like I needed my daughter. I shook my head. My throat was too tight to swallow even a sip.

"Who picked up Grace?" Anarchy wore his cop-face. All business. Not a shred of warmth in his expression. For once, I was glad to see it.

India turned and called, "Donna."

A pale-faced Donna appeared. Tears stood in her eyes and her chin quivered. "I thought it was okay. Mom didn't tell us there was a problem." She sent a reproachful glance in India's direction. "If I'd known Grace was in trouble I wouldn't have let her leave."

Anarchy's hand closed around my elbow, keeping me steady, keeping me on my feet.

"It's true. I didn't tell the girls about your call, Ellison. I thought it best that you, not I, tell Grace what was happening."

I didn't blame her.

Blame didn't matter. Not now. The only thing that mattered

was Grace. Where was she? The question reverberated through my body but my voice-box rebelled.

It was Anarchy who said, "Tell us about the girl who picked her up. Where did they go?"

"She was just a girl. Grace knew her. She called her Jane."

Where did they go? My mouth opened and closed and I squeaked.

Anarchy glanced at me then asked, "What kind of car was she driving?"

"Light blue."

There were probably a hundred thousand light blue cars in metropolitan area.

"Make? Model? License plate number?" Anarchy's no-nonsense tone made Donna blink. Multiple times.

She shook her head. "I don't know much about cars. I don't pay attention to them. I do remember the license plate was red with white letters and numbers."

A Kansas plate?

Anarchy leaned forward. "You're sure?"

"Yes."

Not Missouri. Missouri plates were white with black letters and numbers. Living near the state line as we did, we saw an equal number of both.

"Anything else? Do you remember any of the letters or numbers?"

"J and A."

"That's it?"

"I only remember those because the girl said her name was Jane and I thought it was cool that the first two letters of her plates matched her name."

"How many doors did the car have?" Now Anarchy's tone was patient.

We didn't need patience. We needed urgency. Jane could have already delivered Grace to one of those awful bars.

"Two doors." Donna rubbed her chin and closed her eyes. "I

think. Maybe four."

I pressed the back of my hand against my mouth, stifling a scream.

"Did she say where she was going?"

"I'm not sure. I think I heard Jane say something about home and a grandmother."

"My mother?" My voice creaked like the third step on the backstairs—the one Grace avoided when she was late for curfew. She had to be all right. Had. To. Be.

"We should check your parents' house." said Anarchy.

"I can't imagine why they'd go there."

"Jane's grandmother?"

Jane's grandmother. Who knew it was possible for my stomach to sink even lower? "We don't know who—" my voice died as a tiny sliver of mental acuity slipped past the wall of terror in my mind—the woman who'd sent me looking for Jane in the first place. What if she'd lied? What if there was no restless spirit begging for my help? What if there was just a desperate grandmother? One who'd do anything to rescue her granddaughter? I cleared my throat. "Madame Reyna's. We should go there." My voice was strong and sure.

Anarchy's brows rose. "Why?"

"I have a feeling." More than a feeling. Certainty blossomed within me. Madame Reyna and Jane were related by blood. And the men Jane had been involved with had threatened her grandmother if she dared go home. But now, she had no place left to run. I rushed toward the door, toward the car, toward Prairie Village and Madame Reyna's little ranch house.

"Ellison." India's voice slowed my steps. "Please keep us informed."

"I will." I looked over my shoulder and attempted a smile (a smile that felt like a grimace). "I promise." Jane and Grace were at Madame Reyna's. They were. They had to be. I'd be calling with good news in no time.

Anarchy clutched the wheel as we drove. Ten and two. I

clutched my hands together and prayed.

He parked at the curb in front of the house. "I don't suppose you'd wait in the car."

I snorted and opened the car door.

We hurried up the short front walk, the rain dampening our hair, and, for me, sneaking past the collar of my trench coat.

The front door stood ajar.

Anarchy reached inside his coat and pulled out a gun. He looked at me, his face serious as death. "You won't go back to the car?"

"No." Not now. Not when Grace might be inside. Might need me.

"Then stay here." His tone brooked no arguments.

I nodded and pulled the collar of my trench tighter around my neck.

"I mean it, Ellison. Stay. Here. Do not set foot in this house until I tell you it's clear."

"Okay."

"Promise."

"I promise."

He gave me a look that said he didn't quite believe me. A look that said if I broke my promise, there would be hell to pay.

I gave him a look that said I wouldn't move a muscle. I blinked back raindrops. Mascara ran down my cheeks. I was sure of it. "I won't move."

Giving me one last cop-like stare, Anarchy used the tip of his gun to push on the door. It swung open and he stepped inside.

The temptation to follow him was overwhelming. Grace might be in there.

But, if Anarchy needed to use his gun to save her, I might get in the way. I wiped my mascara-blackened cheeks and waited.

Not patiently.

I leaned over Madame Reyna's neatly trimmed hedge and peeked through the rain-streaked windows into the living room.

Madame Reyna's gold brocade living room set had been

upended, the macramé hangings ripped from the walls, and her crystal ball lay in pieces on the shag rug.

Oh dear Lord.

I straightened and stuck my head through the front door. "Anarchy!"

"Stay outside, Ellison." His voice carried from the back of the house.

No one was home. Worse than that, someone had destroyed what home there was. I couldn't wait. I lifted a sodden loafer. I had to find Grace. Now.

Wham!

My bum hitting the concrete reverberated up my spine.

And the man on top of me didn't seem to appreciate that I'd broken his fall. He struggled—violently—to free himself from the tangle of our limbs.

I gasped for air and my lungs filled with the scents of wet wool and tobacco.

"Son of a bitch." He was almost free.

I grabbed the front of his sweater and held onto the wool as if Grace's life depended on it. "Anarchy!" My voice echoed in the damp air.

"Let go, lady." The man struggled against my hold.

I threw my calf over the bend in his knee. "Anarchy!"

The man raised up, his hand closed into a fist—a fist the size of Rhode Island—and he drew his arm back.

I winced in anticipation of the coming pain. No matter what, I couldn't let go. My grasp on his sweater tightened. I closed my eyes.

His weight disappeared and I was half-dragged off the pavement by my hold on his clothing.

"Let go, Ellison." I opened my eyes and saw Anarchy.

Per his instructions, I released the man's sweater and thudded against the concrete.

An enormous, craggy man scowled down on me.

Anarchy had twisted the man's arm. The hold looked painful.

"Can you get up?" Anarchy asked.

I nodded and rose slowly to my feet.

"There are cuffs in the car. Go get them."

I nodded and hurried toward the car parked on the street.

"They're in the glove box," Anarchy called after me.

I yanked open the glove box, grabbed the cold metal, and raced back up the walk.

Anarchy closed the handcuffs around the man's wrists. "Let's get out of the rain."

With Anarchy propelling him, the man stepped back inside. I followed.

Anarchy pushed the man into the kitchen.

Someone had destroyed Madame Reyna's home. And not just the living room. The kitchen drawers had been emptied onto the rust-colored linoleum floors, plates and glasses had been pulled from the cupboards, and the avocado-green oven door hung at a drunken angle. Miraculously, Madame Reyna's Mr. Coffee had survived.

Anarchy caught me looking. "Crime scene. You can't make coffee."

I sighed.

He forced the man into a kitchen chair. "Meet Rocky O'Hearne."

I'd heard that name before.

Anarchy, who stood behind O'Hearne, mouthed, "Bookie."

A bookie? Now I remembered, Anarchy had told me about him. Rocky O'Hearne wasn't just a bookie. He had his finger in every illicit pot in the city. I shifted my gaze to the man in the chair. My first impression had been spot on. He was craggy. His face was deeply lined and his faded red hair looked wind-swept as if he'd just returned from a walk on the moors. He wore a shapeless, moss-colored sweater (the sweater probably had more shape before I grabbed hold of it), a leather jacket spotted with damp, and corduroy pants. He also wore a bored expression—as if getting cuffed by a homicide detective was nothing more than a tedious inconvenience.

Did Rocky O'Hearne know where Grace was?

Flying across the table and choking Grace's whereabouts out of him probably wouldn't work. Mother, who seldom followed her own advice, often told me that I'd catch more flies with honey than vinegar. Honey was worth a try. "Pleased to meet you, Mr. O'Hearne."

Both Anarchy and Mr. O'Hearne blinked.

"I'm sorry I ruined your sweater."

They blinked again.

The panic that had subsided on the drive over, when I'd been sure we'd find Grace at Madame Reyna's, was building again. Deep breath. "We're looking for my daughter."

Rocky did not reply.

"She's sixteen."

Rocky did not look interested.

"She disappeared this morning."

Rocky looked terminally bored. His gaze traveled the kitchen, catching on Mr. Coffee as if he too wanted a cup of liquid heaven.

"She's with a girl named Jane—Starry."

I had his attention now. His gaze—the cold, pale blue of a January sky—locked onto me. "You know Starry?"

"I do."

"Smart kid."

"She worked for you?" I asked.

Rocky O'Hearne glanced over his shoulder at Anarchy then settled back into silence.

Now it was my turn to look at Anarchy. I pleaded with my eyes. Was there nothing he could do to make this Rocky person tell us where the girls were?

Anarchy righted two additional chairs. "Sit."

I sat.

He took the other chair. "This lady is worried about her daughter."

Rocky swung his bored gaze my way. "The kid ran away?"

"No!" My voice was too loud in Madame Reyna's small

kitchen. I adjusted the volume. "She didn't run away." Tears filled my eyes, blurred my vision. "Grace went with Jane—probably because she thought she could help her."

"With what?"

"I don't know. I just know she's in trouble. Ray's dead—"

Rocky's eyes widened and he rose from his chair. "Ray's dead?"

"Sit down," instructed Anarchy.

Rocky sat and lowered his head so the fall of his hair and his wild brows hid his eyes.

"Ray was murdered," I said quietly. "Last night. At my house."

Rocky's head didn't move.

"Someone threatened my daughter." If I fell to my knees on Madame Reyna's linoleum, would Rocky listen to me? Would he tell me what I needed to know? Did he even have the answers?

Like Rocky, I lowered my head. Unlike Rocky, I was not silent. A sob ripped from my chest. The first sob was followed by a second and a third.

"Shut up."

No one had told me to shut up since I was five. My sister, Marjorie, yelled at me when I sang "Marjorie and Chet sitting in a tree" one too many times. Marjorie didn't count. Rocky's rudeness surprised me enough to quiet my crying.

"I can't stand it when women cry."

Then he was in the wrong business. There couldn't be too many happy women at strip clubs.

"She's sixteen." My voice was still choked with emotion.

"She made a choice."

"Were all the decisions you made at sixteen wise ones?"

"When I was sixteen, I was in juvie."

"There you go. You'd made a bad decision."

"I turned out fine."

He'd turned into a monster. "No one was feeding you drugs. No one accepted money to let men rape you. No one made you dance around a pole. No one—"

"Shut up!" He lifted his head and we stared at each other.

"Why are you here, Mr. O'Hearne?" I asked. "At this house?"

He couldn't cross his arms—not with his wrists cuffed—but he extended his legs and slouched in his chair.

"You have the right to remain silent," said Anarchy. "Anything you say can and will be used against you in a court of law. You have the right to an attorney. If you cannot—"

"You're arresting me?" Rocky O'Hearne sounded annoyed (bothersome-mosquito annoyed) "On what charge?"

Anarchy's gaze traveled the destroyed kitchen. "Breaking and entering. Destruction of property." He looked at me. "Assault."

"I'll be out in an hour."

"If you cannot afford an attorney, one will be provided for you. Do you understand—"

"Yeah, I understand 'em."

"Why are you here, Mr. O'Hearne?" Every bit of sadness and hope and exhaustion and yo-yoing emotion I'd felt that day came through in my voice.

He stared at me, his face impassive.

I wiped a tear from my cheek and my gaze dropped to my lap. He wasn't going to tell me anything. Not one thing.

"I didn't wreck this place," said Rocky. "It was like this when I got here."

I lifted my head in time to see Anarchy nod as if he'd expected as much.

"Why are you here?" I asked.

The expression on Rocky's face was almost wry. "I'm looking for Starry."

"Why?" I insisted.

"She witnessed a murder."

NINETEEN

"Whose murder?" Anarchy's cop-face was firmly in place.

Rocky took a moment and glanced around Madame Reyna's trashed kitchen. Without the broken plates, emptied drawers, and destroyed appliances, it probably looked much like the kitchens in the neighboring houses—cabinets stained an orangey shade of brown and avocado green everything else. A small table sat in front of a window with a view of the bleak backyard. A beehive lantern (also avocado green) hanging above the little table cast sickly light on everything in the room.

"Whose murder?" Anarchy repeated.

"Girl named Leesa. Starry saw the guy who killed her."

She had? She'd never said. Never even hinted.

"Did she describe him?" I asked. Surely the girl would have told me something.

"Nah. She didn't have to."

Anarchy crossed his arms and watched me as if he was curious about what I might say next.

Rocky's lips pulled back into a thin-lipped smile and his eyes narrowed until they were mere slits with pouches beneath them.

"You know who killed Leesa," I said. A statement not a question. No one could look that smug and not know.

"I got a pretty good idea. They want us outta downtown. They think the neighborhood looks seedy enough—" he added a Gallic shrug, complete with not-my-fault pursed lips and a tilt of his shaggy head "—the public will force us out early."

"They?" Better to pursue *they* than point out that if the

neighborhood was seedy, he'd definitely had a hand in making it that way.

"Developers." Rocky twisted the word into something ugly.

"You're saying a real estate developer killed Leesa?" Disbelief colored outside the lines of my words. Rocky was delusional.

"They got millions invested in building that new hotel. It don't get built on time, they lose. Big."

I wasn't about to argue the ins and outs of real estate investing with a hand-cuffed thug, but the real estate developers I knew wouldn't risk spending the rest of their lives in prison for one hotel.

Rocky must have read the doubt on my face because he added, "They killed all those girls. The lawyer too."

A shot of adrenaline hit my system and my mouth dried. "The lawyer? Patrick Conover?" That couldn't be right. Patrick Conover worked for the development company. Now I knew where Rocky got his name. The man had rocks for brains if he thought I'd actually believe his cockamamie story.

"Why would a development company have their lawyer killed?" Anarchy didn't believe Rocky's story either.

Rocky's smile was tight and mean. "Maybe the lawyer had more than one client."

Patrick Conover had put his law license, his livelihood, and his family on the line for a man like Rocky O'Hearne? I thought not. "You're saying Patrick worked for you?"

"I ain't sayin' nothin'." There was a truth.

Of course he wasn't. For all he'd told us, he'd said nothing incriminating.

"But—" Rocky shrugged again (almost Gallic, not quite) "—maybe he had a weakness for young girls."

A weakness for young girls? My stomach tightened into a hard, angry knot.

"And you provided young girls." Anarchy sounded as disgusted as I felt.

Those poor girls.

Grace was a young girl.

The man in the chair was a monster. Plain and simple.

"I didn't say that." Rocky crossed his ankles. "Can't blame me some guy likes 'em on the young side."

I did blame him. He made the young girls available.

I stared into Rocky O'Hearne's blue eyes. They had all the warmth of ice and all the humanity of diamond chips. The man didn't care about who he damaged—not the girls, not their families. Teen-aged girls forced into prostitution and drug addiction meant nothing to him. The man lacked a soul.

My shoulders shivered with a coldness that had nothing to do with the weather.

"Course, there's some guys like 'em past first bloom." He chuckled. "Like Jones back there."

Anarchy and a prostitute? Impossible. Then it dawned on me. Rocky was talking about me. Me. I was past first bloom.

I couldn't argue. Not with the skin on the underside of my arms starting to sag, incipient laugh lines, and thinning lips (why did no one tell me that would happen?).

But women past first bloom knew a few things their younger (still in bloom) sisters did not.

Something other than humanity propelled Rocky through his days. Greed? Lust for power? Or maybe life was just a game to him—a game where he won and the girls he exploited lost.

He'd told us nothing. Nothing we could verify. Nothing that rang true. All he'd done was cast suspicion elsewhere.

The reality was the girls who'd been murdered were probably causing him trouble. Just like Patrick Conover had probably caused him trouble by advancing the eviction schedule for 12th Street.

Rocky's relaxed pose hadn't changed. He still lounged in a straight-back chair. "I got places to be. You want to take off these cuffs?"

Anarchy snorted.

"What are you charging me with?"

"Breaking and entering," Anarchy replied.

"Prove I wasn't invited." Rocky looked around the destroyed

kitchen and his shaggy brows rose, the very picture of wronged innocence. "I came to visit a friend, get my fortune told, and the place was like this when I got here. Looks to me like the house was burgled."

No one was buying Rocky's wronged innocence schtick. Least of all, Anarchy. "Looks to me like someone was looking for something."

"Like I said, the place was like this when I got here. Maybe the lady of the house is a lousy homemaker."

Rocky O'Hearne was wasting our time. Was he frittering away minutes on purpose?

We could waste hours questioning him and learn bupkis. I rose from my chair.

"Where are you going?" Anarchy asked.

"I'm going to find my daughter."

"Wait."

I waited, but only because I had no way to leave.

"I'll call patrol and we'll have someone pick him up."

"You're arresting me? Seriously?" Rocky sounded put out.

"Seriously." Anarchy sounded serious as a heart attack. Serious as a missing daughter. He picked up the avocado-green (to match the appliances) phone, called the Prairie Village Police Department, explained who he was, and requested a patrol car come pick up a suspect.

We waited with Rocky, who'd acquired a fatalistic you-ruined-my-Sunday-but-what's-a-man-to-do air.

When the police officers came, they conversed quietly with Anarchy in the corner. I leaned toward them but couldn't hear a word. Really, missing their conversation wasn't important. The looks the two Prairie Village officers gave Rocky spoke volumes. They weren't happy about taking a notorious (locally, at least) criminal into custody.

Anarchy seem to share their concerns. He scowled at Rocky and the police officers. "We'll get the paperwork to move him to Missouri filed first thing in the morning."

That I heard.

So did Rocky. He chuckled. We might be ruining his Sunday, but he planned on making it home in time for dinner.

The two officers led Rocky away.

Anarchy and I followed—at least to the curb.

He opened my door and I climbed into his car.

He circled the front of the car and took his spot behind the wheel. "Where to?"

I had no idea. If I was in trouble and afraid to go home, where would I go? I'd go to Mother's because she was scarier than anyone. "Let's try my parents'."

Anarchy put the car in gear.

"Unless you've got a better idea."

He shook his head and pulled away from the curb.

"What do you think happened to Madame Reyna?" I asked. I'd been so worried about Grace, I'd barely given the missing madame a single thought.

"No idea. Maybe, if we're lucky, she's at the market or out with friends. At least we know Rocky's people don't have her. He wouldn't have been there if they did."

"Tell me about Rocky O'Hearne."

He shifted his gaze away from the wet road. "You saw him. He's a bad guy. If you see him again, and I'm not with you, run."

"You just sent him to jail."

"He'll be out in time for cocktails."

"Then why arrest him?"

"He broke the law." And Anarchy followed the rules. Starry had broken the law. She'd stolen a car. Would Anarchy arrest her when (not if) we found them? I stared out the windshield at a day that grew more gray and sullen with each passing moment. Anarchy could arrest Starry, but I would not press charges.

"Is he from here? Kansas City, I mean?"

Anarchy answered with a short nod.

"How—" how to phrase the question? "—how did he end up a criminal?"

"Family business."

Ah. "Turn here." I pointed to the left.

A few minutes later we pulled into Mother and Daddy's drive.

Anarchy stared at the house. "Nice place." His tone was dry.

Mother and Daddy did have a lot of house for two people, but Mother entertained. And kept things. And God help me if they ever decided to move.

I dug my keys out of my purse, unlocked the door, and stepped inside.

One of Daddy's coats hung over the newel post (a thing that would never happen if Mother was home) and a few of the flowers in the arrangement on the circular table in the foyer drooped (Mother would have pulled them immediately).

"Grace," I called.

There was no answer.

I walked toward the kitchen. "Grace!"

"Hold on." Anarchy pulled a pager off his belt and read the number. "May I use the phone?"

"This way." I led him into Daddy's study. Unlike the study at my house, Daddy's didn't feel like a cave. The walls were a soft shade of gold, a Mahal rug in light shades of blue, gold, and terracotta covered the hardwood floor and attractive drapes hung at the windows.

Anarchy picked up the phone and dialed. "Jones."

I paced. Had Grace gone home? Was the message from Daddy? I paused my steps and stared at Anarchy. Surely if I stared hard enough, his expression would tell me something. Nope. His face gave nothing away.

I paced some more. My skin—well, under my skin—itched. I bit my lip. I stared at the ceiling. I stared at Anarchy. Who was he talking to? What had happened?

"I understand," he spoke into the phone but looked at his pager. "Yes, sir."

He hung up the phone then picked it up again. Immediately. Without answering a single one of my unanswered questions.

"What's happening?" I demanded. Frustration added a sharp edge to my voice.

"Prairie Village doesn't want to hold Rocky O'Hearne. Hold on."

Hold on?

He dialed, waited, then spoke into the phone. "It's Jones." His gaze shifted from the black telephone to me. "I'll call him. Thanks."

"What?" The sharp edge of my tone was now a razor.

"Your father called." He held the receiver out to me.

I wrapped my fingers around black plastic already warmed by Anarchy's hand and called home. "Daddy?"

"Ellison, Grace phoned."

"Where is she? Is she all right?"

"She's at Peggy's."

"Peggy's?" Why Peggy's? Why hadn't she come home? Was she with Jane? A thousand questions ran through my head.

"Call her."

I had a better idea. "Thanks, Daddy. We'll be home soon."

"Who's Peggy?" Anarchy asked.

I dropped the receiver into its cradle. "A friend of Grace's."

He didn't ask any of the myriad questions floating around my brain. He simply said, "Let's go."

I could have kissed him.

We hurried back to the car and I gave him directions to Peggy's house.

I sat in the passenger seat with my hands clasped in my lap. My arms ached to hug Grace (then shake her till her teeth rattled). "Two blocks then a left."

Anarchy drove without comment. Perhaps he could tell I was composing a rant in my head.

"There." I pointed to a red brick colonial.

Anarchy parked. "Ellison."

I paused, my hand on the door handle and one foot already out the door.

"Grace was trying to help someone."

"And?"

"You would have done the same. You have done the same."

True. But I was an adult. Presumably, I was better equipped to understand and deal with threats. My lips thinned.

"You've put yourself at risk for people who were in trouble. And, if anything happens to you, Grace will be an orphan. She's never yelled at you for that." He reached out and his fingers grazed my arm. "The apple doesn't fall far from the tree."

I clenched my jaw and said not one word.

"Would you rather she not step in when she's needed?"

I'd rather she not put herself in harm's way. Apple. Tree. I saw the irony.

"Just think about it," Anarchy's voice was gentle.

I nodded and got out of the car.

Anarchy did not.

"Aren't you coming?"

"You're sure?"

"We're in this together."

Anarchy's smile chased every cloud out of the sky.

Together, we hurried up the front walk.

The door opened before we had a chance to knock. Dee, Peggy's mother, stepped outside. She wore corduroy pants, a barn jacket, and a fearsome expression. "Ellison, do you know who Grace brought into my house?"

Oh dear Lord.

"I'm here to take them home."

That wasn't good enough. "She brought a stripper into my house!" Dee's outrage echoed down the block.

I held up my hands in a gesture meant to be calming. "Dee—"

"Maybe you think that girl is a suitable companion for Grace, but I won't have it! Not for Peggy."

That girl? "That girl is sixteen and life has already beat her up."

"She wouldn't be in trouble if she hadn't made bad decisions."

"You're saying a sixteen-year-old child deserves to be a

stripper?"

"I'm saying she's seen things and done things I don't want Peggy exposed to."

I opened my mouth, ready with a scathing (in my dreams) retort, and stopped. Dee was protecting her daughter the best way she knew how. I might not agree with her, but I wouldn't argue with her. "We'll take them home. Now."

"Has your daughter ever gone out on a date with a boy you don't know?"

Both Dee and I turned and stared at Anarchy.

"Maybe she met him on the Plaza, or one of her friends introduced her, or maybe she was sitting in a booth at Winstead's and he asked for her number."

"Peggy would never do that." Peggy's mother crossed her arms and donned a stubborn expression (a head-in-the-sand expression). Life was easier if she pretended it wasn't there. I pretended the same for years. But I felt it when I first touched a corpse. I heard it when a dominatrix gave me a safe-word I neither wanted nor needed. I saw it in the soulless depths of Rocky O'Hearne's eyes. What Dee refused to acknowledge was a morass of murk and chaos and uncertainty. Dee could hide behind a manicured lawn and manicured nails and a man who took care of her but it was waiting for her. It was waiting for all of us.

"Are you sure that she wouldn't?" asked Anarchy. "Let's say the boy is really handsome and she knows you won't approve of him. It's just one date. What could it hurt?"

"Stop it." Dee's voice was strident and she positively glared at Anarchy. Finally, a woman who didn't melt at the sight of him. "Who are you?"

"Dee, this is Detective Jones."

She did not extend her hand.

Neither did Anarchy. Instead, he said, "The girl agrees to go out with the boy. She lies to her parents—tells them she's spending the night with a friend. But the boy works for unpleasant men. One bad decision and she's gone."

"That doesn't happen." Dee shook her head. "It doesn't."

"It does," said Anarchy. "It happens every day. The girl gets trapped."

"She could leave." Dee sounded so certain.

"No, she can't." Anarchy's tone brooked no arguments, no doubt. "If she's not addicted to drugs—"

Dee curled her lip.

"If she's not addicted to drugs," Anarchy continued, "she's too scared to leave."

"Scared?" Dee didn't believe him. I did. I'd seen Rocky's dead eyes.

"The people who control the girl—they tell her they'll hurt her family if she runs."

Dee's lips thinned to nothing and she fisted her hand and tapped it against her forehead. "I want that girl out of my house."

"That's what we're here for," I reminded her.

Dee yanked opened the front door and bellowed, "Grace, your mother is here."

I waited, my breath fogging the air in front of me. Hug her? Shake her? Both?

Grace appeared and my decision was made. I folded her into a never-let-you-go hug. "I was so worried."

"I'm sorry. We didn't know where to go. And we weren't near a phone. Mostly we just drove around."

I shifted my gaze to Jane. She stood on the front steps with a hand on her hip and a jaunty jut to her chin that looked too confident. I wasn't fooled. "I'm so glad you're all right." I opened my arms wider, inviting her into a group hug.

She blinked. Rapidly. "I'm always all right."

Now Grace opened her arms.

Jane stood on the stoop looking at us as if we'd taken leave of our senses then—finally—she stepped forward.

Dee covered her mouth with her hand and returned to the comforts of the indoors. "Good-bye, Ellison."

"Bye, Dee." My words might have lost their way in the Tame-

Crème-Rinse scent of Grace's hair.

We wrapped Jane into our hug.

She endured, stiff with an I-don't-need-anyone attitude.

We held her anyway.

And, after a moment, she relaxed. Her eyes misted. She whispered, "I heard what you said. Thank you."

"I hate to break this up—"

All three of us shifted our attention to Anarchy

"But I have to ask." He looked at Jane. "Did you witness a murder?"

TWENTY

Anarchy insisted on taking Jane into custody. Insisted.

The cold and rain had nothing on the temperature of my digestive organs. "I'm not pressing charges."

"Charges?" He tilted his head slightly. "Oh, the stolen car. I didn't figure you would."

"Then why—"

"Protective custody," he explained. "She saw a murderer. She's in danger."

"I didn't really see him." Jane shook her head. "It was dark and he was in a car, and Leesa was talking to him through the passenger's window. I wouldn't recognize him if he was standing right in front of me."

The skin at the corner of Anarchy's left eye twitched.

"I say we get out of the rain." No one could argue with my suggestion. A chilly drizzle was slowly soaking us through.

We left Dee's house with Anarchy behind the wheel, me in the passenger's seat, and the girls in the back.

I turned and asked, "Jane, who is Madame Reyna?"

Her lips thinned and she turned her head—away from me—and looked out the rain-streaked window. "My grandmother." The raindrops moving across the glass must have been fascinating because her gaze remained fixed on them. "We thought about going to her house but I didn't want to put her in danger."

Anarchy reached across the seat and squeezed my hand tightly, his meaning clear. I was not to tell Jane about the wreckage at her grandmother's home. I was not to tell her that her grandmother was missing.

"I'm just glad you're safe now." I turned and stared out the windshield. The wipers swished away the light rain.

Anarchy drove to my house and the four of us piled out of the car.

Daddy opened the front door immediately—as if he'd been waiting by the window. He shook his finger at Grace. "You put your mother through hell, young lady."

"I know." Grace actually sounded contrite. "And I'm sorry."

That was all it took for him to forgive her. He grinned. "Come on in out of the rain."

We tromped inside.

I took off my coat and folded it over my arm.

Anarchy did the same.

"Are you staying? I thought you were taking Jane into custody."

"I'm not going anywhere. Not until I can get a patrol car parked in your driveway. Not until I know you're safe."

A warmth that had nothing to do the heat vents in the foyer suffused me. Gulp. "Daddy, is there coffee?"

"We'll make some fresh."

The kitchen felt homey and comforting. A feeling only enhanced by the heavenly smells of Mr. Coffee brewing ambrosia.

I wrapped my cold fingers around a mug and settled onto a stool. If Jane was only going to be around for a few minutes, I'd better get my questions in quick. "What happened last night?"

Jane, who also held a cup of coffee, paled. "He's dead, isn't he?"

I donned a sympathetic face and nodded.

"Ray wasn't so bad. He treated me like a human being and not a piece of—" she glanced at my silver-haired father "—and not like a product." She shifted her gaze to the contents of her mug. "I wanted to return Grace's car. I felt bad about stealing it."

No one said a word. The only sounds were the ticking of the

clock and Max's yawn (we were disturbing his late morning nap).

"I'm not great at driving a stick, so I asked Ray to drive Grace's car and I drove his Impala."

She looked up from her coffee and stared at the wall. "He parked in the drive. I heard a shot. Then someone ran toward me. I knew it wasn't Ray. He was too bulky. Too slow. I got scared and took off."

"And after that?" I asked.

"I drove around. I didn't know where to go." Now she looked at Grace. "I remembered that Grace had told me she was spending the night with a friend, so I stopped at a gas station, looked the address up in the phone book, and went there this morning."

"Why didn't you stay at Donna's?" My voice was sharper than strictly necessary.

"We should have," said Grace. "I was kinda freaked out and I didn't know what to do."

"I'm glad you're safely home now." Glad I could banish that awful threat. Glad Anarchy had been there—not to solve my problem, but to help me solve it. I abandoned my stool and wrapped Grace in another hug.

Ding dong.

"I'll get it." Anarchy disappeared down the hallway before I could point out that I answered the door in my house.

He was back in a minute. "The patrol car is here. Are you ready, Jane?"

Jane put her mug down on the counter and nodded.

I walked with them to the front door.

Jane slipped her arms into her coat.

Anarchy slipped his arms around me. "I'll be back. Don't do anything dangerous."

Like letting Anarchy Jones into my heart? I looked up at him and said, "I never do."

He snorted, dropped a chaste kiss on my forehead, and released me.

I stood in the doorway and watched the two of them drive

away.

When I returned to the kitchen, Grace was peppering Daddy with questions.

"What's up with Granna? When's she coming home?"

Daddy peered into his coffee mug as if he was genuinely surprised to find it empty.

"You know—" I refilled my coffee mug "—it's been so cold and gloomy here, maybe Granna just needed some warmth and sun."

"Piffle." The word sauntered off Grace's tongue, as sassy as could be.

I raised my brows. "Piffle?"

"She needs to get down off her high horse."

Daddy and I stared at her.

"Unless there's something you're not telling us."

I shot Daddy a look. "May I get you more coffee, Daddy?" I asked so sweetly he wouldn't need sugar.

He pretended not to notice my glare. "Yes. Please."

Grace, her grenade thrown, tossed her hair. "I need a shower."

My stomach rumbled and I glanced at the ticking wall clock before taking possession of Daddy's cup. "Are you hungry, Grace? Aggie left some soup. I can warm it up."

"Fine." She tossed her hair a second time. "I won't be long." Then she ran up the backstairs.

"Are you hungry, Daddy?"

"I could eat," he allowed. "Aggie made the soup?"

"Italian wedding." I added coffee to his cup. "All I have to do is pour it into a saucepan."

"Sounds good."

I returned Daddy's coffee mug then fetched a sauce pan from the cabinet and the soup from the fridge. When I heard the water running upstairs, I asked, "Have you heard from her?"

Mother not talking to him was novel—and unpleasant. The corners of his mouth drooped. "No."

I poured the soup in the pan and turned on a burner. "Maybe you should call her."

"She's very angry." He regarded the pan on the stove. "Warm the soup on low, honey."

Everyone was a critic. I turned down the heat. "What happened?"

"This isn't something a man wants to discuss with his daughter."

"Mother left you. I think we're past that objection."

He went back to searching the depths of his coffee mug for answers. "Your mother was not my first love."

Oh dear Lord. Be careful what you ask. I abandoned the soup, and settled onto a stool.

"My senior year at Stanford, I met a girl. She was different from the girls back here. A free spirit." He shifted his gaze from his coffee to the past. The expression in his eyes was soft and gentle—as if he was looking as his younger self and the girl. "We fell in love and she got pregnant."

I swallowed. My mouth suddenly dry. Coffee! I needed more coffee. I got up and poured myself another cup. And, just to prove my cooking prowess, I stirred the soup. "What happened next?"

"I asked her to marry me, told her we'd come home to Kansas City and have a marvelous life."

"She said no?"

"She said no." Forty-plus years later, Daddy still looked sad. He even wiped under his eyes with the knuckles of his right hand.

"She had a daughter." I wanted to know more about this mysterious half-sister.

"Karma."

I sat down again. I had to. I had a half-sister named Karma? "And you never told us?"

"I told your mother."

There was a conversation I was glad I missed.

"I told her before we married. A child isn't something you can keep from your wife. We agreed—" he shifted his gaze to the soup "—we agreed we were starting a new family and we'd keep what was in my past separate from our future."

Classic Mother. An undiscussed problem or issue or sister, was a problem or issue or sister that didn't exist. I, for one, would have appreciated knowing about Karma.

"All those golf trips to California. That's where she is, isn't she?"

He nodded.

"Do you see her?"

"Yes."

"Does she know about us?"

"Yes."

He'd kept secrets from us, but not from Karma. Something inside me deflated. Deflated even as jealousy ran acid green in my veins. My father. He was *my* father. You'd think at almost forty I'd be past juvenile, emotional responses. Apparently not.

"Your mother—"

"You don't have to explain." Mother hadn't wanted us to know. He could have overruled her.

The sound of running water ended. Of course it did. Grace's showers usually lasted longer than an episode of *All in the Family*. But now, when a private conversation with Daddy was all I wanted, she turned into Speedy Gonzales?

I glanced at the ceiling. "Call her."

Daddy's answering sigh belonged to a man who'd spent forty years married to a woman who could inspire fear in Attila the Hun. A sigh that belonged to a man who knew his wife wouldn't be coming home without serious groveling. Although—

"If Mother knew about Karma all along, why is she angry now?"

"When Sylvia died—" he rubbed his mouth with the back of his hand "—losing her mother was hard on Karma. They were very close. I spent more time in California. Your mother contends I wasn't around when you—you and Frances—needed me most."

"When we needed you most?" Daddy and his shoulder had been there when Henry died. He'd held my hand through the funeral. Stood next to me at the reception afterwards. He'd silenced

Mother with a look when she said the flowers were too bright. He'd been there. "What do you mean? You were there."

"Not for all of them."

"All of them?"

"The bodies, Elli. You found bodies when I was out of town. Your mother is traumatized by all the bodies."

Mother? Traumatized? "She's not the one who finds them." A small point, but an important one.

"How would you feel if it was Grace who found all those bodies? Here. There. Everywhere."

A smart answer stalled at the tip of my tongue. How would I feel? "I'd worry myself sick," I admitted.

"And you think your mother is any different?"

Of course she was different. She was Mother. Mother wasn't upset because Daddy missed all those murders. She was livid because he spent too much time with Karma. Time that should be spent with his family in Kansas City.

Besides, the whole argument was moot. I'd had a nice long stretch—months—of not finding bodies. Until Ray got himself murdered in my drive.

"Mother may be worried about the bodies," I conceded without meaning it. "But the ashes in the closet were what set her off. Why would she think you'd left Sylvia's ashes in the hall closet?"

Daddy took a moment and refilled his coffee mug. He also stirred the soup. "Sylvia was cremated and Karma wants me to be there when she releases the ashes." He stirred again. "I think this is ready."

I fetched three plates and three bowls from the cabinet. "Do you mind if we eat in the kitchen?"

"No."

"Good." I grabbed spoons. "Crackers or baguette?"

Daddy eyed the soup. "Baguette."

"I'll get the loaf from the pantry." I called up the stairs. "Grace, lunch is ready."

A moment later, the three of us were seated at the kitchen

island with bowls of Aggie's wonderful soup and crusty bread in front of us.

"So?" Grace's gaze traveled from me to Daddy. "Are you going to tell me?"

Daddy's soup spoon froze half-way to his mouth.

Secrets weren't doing our family any favors. I fixed Grace with a severe stare. "Family matters stay within the family. If we tell you, this goes no further. You don't tell your friends. You don't write it in your diary. You don't whisper it in your dreams."

"Geez, Mom. You sound like Granna."

I winced. "Sometimes Granna gets things right."

"Fine. Okay. Vault." She mimed locking her lips and throwing away the key.

"Daddy? You want to tell her?"

He shook his head. "This one's on you."

"Before your grandparents were married, while your grandfather was away at college, he fell in love and—"

"Wait." Grace held up her hands and wrinkled her nose. "Are you saying?"

"You have another aunt."

She sat for a moment, her expression stunned. Then an impish grin spread across her face. "No way."

"Way."

Grace gave us her best Diana Ross impression.

Mother would not have appreciated Grace's rendition of "Love Child."

Daddy simply choked on his soup.

I handed him my napkin.

Grace stopped singing. "Is she married? Does she have kids?"

Daddy wiped soup from his chin. "Yes and yes."

"Cool." At least Grace, unlike her mother, was unfazed by the prospect of unknown relatives. "Can I meet them?"

Because we needed more dysfunction in our family. "Let's not get ahead of ourselves."

One could only imagine a family gathering that included

Mother and Daddy's illegitimate daughter. The mind boggled.

We finished Aggie's delicious soup without further discussion of Karma and without Grace reprising her Diana Ross impression.

When we'd scraped the last drop from the bottom of our bowls, Grace disappeared.

Daddy stood. "Elli, you're fine here. I'm going home."

I hugged him. "Thanks for all your help today."

"Thank you for being so understanding about Karma."

He was giving me too much credit. I wasn't understanding, I was overwhelmed. "Of course." In our family, skeletons falling out of ash-filled closets should come as no surprise. "I love you, Daddy."

I let him out the front door, waved at the patrol officer parked in my driveway, and went upstairs to my studio.

Painting—the restorative act of adding color to canvas—took up my afternoon.

I descended the stairs when the afternoon's murk ceded to darkness. "Grace," I called. "Are you hungry?"

"Yeah."

I tracked her down to the family room. She sat on the couch cocooned in a fuzzy blanket watching an afternoon movie on channel forty-one. "What are you watching?"

"Some movie. There's nothing on but sports."

"Do you want a pizza?"

She nodded.

So did Max.

"Pepperoni or combo?"

"Combo."

Max didn't argue.

I picked up the phone, dialed the number I knew by heart (calling for take-out was what I cooked best), ordered the pizza, then joined her on the couch.

The movie she was watching was in black and white. A terrified woman was running from a house.

"You know—" Grace's gaze shifted from the frightened woman

to me. A frown wrinkled her forehead (Grace's, not the fleeing woman's) "—I get the weirdest feeling this isn't over."

I frowned too. I had the same feeling.

TWENTY-ONE

Bad was too kind a word for Grace's movie but we sat and watched and waited for the hero to save the heroine until six.

"I can't stand any more of this. How about we switch to *60 Minutes*?" I asked.

"Fine with me." Grace exited her cocoon and and flipped the television dial.

Morley Safer filled the screen.

Ding dong.

"That'll be the pizza." I hauled myself off the couch, stopped in the kitchen, and grabbed my billfold from my purse.

The patrol office and a very nervous pizza guy waited on the front stoop.

"You ordered pizza?" the officer asked. He was the approximate size of a mountain and his face was hewn from granite. No wonder the pizza guy was shifting from foot to foot and looking over his shoulder at his still-running car.

"I did." I paid the delivery man and he hurried down the drive to his car.

"Are you hungry, officer?"

"No, ma'am."

"You're sure? We've got plenty. It's combo." The man could guard us just as effectively from inside the house as he could from his car.

"I'm on duty, ma'am."

It wasn't like I was offering him a tequila shot.

The smell of hot tomato sauce and melted cheese wafting from the box made my mouth water. "Fine. Let me know if you change your mind or if you want hot coffee or a bathroom or—"

"I'm on duty, ma'am."

Who was I to argue with hewn granite?

I closed the door. With Max at my heels (the pizza smell had attracted him like a moth to a flame), I returned to the kitchen. Plates, napkins, and a knife to separate the slices—I stacked them all on top of the box. "Grace," I called. "What do you want to drink?" I poured myself a glass of wine and waited for her answer.

"Grace, honey—" louder this time "—do you want a drink?"

Her response was garbled.

I pulled a Tab from the fridge and added it to the top of the pizza box. If she wanted something else, she could get it herself. Then, with balancing skills I didn't know I possessed, I centered the box on my left hand and grabbed the wine glass with my right.

If I didn't trip over Max (who was underfoot with a pizza-induced spring in his doggy steps), dinner was served.

Together we two-stepped toward the family room.

Until Max stopped dead in his tracks. Of course I tripped over him but the only casualty was sloshed wine.

"Max," I snapped. "What are you doing?"

Max growled.

"What is it, buddy?"

I stepped around him and wished I hadn't.

A bedraggled—wet, dirty, with leaves in his hair—Bruce Petteway had joined Grace in the family room. Not just joined her. Seized her. The two stood in front of the television, facing me. Bruce held a gun. A gun he pressed against Grace's ribcage.

I didn't drop the pizza. I didn't drop the wine. Mainly because a strange been-there-done-that calm washed over me. I deposited dinner on my desk. "What are you doing, Bruce?"

Next to me, Max growled. Deep in his throat. He'd been-there-done-that too.

Bruce didn't answer me.

"How did you get in here?" I demanded.

"The back door was unlocked."

I gave Grace the look. The look Mother usually saved for my worst transgressions—finding bodies, dating a homicide detective, wanting to meet my half-sister.

Bruce settled his gaze on me. His irises were pinpricks and he seemed to vibrate like a human tuning rod. What kind of drugs was he on?

"I'm sorry. I forgot to lock the door when I let Max in."

Max growled. Deeper this time. His lips drew back from his teeth. He looked truly fearsome.

"Control your dog!" Bruce shifted the gun away from Grace and pointed it at Max.

With Bruce's gaze fixed on Max, I slipped the knife on the pizza box into my sleeve. What good was a kitchen knife against a gun? Not much, but the knife was all I had. I clutched the handle tightly. "Grace has nothing to do with this."

Grace made a tiny mewling sound in her throat.

"Let her go. Please."

Bruce pointed the gun at Grace's ribs again.

I held up my free hand. I give up. You win. Let go of my daughter! I hadn't seen this coming. Bruce, a killer? I hadn't credited him with enough gumption. Quite clearly I'd been mistaken. Was he the real estate investor who'd killed Leesa? Had he killed Ray? Jane had described the man as bulky. Bruce was definitely bulkier than Ray. I was bulkier than Ray.

I inched closer to the man with the gun and my daughter.

"Stay where you are!"

I froze. "Let Grace go. Please."

He shook his head. "It didn't have to be this way."

"Mrs. Russell—" a strident voice carried from the kitchen "—I have had quite enough of you and the shenanigans in your house. They affect my property. Do you know some man just snuck through my backyard?" The voice grew louder and louder until Margaret Hamilton was framed by the doorway.

Bruce shifted the gun's aim from Grace to my next-door neighbor.

I pulled out my knife.

Max launched himself at the stranger in his house. Teeth bared. Hair raised in a ridge on his back. Max was a terrifying beast. Fortunately, the stranger he went for was Bruce and not Margaret.

Bang!

"Eeeeeeee!" High-pitched. Ear-splitting. Coming from Margaret or Bruce? Impossible to tell.

Bruce was on his back with Max planted on his chest.

Max's gleaming teeth were less than a quarter-inch from Bruce's throat.

Margaret was on the floor clutching her upper arm.

Grace was shaking, but not so much she couldn't kick the gun Bruce had dropped under the couch.

Bruce pushed at Max.

Max bit him. Hard. In the fleshy part of his hand.

Blood dripped onto Bruce's face and he gasped. "Get him off! Get him off!" His voice was a falsetto.

"I'm shot." Margaret's voice was a deep bass.

I held up my knife. "Grace, go get that knucklehead cop."

Grace took off at a run.

Margaret dragged herself off the floor. Blood welled through the fingers clasped on her arm.

"Mrs. Hamilton, how badly are you hurt?"

She firmed her chin and leveled her witchy gaze at Bruce—and Max. "Only a scratch thanks to that beast."

Max looked over his shoulder and grinned at her.

"Don't," she warned, "think you're forgiven for that squirrel."

Max grinned bigger.

Bruce groaned.

I had no sympathy. It was one thing to threaten me and something entirely different to threaten Grace. I pointed the knife at him.

Officer Hewn rushed in, his steps slowing as he took in one shot next-door neighbor, a dog that might or might not be vicious, a woman with a knife, a man on the floor, and a fast-cooling pizza.

"What happened?" he demanded.

"He shot me."

"He grabbed me off the couch."

"He threatened my daughter."

Bark.

"The dog attacked me."

We all spoke at the same time.

The first cracks appeared in Officer Hewn's hewn face. Worried   cracks.   How-do-I-explain-half-the-neighborhood-waltzing-through-the-back-door-while-I-sat-in-my-patrol-car cracks. He swallowed loud enough for us all to hear him. "I called this in. Detective Jones is on his way."

Thank God for small favors.

"This is the man who's been sitting in your driveway watching your house all day?" Margaret's tone let us all know she wasn't impressed.

"It is."

Margaret Hamilton sniffed. "They would have been better served paying Marian Dixon."

My nosy, across-the-street neighbor had probably spent her afternoon and evening watching the man paid to watch my house. And she'd done it for free.

Officer Hewn scowled at us. For about a half-second. "You're shot?"

"I already told you that." Margaret sounded mightily put out. If I were Officer Hewn, I'd be worried she'd turn me into a rock. Or worse.

"He shot you?" Office Hewn pointed at Bruce.

"Yes."

"Where's the gun?"

"Under the couch." Grace's voice was small.

For the first time, Officer Hewn seemed to notice the knife in my hand. "What are you doing with that?"

"It's for the pizza." I dropped the knife on the box.

Margaret Hamilton cackled.

"Max, come here."

Max surveyed Officer Hewn, decided the police officer was up to the task of controlling Bruce, and came to my side.

Bruce didn't move. Max had knocked all the stuffing out of him.

The whine of sirens reached us in the family room then came, "Ellison!" Anarchy's voice boomed throughout my house.

"Family room," I called.

The pound of running feet on hardwoods came next.

Then Anarchy.

He skidded to a stop in the doorway "You're all right?"

"I'm fine. Mrs. Hamilton has been shot."

Mrs. Hamilton leaned against the white wall and the wall had more color than she did. "He just grazed me." Margaret Hamilton might fly a broom whenever the moon was full, but she was a brave woman.

"You need to sit down." I led her to a chair.

She refused to sit. "Your upholstery."

"To hell with the upholstery. Sit down."

"An ambulance is on its way," said Anarchy. "Grace?" His gaze landed on my daughter. "You're all right?"

She nodded.

Anarchy shifted his gaze to Bruce and his eyes narrowed. His lips narrowed. His focus narrowed.

Bruce shuddered.

A uniformed officer appeared in the door. "The ambulance is here."

"I don't need an ambulance," Margaret objected. "I'm fine."

She'd been shot. In my home.

"I'll follow you. We'll have the doctors look at you then I'll drive you home."

She looked as if she meant to object. Strongly.

"Please, Mrs. Hamilton," said Grace. "I won't be able to sleep unless I know you're okay."

"You don't need to follow me. I'll catch a cab when they're done with me." She sounded brave and strong but I wasn't buying it.

"Are you kidding?" I asked. "You saved us." Besides, it had been months since I'd been to the emergency room. If I didn't put in an appearance soon, they might forget me.

"Hmph."

We followed her to the hospital. In the Mercedes. Not thinking about what had happened in the passenger seat where Grace sat was the best policy. I needed a new car.

"I'm really sorry, Mom. About the back door."

"It's okay, honey. I'm just glad you're safe."

"Why—" she looked down at her hands. They were clasped together in her lap.

"Why did Bruce invade our home and point a gun at you?" Just thinking about it made my fingers tighten on the steering wheel.

She nodded.

"Either he's a murderer or he's having a very bad divorce."

"I hope it's the divorce. It's too scary to think about a multiple murderer digging a gun into my ribs."

It was too scary to think of anyone digging a gun into her ribs.

I needn't have worried that the staff at the hospital would forget me. They greeted me like a long-lost family member. "Mrs. Russell, how are you? Mrs. Russell, it's nice to see you. Mrs. Russell, who did you bring in tonight?"

"Fine. Nice to see you too. I'm here about Margaret Hamilton."

They put her on the fast track. And I didn't even mention Mother's name.

Two hours later, Mrs. Hamilton was in the passenger seat of the Mercedes. "I told you it was just a scratch."

"You were right." I wasn't about to argue with her.

"It was nice of you to follow me—and to wait. Thank you."

"You're welcome." I fixed my gaze on the road ahead of us. "Thank you. You saved us."

"Hmph." Mrs. Hamilton turned away, her gaze fixed on the darkness outside the passenger window.

I drove in silence.

Grace, who sat in the backseat, had the good sense to stay quiet.

I pulled into Margaret Hamilton's drive, stopped under the porte cochere, and hurried around to the passenger's side to help her out.

She opened the car door herself. "Thank you." She regarded me with beady black eyes. "Thank you, Ellison."

She'd never called me by my first name. Never invited me to use her first name.

I took a breath. "It was my pleasure, Margaret."

We stared at each other for a moment then she opened the door to her home and sent me on my way with a firm nod of her chin. "Keep that dog out of my yard."

"I will."

"And buy him a bone from me."

"Consider it done."

Grace and I pulled up our own drive, parked behind the house, and entered through the back door.

Grace looked around the empty kitchen. "I want cocoa. Do you want cocoa?"

"Sure. Give me a minute and I'll make it for you." I walked toward the family room.

"I'll make it," she offered.

"Thanks."

I stepped into the family room.

Bruce was gone.

Officer Hewn was gone.

The smear of Margaret's blood on the wall was gone.

The pizza was gone.

Anarchy was there.

We stared at each other. Lord only knew what I looked like. He looked perfect. Coffee-brown eyes, slightly sardonic grin, his hair mussed as if he'd been running his fingers through it as he waited for me to come home. Be still my heart.

"How's your neighbor?"

"She'll be fine. How's Jane?"

"She's safe." A twitch at the corner of his mouth threatened to turn his sardonic grin into a genuine smile. "I'll need to take statements."

"Can it wait till tomorrow?"

"I'll be here."

He would? "Oh?"

"I'm spending the night."

"The neighbors will talk."

"The neighbors are already talking."

I couldn't argue that. "Grace is making cocoa. Would you like some?"

He gifted me an actual smile. "I would. Thank you."

We walked back to the kitchen with his fingertips burning a hole in the back of my sweater.

Grace looked up from the stove and smirked at us. "I made enough for three."

We sat around the island in companionable silence and drank hot cocoa.

Grace finished first. "I'm tired." She stood, rinsed her cup, and put it in the dishwasher. "I'm going to bed. See you in the morning."

"Wait." I rose from my stool and hugged her tightly. "I am so, so glad you're okay. I love you."

"Love you too, Mom. And don't worry, I'm not like traumatized or anything. Mr. Petteway wasn't nearly as scary as some of the people we've faced."

Oh dear Lord. How many evil people had we faced? I'd lost count. Apparently, Grace had not.

Mother was right. My finding bodies had to stop. I could

retreat to my studio, paint, and keep my nose far, far away from other people's problems. Then Grace wouldn't have to deal with guns and blood and fear. "I am so sorry."

"It's not your fault." She grinned. "Besides, life at our house is never boring." With that, she kissed my cheek and disappeared up the backstairs.

"She's a great kid."

"She is," I agreed.

"She's got a great mother."

I shook my head. "There's nothing wrong with boring. Grace's biggest worry should be her date for next weekend, not getting shot in the family room."

Anarchy stood. Anarchy wrapped an arm around my back, pulling me close. Anarchy traced my cheekbone with the pad of his thumb. "Don't worry about Grace. That kid has more bounce to her than a rubber ball."

My word-forming ability fled.

He leaned down and brushed his lips across mine.

Fire.

"Want to grab those blankets and pillows?"

"What?" There. I'd formed a word.

"I'm spending the night on the couch."

"You don't have to do that. We're fine."

"I'm not convinced Bruce killed Ray." He released me. "I'm not convinced Bruce killed anyone."

I wanted to disagree—life could return to normal if Bruce was the killer—but I couldn't. "I'll get them."

A moment later I stood in the family room handing over a stack of bedding. "What if Rocky was telling the truth? What if the killer is a real estate developer?"

"Rocky telling the truth?" Anarchy raised his brows. "Not a snowball's chance. Why don't you let me worry about killers and—" his voice died.

Something in my expression killed it. "Let me worry about killers—"

"That sounded patronizing, didn't it?"

Uh, yes. Incredibly so. I nodded.

"That's not how I meant it. Catching killers is my job."

"And my job is painting pretty pictures."

"Ellison—" with his free hand, he raked his fingers through his hair and his brow furrowed "—I'm making a mess of this. I apologize." He dropped the bedding on the back of the couch and stepped closer to me. "You are a brilliant—" he leaned forward and brushed my cheek with a kiss "—capable—" now a kiss tickled the corner of my mouth "—brave woman."

How could I possibly stay annoyed with a man who kissed me like that? Especially when his eyes told me he meant every word he said?

"I'm just old-fashioned enough to want to protect you."

I nodded and took a step away from him. I had to. If I didn't, I'd melt into his arms like some old-fashioned damsel who needed protecting. I shifted my gaze to the stack of sheets and blankets and pillows. "You've got everything you need?"

"Not by a long shot."

I wanted that instant—the sudden joyous leap of my heart, the warmth in Anarchy's gaze, the electricity arcing between us—caught in amber. A precious jewel of a moment to be treasured forever.

"Good night." The only words I could manage.

I climbed the stairs slowly. The weight of my thoughts affecting my feet.

Anarchy and me? A future?

I considered the possibility as I washed my face, as I brushed my teeth, as I selected a silk nightgown the shade of midnight instead of flannel pajamas. I considered and reached no conclusions.

One thing I did know, Anarchy's antagonism toward Rocky O'Hearne had colored his judgment. The things Rocky had told us—they'd stuck with me—they had the ring of truth. And if Rocky was telling the truth, then I knew who'd killed all those people.

If. A big if. One I couldn't hope to prove.

I pulled back the comforter and climbed into bed.

Max circled three times then settled onto his bed with a tired sigh. Being a hero was exhausting work.

"Thank you, Max. I love you."

He didn't reply. He didn't have to.

I settled into my pillows and closed my eyes.

I opened them again five minutes—two hours—later. Something was wrong. I felt the wrongness in my bones.

I lay in bed and listened—the heat blew through the vents, the wind outside rushed through the trees and flung an occasional leaf or twig against the house.

Nothing amiss.

But something didn't feel right.

I reached into the drawer of my bedside table, picked up my gun, and slid out of bed.

Max lifted his head.

"Am I imagining things?" I whispered.

He rose to his paws.

Together we tiptoed down the hall. Together we paused at the top of the stairs.

Voices.

I heard voices.

I tightened my grip on the gun and descended the stairs. Maybe Anarchy was watching television—except there was nothing on past midnight on a Sunday night.

Maybe Anarchy was talking to Grace—except the timbre of the voices was too deep.

Maybe—maybe there was a stranger in my house.

I sidled down the hallway toward the family room.

"Where is she?" A man's voice. Not Anarchy's.

My mouth was sand-trap dry.

"You won't find her. Besides, she can't identify you."

"I guess that means you're the only one."

I was glad of that dark nightgown.

I hid in the shadows just outside the doorway to the family

room.

Anarchy, sleep-mussed and unarmed, stood with his hands raised.

And—dammit, I hated being right—Bill had a gun pointed straight at Anarchy's heart.

TWENTY-TWO

Outside, the March wind shredded clouds and bent tree branches. Their shadows danced—waltzed through the family room—with the furniture, the walls, the men.

My heart danced in my chest. Not a waltz. More like a quick-step. One that left me breathless.

I gasped for air. "Put down the gun, Bill."

"Dammit, Ellison." Given that Bill had a gun pointed at his chest, Anarchy ought not curse at me.

I took a breath. A deep one. "I mean it, Bill. Put down the gun."

"Or what?" Bill was not taking me seriously.

"Or I'll shoot you." Somehow, I kept the tremble in my throat out of my voice.

"I wish you would have stayed in bed, Ellison." Bill's voice was tinged with regret.

Anarchy nodded as if he agreed.

"It didn't have to be this way." Bill shook his head sadly.

The shadows danced again and for an instant, Bill stood in the light, the expression on his face clear as day. He meant to kill us both. The gun in his hand was still pointed at Anarchy.

I closed my eyes for an instant. "Please, Bill. I don't want to shoot you."

"You won't shoot." He sounded so certain.

"Last chance," I warned.

"If you were going to shoot me, you'd have done it by now." Another man—this time a dangerous man—underestimating my resolve.

His mistake.

Bang!

Bill went down and his gun skittered across the floor.

Anarchy lunged for the fallen weapon.

I lunged for the light switch.

Bill didn't lunge at all. Bill didn't move.

Oh dear Lord. Why couldn't I breathe? I'd shot countless targets. Even won medals. Shooting a person was different. My stomach heaved. Thank God I'd never had a chance to eat any pizza. I swallowed bile.

"Is he—?"

Anarchy scowled down at the man on the floor and the fast-growing pool of blood. "You shot him in the arm, Ellison. He'll live."

I pressed my hand against my mouth and leaned on the wall. I'd shot someone.

Bill groaned.

Anarchy strode across the room, grabbed the receiver from its cradle, and jabbed his finger into the dial.

Max stood at attention next to me, ready to lunge if Bill so much as moved.

Anarchy barked into the phone.

Bill groaned. Again.

Grace ran into the family room (she wore flannel pajamas). "Mom?"

"Everything's all right, honey."

She looked at Bill bleeding on the floor. Obviously I was lying.

"No. It's not. You're shaking."

I was?

I held my free hand in front of me. It quivered like an Aspen leaf.

Grace glanced at Anarchy. "Come on, Mom. Sit down for a minute." She led me to a chair and asked, "What happened?"

"Bill broke in—" he must have broken in. Surely Anarchy

didn't open the door for him "—and threatened Anarchy. I shot him. Everything's all right, now." And would be until I told Libba I shot her boyfriend.

"I think you're in shock. Anarchy? Some help?"

No. No, no, no. I was not a damsel in distress. "I'm fine, Grace."

She regarded me with doubt in her eyes. "Why did Bill threaten Anarchy?"

"Bill is the killer."

"What?" Her brow wrinkled.

I nodded. "As near as I can tell, Bill had a lot at stake in getting the new convention hotel built on time. The businesses on 12th Street have been slow to move out. Bill thought he could get the strip clubs closed down sooner if there were enough murders associated with them."

"He killed Jane's friend?"

I nodded.

Grace stared long and hard at the man on the floor. "And he came here to kill Anarchy?"

Killing Anarchy hadn't been his purpose—more of a bi-product. "He came here looking for Jane."

Anarchy stopped barking and hung up the phone. He turned, looked at me, and his eyes widened.

Midnight silk. I should have gone with the flannel pajamas.

Or not.

He crossed the space between us in a heartbeat, knelt next to me, and took the gun from my hand. "Are you okay?"

I thought a moment. "No. But I will be."

"There are more officers on their way."

I didn't fancy welcoming a bunch of police officers in my nightgown. "I'll get dressed." I pushed myself up and out of the chair and swished down the hall with Max and Grace at my heels.

Dressed meant jeans, a sweater, and loafers.

Then I made coffee. I even whispered to Mr. Coffee, "Two shootings in one day. It's a good thing Mother is in Palm Springs."

He offered me a sympathetic gurgle.

Ding dong.

I opened the door to Detective Peters. He looked like the call to my house had pulled him from bed. Stubble, wrinkled clothes, cranky expression. Of course, that was his usual appearance, so maybe he'd been sitting by the phone.

"What the hell happened here?" he demanded.

"I shot an intruder."

"An armed intruder?"

"Yes."

Detective Peters' habitual scowl deepened. It would have pleased him greatly to charge me with assault. Since Bill was armed, shooting him was self-defense.

"Everyone is in the family room," I said.

He knew the way.

I planted myself in the kitchen in close proximity to Mr. Coffee.

A string of policemen paraded through my kitchen. I offered all of them coffee.

None of them accepted.

More for me. I gripped the handle of my mug and waited.

Grace waited with me. "I have a question."

"Shoot." I winced. "Poor choice of words. What's your question?"

"Mr. Petteway wanted to stop you from talking to his wife's divorce attorney, right?"

"Right."

"What were you going to say?"

No. No, no, no. No way was I telling Grace about the happenings in the passenger seat of the Mercedes. "I don't think it matters now."

She stared at me. "You're not going to tell me, are you?"

"No." I smiled at her. "I'm not."

She didn't argue. She yawned.

"You should go to bed, honey."

Grace shook her head. "I don't want to leave you."

My heart swelled with love. "I'm fine."

She didn't look convinced.

"You go on to bed. This is the boring part." I knew from experience. "They'll be tromping through here for hours." I sipped my coffee. "Besides, it'll be hell getting up for school tomorrow if you don't get some sleep."

"School?"

"Tomorrow is Monday." I looked at the wall clock. "Today is Monday."

Grace, God love her, rolled her eyes. If ever there was indicator for all being well in a teenager's life..."Fine." A huff not a word. She stomped over to the base of the staircase. "Love you, Mom."

"Love you, too." More than anything.

She disappeared up the stairs and I sipped my coffee.

I gave my statement to a uniformed officer.

I drank more coffee.

The police led Bill away in handcuffs.

I drank more coffee.

I gave my statement to Detective Peters and confirmed my gun was my gun.

I drank more coffee.

The house emptied.

I drank a glass of water.

"You're still up." Anarchy's voice soothed my over-caffeinated nerves.

"I am." I'd been waiting for him.

"I'm going to the station. The captain wants a report."

I nodded. "Will I see you later?"

His grin was like dawn breaking on a dark winter's morning. "Count on it."

"Mrs. Russell, I'm sorry to disturb you." Aggie stood in the door to my bedroom with a cup of coffee in her hand.

I struggled to sit. "What time is it?"

"Almost noon."

"Noon?"

"Your mother has called six times."

"She has?"

Aggie hurried across the room and handed me the coffee.

I closed grateful fingers around the mug and took my first sip. Heaven.

I'd dragged myself out of bed to get Grace off to school then immediately crawled back into bed. Without coffee. Hours ago.

"Six times?" I'd unplugged the phone in my bedroom after I waved Grace good-bye. I hadn't heard a single ring.

Aggie nodded. "What happened here this weekend? I knew I shouldn't have gone away with Mac."

I told her everything. Ray's dying in the driveway. Bruce shooting Mrs. Hamilton. Me shooting Bill.

"I missed a lot." Her voice was dry, as if a lot was an understatement.

"Lucky you."

Brnng, brnng. The sound was far away.

"I guess I should plug in my phone." I made no move to do so.

"You take it easy. Drink your coffee. After the weekend you've had, the least I can do is run interference." She disappeared into the hallway and the ringing stopped.

Six calls? Mother must be on the warpath.

I leaned back against the pillows and drank my coffee. In peace. Mother and her warpath were in California.

Tap, tap.

"Come in."

"Those six calls." Some of Aggie's bounce had bounced away.

"Yes?"

"The first three were early this morning. Then there was a break and I took three more."

I didn't like where this was headed. "She's on a plane isn't she?"

Aggie nodded. "That was your father. He's picking her up at the airport shortly after one."

"Her head is going to explode. In front of me. And after her head explodes, she's going to make sure mine does too."

"I'll fix you brunch. You'll feel better once you've had something to eat."

I'd feel better if Mother was still safely in Palm Springs. Although, it was a good sign that she'd called Daddy to pick her up.

By the time Mother and Daddy arrived, I'd been fortified with three additional cups of coffee, two slices of Aggie's cinnamon crumble coffee cake, and a heaping plate of eggs and bacon.

I felt almost human.

Mother blew into my kitchen like an F5 tornado. "Explain yourself."

I'd grown up on the edge of the plains. I knew what do in case of tornado. Take cover, let the storm blow, and, when it was over, clean up the debris. That had been my life-long plan for dealing with Mother. Not today.

"Pardon me?" My tone was polite, even sweet.

"What has been going on in this house?" she demanded.

"I'm so glad you arrived safely. It's nice to see you. Would you care for coffee?" I stood and entered Mr. Coffee's comforting orbit. "Daddy? Coffee?"

"Ellison!"

"That's a no? Daddy?"

"I'd love a cup, Elli."

"Of course, Daddy." I pulled a cup from the cupboard and filled it for my father. Then I refilled my own.

Mother gnashed her teeth and clutched the side of her head. Like Grendel. "Ellison!"

"Yes, Mother?" My voice was mild.

She gave me the look. The one meant to turn me to stone. "Was someone murdered in your front yard?"

"Uh-huh." I nodded, still pleasant.

"Were two people shot in your family room? In separate

instances? On the same day?"

I cocked my head. "It sounds so awful when you say it that way."

"Did that detective spend the night at your house?"

"That is none of your affair."

Mother's mouth opened and closed but no words came out. She couldn't have been more shocked if I'd slapped her.

I was not going to discuss Anarchy with Mother. Not under any circumstances. "You're sure you don't want coffee?"

"I'm sure." Good thing her glare couldn't actually melt flesh off bones.

I resumed my seat. "It's so nice to see you and Daddy together."

Mother blinked. She wasn't done talking about Anarchy.

I was. "Daddy missed you."

Mother blinked again.

"I missed you, too." It was true. For all her sound and fury, Mother was the one I wanted in my corner when the going got tough. I sipped my coffee. "How about we all just forgive each other? Water under the bridge? All's well that ends well?"

Mother's gaze was stony. Her face was stony.

"To err is human, to forgive, divine."

The stone façade crumbled. A bit. "I can't leave town for a day without disaster striking."

"Believe me, Mother. You couldn't have stopped this disaster." But she could have added color commentary. She would have added color commentary. "The real disaster is the rift in our family." I leveled a stare at her over the rim of my coffee cup. "It's time to move forward."

For a moment no one moved. No one except Max. He yawned.

Mother glanced at Daddy and her expression softened. "You might be right."

I nearly fell off my stool.

She reached up on her tip-toes and kissed Daddy's cheek. "I'm sorry, Harrington. I don't know what got into me."

A two-hundred-mile-per-hour wind.

The stress Daddy had been carrying on his shoulders all week slid right off. He straightened. His eyes twinkled. "I'm glad you're home, Frannie."

Mother smiled.

I'd done it. I'd faced down a tornado and won. This called for a celebration. I refilled my coffee cup.

Ding dong.

I hurried to the front door, pausing to smooth my hair before closing my fingers around the handle.

Deep breath.

I pulled the door open.

Anarchy stood on the other side holding a pizza box. "Combo, right? It's Minsky's. Grace says that's your favorite."

My stomach rumbled and my mouth watered. That pizza smelled like heaven. Heaven I'd been denied last night. At that moment, there was nothing I wanted more than a slice of pizza—not even coffee.

Anarchy stepped inside and dropped a kiss on my cheek. His eyes searched mine. "Feeling better?"

"Much. How's Jane?"

"At home with her grandmother."

"Madame Reyna? Where was she?" I'd forgotten to worry about Madame Reyna.

"Apparently she had a premonition and went to stay with a neighbor."

Maybe she really was psychic. "I'm glad she's okay." I should have worried for her.

"I'm glad you're okay." He stared down at me. A woman could drown in the depths of his coffee brown eyes.

I swallowed (gulped). "Let's take that to the kitchen before it gets cold." We took a few steps. "I'll get us some plates. Maybe some wine." A thought stopped me dead in my tracks. "What about

Bill? What will happen to him?"

"He confessed to five murders. He'll be going away for the rest of his life." Again Anarchy's eyes searched my face. "You didn't seem surprised to see him."

"I wasn't."

"How did you know?"

"I believed Rocky and I figured it had to be Bill or Wright and, frankly, one hotel deal going south didn't seem like it would matter to Wright."

We walked the rest of the way to the kitchen with Max at our heels (pizza). I didn't blame him. The scent was tantalizing. My stomach growled.

"I've been thinking." Anarchy dropped the Minsky's box on the counter.

"About?" I reached up into the cupboard and grabbed two plates.

"You saved me."

"I did, didn't I?" I put the plates on the counter.

"I didn't thank you."

"You didn't."

He pulled me into his arms. "Thank you." He kissed me then. Turns out, there was something I wanted more than pizza.

TELL THE WORLD THIS BOOK WAS

GOOD	BAD	SO-SO

AUTHOR'S NOTE

In 1974 and 1975, Kansas City did tear down the strip clubs on 12th Street and replace them with a convention hotel. Any skullduggery is purely a product of my imagination.

As for Leesa and Jane, what happened to them happens every day. I encourage you to visit www.state.gov/j/tip/id/help/ to learn more.

JULIE MULHERN

Julie Mulhern is the *USA Today* bestselling author of The Country Club Murders. She is a Kansas City native who grew up on a steady diet of Agatha Christie. She spends her spare time whipping up gourmet meals for her family, working out at the gym and finding new ways to keep her house spotlessly clean—and she's got an active imagination. Truth is—she's an expert at calling for take-out, she grumbles about walking the dog and the dust bunnies under the bed have grown into dust lions.

The Country Club Murders
by Julie Mulhern

Novels

THE DEEP END (#1)
GUARANTEED TO BLEED (#2)
CLOUDS IN MY COFFEE (#3)
SEND IN THE CLOWNS (#4)
WATCHING THE DETECTIVES (#5)
COLD AS ICE (#6)
SHADOW DANCING (#7)

Short Stories

DIAMOND GIRL
A Country Club Murder Short

Henery Press Mystery Books

And finally, before you go...
Here are a few other mysteries
you might enjoy:

KILLER IMAGE

Wendy Tyson

An Allison Campbell Mystery (#1)

As Philadelphia's premier image consultant, Allison Campbell helps others reinvent themselves, but her most successful transformation was her own after a scandal nearly ruined her. Now she moves in a world of powerful executives, wealthy, eccentric ex-wives and twisted ethics.

When Allison's latest Main Line client, the fifteen-year-old Goth daughter of a White House hopeful, is accused of the ritualistic murder of a local divorce attorney, Allison fights to prove her client's innocence when no one else will. But unraveling the truth brings specters from her own past. And in a place where image is everything, the ability to distinguish what's real from the facade may be the only thing that keeps Allison alive.

Available at booksellers nationwide and online

Visit www.henerypress.com for details

BOARD STIFF

Kendel Lynn

An Elliott Lisbon Mystery (#1)

As director of the Ballantyne Foundation on Sea Pine Island, SC, Elliott Lisbon scratches her detective itch by performing discreet inquiries for Foundation donors. Usually nothing more serious than retrieving a pilfered Pomeranian. Until Jane Hatting, Ballantyne board chair, is accused of murder. The Ballantyne's reputation tanks, Jane's headed to a jail cell, and Elliott's sexy ex is the new lieutenant in town.

Armed with moxie and her Mini Coop, Elliott uncovers a trail of blackmail schemes, gambling debts, illicit affairs, and investment scams. But the deeper she digs to clear Jane's name, the guiltier Jane looks. The closer she gets to the truth, the more treacherous her investigation becomes. With victims piling up faster than shells at a clambake, Elliott realizes she's next on the killer's list.

Available at booksellers nationwide and online

Visit www.henerypress.com for details

FIT TO BE DEAD

Nancy G. West

An Aggie Mundeen Mystery (#1)

Aggie Mundeen, single and pushing forty, fears nothing but middle age. When she moves from Chicago to San Antonio, she decides she better shape up before anybody discovers she writes the column, "Stay Young with Aggie." She takes Aspects of Aging at University of the Holy Trinity and plunges into exercise at Fit and Firm.

Rusty at flirting and mechanically inept, she irritates a slew of male exercisers, then stumbles into murder. She'd like to impress the attractive detective with her sleuthing skills. But when the killer comes after her, the health club evacuates semi-clad patrons, and the detective has to stall his investigation to save Aggie's derriere.

Available at booksellers nationwide and online

Visit www.henerypress.com for details

CROPPED TO DEATH

Christina Freeburn

A Faith Hunter Scrap This Mystery (#1)

Former US Army JAG specialist, Faith Hunter, returns to her West Virginia home to work in her grandmothers' scrapbooking store determined to lead an unassuming life after her adventure abroad turned disaster. But her quiet life unravels when her friend is charged with murder – and Faith inadvertently supplied the evidence. So Faith decides to cut through the scrap and piece together what really happened.

With a sexy prosecutor, a determined homicide detective, a handful of sticky suspects and a crop contest gone bad, Faith quickly realizes if she's not careful, she'll be the next one cropped.

Available at booksellers nationwide and online

Visit www.henerypress.com for details

CPSIA information can be obtained
at www.ICGtesting.com
Printed in the USA
LVOW13*0227200618

581349LV00008B/52/P